ANNIE POTTS
IS DEAD

M Y ALAM

SPRINGBOARD FICTION

Published 1998 by **Springboard Fiction**
Yorkshire Art Circus, School Lane,
Glasshoughton, Castleford, WF10 4QH
Tel: 01977 550401
Fax: 01977 512819
e-mail: BOOKS@ARTCIRCUS.ORG.UK

© Text: M Y Alam, 1998
Editor: Danny Broderick
Extra Editorial Support: Adrian Wilson

Support: Ian Daley, Isabel Galan, Jo Henderson, Lorna Hey

Cover Design: Paul Miller of Ergo Design
© Photograph of Author: Kevin Reynolds
Printed by FM Repro, Liversedge

ISBN:1 901927 03 2
Classification: Fiction

Springboard is the fiction imprint of Yorkshire Art Circus. We are a unique book publisher.
We work to increase access to writing and publishing and to develop new models of practice
for arts in the community.
Please write to us for details of our full programme of workshops and our current book list.
Our Website is http://www.artcircus.org.uk
Yorkshire Art Circus is a registered charity No 1007443.

Yorkshire Art Circus is supported by:

For mothers and fathers,
For sons and daughters,
For readers and writers,
For lovers and fighters.

For givers and takers,
For movers and shakers,
For sleepers and wakers,
For makers and breakers.

For purity and for sins,
For losses and for wins,
For heroes and for villains,
For Waterstones and for Dillons.

For those who live and for those who die,
For those with truths and for those with lies,
For those who need it and for those who don't,
For those with hope and for those with none.

"...man is not truly one, but truly two. I say two, because the state of my own knowledge does not pass beyond that point."

The Strange Case of Dr Jekyll and Mr Hyde,
by R.L. Stevenson

right here, right now
part one - paid in full

The second best thing I ever did was coming here. For me, it was about doing the right thing. This idea of return that I'd dreamt of for so long simply had to be fulfilled. That, more than anything, was the best thing.

I was given all those warnings but I didn't really believe any of them. About the food, the climate, the people, and of course, a triple dose of a thug called Culture Shock would leap out from some shit-filled alley and begin to kick my head in. All those warnings came true. This place is totally unexpected in some ways, but at the same time, I think it's me and I was born to be here all along. Over here, I might just be in my element.

Most mornings I rise early. As early as five o'clock, sometimes. When I've been working odd hours, I'll rise a little later. At one time, I used to 'get up' or 'wake up' but these days, I 'rise' because these days, I'm different.

What struck me when I first arrived, was how energetic I felt at such ungodly hours. Back in Bradford I could never get to bed soon enough, and once I was in bed, I could never get enough sleep. I was always late and only got out of bed when someone ripped the sheets off me. But here, even three or four hours a night is enough to keep me going through the day. And then there's the pace of the place. Everybody takes their time and there's no room for anyone who likes to run around like an anxious rat on speed. Here, you have to adapt, and that's okay. I can adapt.

Most mornings my mum makes breakfast, and after eating I have a wander into the bazaar. I listen to the chit-chat from the local business community while I get myself the closest shave ever in the local barber's shop but I never say much. I do what I'm good at. I just watch, listen and take note.

Then I do the daily shopping. If there's meat to be bought, I buy it from the guy who's got a few dozen live chickens cooped up in little baskets held together by ribbons of old cloth and bits of fraying string. Everything is recycled here and that's not because people are conscious of being environmentally friendly like they are back in England, but because it's cheaper to repair things and use them over and over again. The guy who sells the meat usually has a couple of skinned lambs trussed up there, but so far, anything other than chicken or vegetables gives me the shits. It's all very free range over here and the animals, which everybody seems to keep, get to eat whatever happens to be handy. They don't get a shit load of chemicals and various parts of dead cousins rammed down their throats which must be nice. You tell the guy at the stall you want a chicken and he asks you to choose one from his range of death-row cluckers. I go for the ugliest one on purpose because I still can't fully handle it when he grabs hold of a nice looking bird and slits its throat while it's still making a fuss and trying to escape from his firm, unyielding grip. So I be selective about it and figure an ugly chicken hasn't got that much to live for and probably has it coming, anyway.

It's usually sometime around midday when I start working, and working here is brilliant. I just sit down and do it. I managed to bring a computer with me from England. Had to bribe the customs' men with a few thousand rupees at the airport to get it through but that's no big deal. Perpetuating corruption, something that's supposed to exist in all countries like Pakistan, is a small sacrifice to pay. It's been well worth it, though. I don't think I could have survived without it.

So I sit, I think and I work. It's funny but there's still a lot of England, mainly Bradford, in me and that's what I still like to write about the most. It's only been a couple of months since we arrived and I know the fondness or love or whatever it is that I've still got inside me will fade in time. The trouble is, I don't think I want it to.

I haven't got much to do with England these days. Just two things, actually. Shelley and my main man, Gates. I write to Shelley when I'm bored and Shelley writes back when she's got the time or when she feels like it. Gates is always sending me letters and hassling me for some more stuff. I get a kick out of that because usually people like me are the ones who get to be fucked around by people like solicitors. Getting one over on someone like Gates is bound to be a bonus for someone who sees the world like I do.

I'm pretty popular at the moment but I know the novelty of a reclusive-but-suspect writer will soon wear off. So I've got to keep on churning it out while people are still interested and while I can still make something of it.

But what people don't realise is how carefully I worked all of it out, and, for that matter, they don't realise how much is reality and how much is what they'd call fiction. But that's good. That, in fact, was the object of the whole exercise.

Of course, I still think about Annie. Not all the time like I thought I would but she still appears in my mind when I least expect her to. I've got a lot to thank her for and I don't really think of her as dead because nothing's really dead until people stop thinking about it. Sometimes I get close to tears and I wonder how badly I'm going to suffer later on, but I always end up thinking of it as more Annie's choice than mine. Annie was a good person. Annie was a giving person who gave the only thing she had left. It's through me that she'll still live. I know I'm lying to myself when I think these things. It makes me feel a little better if I think of them like that, that's all.

sound of da police

It was about three in the morning and there was this banging going off outside. At first I thought it was just the dippy cunt who lived across the road. He came home pissed on the weekends and resorted to kicking the shit out of his door because either his wife had locked him out, he'd lost his key, or he was simply too fucked to remember how something as simple as a key worked. The first few times it happened it had been pretty funny and we all talked about it the following morning. But once we got used to it and had to hear it twice a week and every bloody week, the novelty of a daft and pissed-up twat making a proper tit out of himself seemed to wear off a bit.

But eventually it dawned on me, in my half-awake state, that this banging was different. It was too loud, and too near to be the banging of a disorientated drunk. So patently distinct compared to the usual and pissed-up banging of everyone's favourite drunk pisshead from number sixty-eight. Orderly and careful, and not accompanied by the usual *"Sheila! Open fuckin' door, willyer! Open fuckin' door, yah bastard!"* as there usually was when dozy bastard did his twice weekly thing.

I got up and looked out of the window, preparing to yell some of my own abuse at the inconsiderate pissed-up cunt. Again it was something we, the surrounding neighbours, did automatically. Whoever was up first would open their window and shout something like,

"Shut yer fuckin' mouth, yer noisy fuckin' bastard! Before I come out and kick yer fuckin' head in!"

He would respond by defensively holding his hands up and then shouting through his letter box,

"Now look what you've done yer dozy bastard! You've gone and woke fuckin' neighbours up, now! Sheila! Sheila, yah bastard! Open fuckin' door!"

Then he'd pause and tell his poor neighbour,

"Sorry mate, she's locked us out, like."

But he wasn't there. I looked again to make sure. He wasn't fucking there! What the fuck was going on around here? Some other noisy, inconsiderate bastards must have been banging away like barn doors at this time of night and not giving a shit about those of us who needed our sleep. The second I looked out of the window, I forgot all about noisy, inconsiderate bastards and the pisshead at number sixty-eight. I looked down and what I saw convinced me I must have still been dreaming. So I went back to bed. But the banging continued. So I got back out of bed and went over to the window again.

It wasn't a dream. There *were* a couple of cop cars parked up. This was no ordinary sight. This could have been one of those weird dreams that seemed to be realer than real. One of those dreams that tricked you into thinking you were awake when you were still asleep. But it wasn't because what I saw outside was still there and, as far as I could tell, still real. The cop cars were outside our house and they were waiting for something, I didn't know what, to happen. Then I got it. Then I remembered what had been temporarily wiped from that roguish memory of mine. I remembered what I'd chosen to forget. I recalled a reason for them being here, at this time of night. I smiled to myself. It was okay. In fact, it was only to be expected. I calmed myself down and got ready, but still, the worrying persisted.

Why the fuck was I being so worried? I'd never done anything to attract the attention of the old bill in my life. Not really, anyway. It must have been something to do with those other neighbours of ours, I decided. That was why the fucking coppers were here. It would have been obvious to anyone who was familiar with our street.

The neighbours who lived next-door-but-one were probably busying around like a load of beavers, panicking and hiding whatever they had that was crooked. I had it all worked out, and tomorrow I'd be able to tell anyone who cared to ask what the story was with the old bill making a racket in the middle of the night. The neighbours in question had probably been fencing a load of dodgy gear, which was of the shittiest quality, as well as knock-off. Some fucker must have grassed them up for either a) undercutting his keen prices or b) selling the grassing bastard some extremely sub-standard clobber. Those people from next-door-but-one were like that. No scruples whatsoever.

Just because shite happens to be bent doesn't mean the consumer has no rights, rights that those Watchdog types are always making a fuss about. Quite the opposite, in fact. Stolen goods are still subject to recourse if proven to be defective or sub-standard. You approach the supplier with the defective item and you sort it out and there's hardly ever any hassle. Receipts? What fucking receipts? Who cares? The supplier is only going to sell the same defective item on to someone else and make that cash work, the same as your cash worked, until the new buyer brings the item back to the seller because it's just as fucked as it was the first time it was sold. This might be a little inconvenient, but everybody gets happy in the end. If you think about it, you can manage to live quite well by selling defective stuff. You get money for the stuff, and you make that money earn for you even though it's not permanently yours, and then you pay it back whenever those disappointed customers come back and start moaning at you. And then, if you're a bit wide, you can always make out that they fucked the item up themselves, but you still give them something as if you're doing them a favour and doing that on its own can be enough to satisfy some people. Best of all are the customers who leave it for ages and really don't expect to be fully refunded for those knackered goods just because they've left it for too long.

But these particular neighbours of ours would sell any knackered old shit and when they got a come-back because their stuff was crap, knackered or both, they'd deny all knowledge of the item as well as the transaction. It didn't matter if they'd only sold the fucking thing the day before. They were just in it for a quick buck and they never gave two shits about refunds or swaps. And that was why someone had grassed them up and that was why, perhaps, the coppers were out there and giving it a bit of the old Ringo Starr with the doors.

I kept looking out and watching for something to happen but I couldn't see too much from where I was up in the attic. All I got was the sound of the cop cars and the noise of the coppers. Then it stopped. Maybe they'd had enough and decided to make their way back to the station. On the way they could hassle some poor cunt who was driving two miles over the speed limit or cop for some poor sod who was breaking a law that was just as heinous.

As he stepped back from our front door, one of the coppers came into view. Our front door. I swallowed. He'd stepped back from our front door, which meant they had come for us. I froze for a moment and it was then that he looked up and saw me looking down at him. I pressed my palm to the cold glass and signalled him to hang on. I was coming down to see just what the fuck was going off with these tits. Who the fuck did these dickheads think they were fucking with? What did they think we were? Crooks like those idiots down the road who sold the dodgiest shit going? No fucking way.

I stepped away from the window and listened. A couple of seconds later I heard my brother jump out of bed and shout something out of his window. I knew what he'd think. It was the shop. Some bastard had robbed his shop again.

I'd better tell you about the shop before I go any further. It's my brother's shop and it's right in the middle of Manningham which is a bit of a shit-tip to some people, but once you've spent a fair chunk of your life there and you've got to know it as well as you can get to know anything, it's all right. One thing I like about it is that you get to see loads of people who are pretty fucked up. I'm not saying I'm glad they have hard lives or anything, it's just that it can be interesting watching the way some of them are.

And now, my brother would be thinking, we'd been done over once again. Some bastards had broken in and took what we, especially my brother, had worked our arses off for. I felt bad for my brother because he'd be thinking everything was over. It was the moment all of us had feared ever since we'd bought that fucking place. It was reasonably secure, with steel shutters and an alarm, but those little defences meant nothing. The bastards had got in once before and we spent some more money making it doubly secure. But still, in the backs of our minds, we knew it could happen again.

Now my brother would be thinking we shouldn't have bothered installing more security locks and shutters because it turned out to be a waste of money. We should have just left the door open for any bastard to get in and take what he wanted. It was accessible because no matter what you did, if the bastards wanted to get in, they'd find a way soon enough. A few weeks earlier a clothes shop had been done over and they'd got in with a car. Ram-raiding was the latest trick. It was the easiest thing in the world. All you had to do was go out, nick a car, smash a way in, take what you want and then drive off. A piece of piss. Thieves couldn't get easier than that and people like my brother couldn't stop the bastards because every time he put something in their way, they just looked at it, laughed at it and then shat all over it.

"Gerrup, something's going on, man," said my brother as I ran down the stairs. "It's the fucking shop!"

"What?"

"The shop! The fucking shop!"

I opened the door and as I waited for the copper to say something to make me feel better, I noticed how big he looked. I wondered why it was that all coppers still looked massive. If it was just the uniform, why was it that other people in uniforms didn't look big? Bus conductors didn't look big. Railway people didn't look big. Firemen didn't look big. In fact, firemen always seemed to look small to me. It was something else about coppers that had intimidated the shit out of me when I was younger. Presence, or just the fact that I knew these people would take me away if I carried on being the naughty little shit that I always was as a kid. Then again, it could have been the same for everyone like me.

"Tahir Mahmood?"

"Yeah? I mean 'no'. What's up?"

"You Tahir Mahmood or aren't you?" said the copper, all fucking attitude and no time for small talk, this prick.

"No, that's my brother, he's on his way. Is it the shop or what?"

"In a manner."

I'd seen these types before and it was always best to let them think they were on a mission from God. It was more than simply having a chip on a shoulder. It was the way people like him saw people like me. I could sense it a mile off because I'd been sensing it for most of my life.

"Bastards! What have they took? Bastards!"

My brother came out.

"What's up?" he said.

"You Tahir Mahmood?"

My brother's only a couple of years older than me and he'd had the shop for about twelve years. Recently, he'd got to thinking it had been twelve years too many. Having said that, it was the only thing he'd ever done for any serious length of time, apart from a couple of training schemes he did when he was a school leaver, back when the Tories first thought it would be a good idea to start doctoring the unemployment figures and what have you. I just couldn't see him working in an office or a factory like I'd done in the past. He never had the temperament for it for one thing and I could easily imagine him getting sacked for telling his superiors to go fuck themselves simply because they might have been stupid enough to tell him what to do. Anyway, it was more of a family business than just his shop, but none of us really cared too much about that. We're okay as far as brothers go, his thing is mine and mine is his. We're kind of cool about shit like that which is nice and pretty rare in this day and age.

"Yeah. What's happened, then?"

"I'm going to have to ask you to accompany me to the station."

"What's that?"

"You heard. You've got five minutes to get yourselves changed. Or we take you as you are."

"What? What for?" my brother said and then looked at me.

"Is it the shop or what?" I asked the copper.

"You'll find out soon enough."

"Just fucking tell us will yer? Is it the shop or isn't it?"

He was a dickhead was this copper. The prick must have watched far too much *Miami Vice* as a kid for his own good.

"Just shut it, you," he said and stabbed me in the chest with his forefinger.

"Fuck you, man. I asked a question, that's all," I said and stabbed the cunt back.

I shouldn't have done that. I should have just took his shit like he expected me to. He moved closer to me.

"And I told you to shut your paki mouth, you black paki shit."

He didn't use his finger this time. He just fisted me one in the gut. I keeled over and fought to get my breath back.

"You okay?" asked my brother.

"I'm all right." I said as I got back up.

"What the fuck is it with you cunts?" my brother yelled. "What the fuck do you want from us?"

"Shut it…"

"Just tell me. What have they took? How much damage?" my brother asked in a calmer voice, doing his best to chill things down. "That shop, it's everything we've got."

"Now, you two black cunts, just shut your fucking mouths and do as you're fucking well told," the copper whispered in a riled but worried tone. I could tell he just wanted to get the thing done without any hassle and suddenly didn't like the way it was panning out for him. But that was his own fault. All he had to do was to be nice about it. I just looked at him in defiance.

"Eat my black paki shit."

"Look," he sighed, "you black cunts give me enough grief by just being here. Shut it and do yourselves a favour, you understand? Or do we have to make you thick bastards understand?"

Bitchy or what? Two could play at that game.

"Fuck you! Fat mother-fucking pig!"

"Right, that's it," he turned around to the cars. "George! Chris! Get the others, we've got a couple of firecrackers on our hands."

Firecrackers? Did he just call us firecrackers? We weren't the firecrackers – these coppers were the firecrackers.

"You've fucking had it now!" he sneered as he turned back around to face us.

Out of the two cop motors trouped half a dozen of these fat rugby playing coppers like bit part players in *The Sweeney*. Every one of the cunts had a moustache of one type or another, as if that was all you needed to be a copper these days. Next thing, they were all over us. Two of them tackled me from the legs and another one got me around the neck and shoulders. I kicked, squirmed and shouted but the cunts weren't letting go. They got me on the floor, face down, one of them digging his knee in my back, another two kneeling on my legs while another one came along and cuffed me.

They were obviously used to holding people down in the middle of these wonderful inner-city streets. Perhaps they were trained for this sort of shit.

They got my brother too, but my brother's mind moves like lightning in situations like those. He manages to pre-empt situations before they happen when he's on fire, like that. He managed to belt a couple of them when he saw what they were doing to me. Well, that's what big brothers are for, right? They gave it to him worse than they gave it to me because he'd managed to hurt a couple of the fat bastards. There's nothing that coppers hate more than being battered by a perp but what they didn't understand was that none of that shit was necessary. All they had to do was to be nice about it. All we were doing was protecting ourselves. You just don't take shit from people like that if you claim to have any self respect. My brother nearly struggled free but then, another two got out of the cars and came over to help restrain him. One from the first team was holding his nose and blood was seeping out from in between his fingers. A good and hard head, has my brother. It was strong enough for any one of these fucking pigs, anyway. It wasn't that he was a hard man or anything. He was just capable of taking care of himself in a world where you needed to be careful. And unlike me, he'd always been able to use his head in more ways than one.

As a result of my brother's actions – what I'd call 'self defence' and the pigs would later refer to as 'resisting arrest' – they thought that it would only be right and fitting if they kicked the fuck out of him. So they did, right there, in the middle of the night and right on the pavement.

Eventually, a few lights began to come on up and down the street and the coppers started calming down with their antics. It wouldn't have done to have a few dozen pakis witnessing a bit of the old and infamous excessive force that wasn't supposed to exist anymore. A crowd began to gather. My little sister was the first to come out of our house, slowly followed by my mum and my dad. And that was the hardest thing to deal with. The kicks in my guts and the licks to my head didn't matter and didn't hurt right then. It was as if the battering I'd just received had never happened because of those looks on the faces of my folks. They all looked like they were crapping it something rotten, like someone had died. Not one of them had encountered anything like this before. A sight that was shocking because what they were seeing outside their own front door was totally alien to them. This sort of thing just didn't happen to people like us. Our folks were more than just worried, but I was okay. I'd done nothing wrong and I'd force that on any bastard who'd try and tell me otherwise.

help the aged - part one

Her name was Annie and she was about seventy or something. When she first moved into the area she used to come in to the shop and bore the pants off whoever happened to be on duty. A couple of years later her health got bad and she used to ring us up and ask whether or not we'd mind dropping an order off for her. I didn't mind too much. She was old and a bit of a dippy twat, but all right at the end of the day. And besides, she only lived a few seconds from the shop, and when you've got a shop you'll do your best to make that extra few pence. Business is business, and sometimes, you just have to go out of your way and kiss arse.

My brother, on the other hand, couldn't stand the sight of her. She just annoyed the tits off him for some reason. I mean, sometimes she'd go on and on without any sign of shutting up, but I just hacked it because that's what I'm like with some people. Besides, it wasn't really her fault, and who was to say I wouldn't be like that when I started getting on a bit? Maybe my brother should have been a little more patient with her, but he's stuck in his ways and I could never convince him she wasn't as bad as he made out. Most of the stuff she came out with was the usual bollocks old people come out with, but sometimes she'd say something to get me interested, like what she thought of literature and stuff like that. Best of all, she'd been an actress when she was young, and she'd tell me how scripts and directions worked in theatres. She also liked a good read and used to tell me about all these writers she knew. Apart from Freddy, she was the only one who ever showed the slightest interest in any of my stuff.

She also seemed to appreciate a good joke now and then, which was nice for an oldie. Most of them spend their time moaning and groaning about one thing or another, but she could come out with some beauties when she put her mind to it. She'd also tell me about her time in the theatre. This one time, she worked with some famous actor who'd fluffed his lines in front of an audience and then she told me, how she'd been quick to cover for him. She must have been a bit of a contender in her day, but for some reason she never quite managed to scale the heights of some of her contemporaries. Maybe she was just shit at acting but wasn't keen on admitting it. Anyway, she was never really bitter about not being dead famous like some of the people she started off with, but, I guess, she must have had some regrets about what could have been. Everybody has some regrets, right?

The thing about this old dear called Annie that really annoyed me though, was her health. Fact was, she brought on these illnesses of hers all by herself. I'm not one to judge people – they can do what the fuck they want as long as they don't try to impose themselves and their ideas on me – but some people just ask for trouble with the way they go about living their lives. There she was, an old biddie who suffered more than most with her asthma, anaemia, diabetes, bronchitis, emphysema and fuck knows what else, but she lived as if she was still young, healthy and super-fit. Forty coughers and half a bottle of scotch every day wasn't going to do her lungs or blood any good as far as I could see, but she went for it nevertheless. And you could tell she was in pain. That mask of a smile and the occasional laugh was just too flimsy to function most days, and I always felt bad about thinking of her as someone who was ready for the knacker's yard.

She'd ring either me or my brother at the shop and go on about this and that – about her asthma, about her tubes being all blocked up again or anything else that might have been giving her trouble. I'd just listen to her without saying a word. After a couple of minutes into a monologue, she'd break off and ask if I was still listening. I'd say I was and off she'd go again, pissing herself laughing at my cheap and shitty banter. When she eventually stopped cackling, she'd place her order for the day, and even then, sometimes it would take ages for her to get off the line. But like I said, she never really got on my tits like she did with my brother. He was just too stressed to take small talk from a semi-senile, incontinent and dying old maid.

The thing is, after a few months of the delivery lark I got to thinking she must have been pretty fucking miserable and lonely to go through the same old shite every day. Imagine having no one else to ring other than the cunts who ran a corner shop in the middle of Shitsville. And we had enough to do without providing her with a twenty-four hour chat-line she could use whenever she felt a bit lonesome. I suppose it was either us or the Samaritans, and maybe that was why I started enjoying spending ten or fifteen minutes with her every now and then. Maybe I did it out of pity. And like I said, maybe I'd be just as bad when my time to start dodging the coffin came along.

My brother ended up hating her more and more as time went on. There were times when he complained he'd had enough of her fucking rambling, so he'd just put the phone down on her and refuse to answer it when it started ringing again. I had to admit, she did have this tendency to go on like that, but it was nothing I couldn't handle. Sometimes I'd just switch myself off once she got going and I'd let her get out of breath, start coughing, and soon enough she'd put the phone down all by herself. The only times she really pissed me off was when I was having a bit of a possessed session with my stuff. When I just went for it like a mad cunt and the words wouldn't stop coming out of me. I'd spend hours at it, but all the time I'd be hoping that the run wouldn't get interrupted by either a customer, or a phone-call from poor old Annie.

Annie got dead one day. And the next day my brother and I were locked up because they thought we had something to do with it. Funnily enough, it was the first time we were ever forced to close the shop. The only day we ever got off before was Christmas Day, and even then we opened up for an hour or two in the afternoon because we bored our tits off sitting at home and trying to watch the shit they put on every bloody Christmas.

As I languished in the cell on the night of our arrest, nothing seemed to matter any more. Not me, not my work, not my brother and not even the shop. Maybe, I thought then, spending a bit of time in a cell would show me a better glimpse of the other life I'd only seen fleetingly, when I was young, bold and naive. A different life from the shop which me and my brother had grown to hate over the years.

Not that the shop was all bad. You might think that working in a shop must be the most boring thing in the world, but there are things that can make it better. For one thing, you get to see a lot of life while you're scratching your balls behind the counter and waiting for people to come in and buy things from you. A lot of interesting people come into a shop, and believe it or not, shopkeepers soon get to become pretty fucking sharp social observers.

That shop was really what started me writing. Initially, I'd just write any old shite to help me speed up my typing skills for a course I was doing at college, but after a while, the bits of text that appeared on the screen would develop into something else. I'd hear a customer say something – anything – and I'd key it in. The next thing I knew, I was half way through a ten-thousand word story, triggered off by next to nothing. There were also many customers who were good people. There were the people we could trust with a few quid, and those we could trust with a little more. That's how shops are. Every shopkeeper has a few customers who are more like friends than customers and sometimes they make life a little more bearable. Like Jamie, the man's got a stomach that's always lined with booze of one description or another, but at the same time, the man's got a heart of pure gold. A heart that's going to get him killed one day. And the knife-man, Gillette, who can be something of psychotic maniac when he wants to be, but will help you out any day of the week with those special skills of his.

At the same time, there were some people who were cunts. Plain and simple. A bunch of fucking cunts. People you'd never trust in a million years. People like Big Joe, the cunt who'd sell his own mother down the river for the price of a wrap. And people like fucking Dominic, who's so out of his fucking head with sex, drugs and rock and roll that he doesn't even recognise his own fucking face in the mirror. People like Mad Colin, who'll threaten to kill you rather than pay you back the few quid he's borrowed for a couple of cans of Special fucking Brew. And Kilo – so-called because he went around telling everyone he smuggled in a kilo of powder every time he came back from Pakistan – who'll back you up to the hilt until it comes to the crunch. There's Mammo, who'll wank you off with one hand and stab you with the other. All bastards. Plain and simple.

Then there are people like Snowy, a 'decent' dealer, Hash Bash, another dealer who hasn't been around for quite so long but who I know to be okay because I went to school with him, and Jake, a middle-aged Welsh joiner who's been a regular and decent customer in the shop for longer than my brother's owned it. Jake's one of the few blokes you should never trust around here but you always end up trusting him because he's such a sincere sounding cunt when he needs to be. Then there's The Woodman, really into that 70s revival thing, but at the same time, a pretty strong anti-American, which is kind of fucked up because the only music he listens to is the stuff from America. He might be a fucked up piece of work but he's all right. He's known my brother for years, and if my brother says he's okay, well, that's good enough for me.

There are also a large number of people who don't fit into any category. People who aren't crooks, cunts or users. People who I like to think of as just friends, who I can hang around with whenever things get too boring.

And then there are people like Freddy. Frederick MacMahon. People like Freddy are the ones I'm never too sure about, the ones who can be dangerous when fucked with. Freddy was almost a friend, but he was just too crooked and unethical to trust in the same way I'd trust Gillette or Jamie, or even Jake the Peg, for that matter. But just one thing drew me towards Freddy. Books. He was one of the few people who I knew of in Manningham who actually read books. Seriously. No fucker ever wanted to know if you tried talking books with them. He even lent me *Catch-22* and we'd talk about it for ages while I was still reading it. Freddy read all sorts of shit and, at first, that was why I thought it'd be a good idea to let him see some of my stuff, just to find out what someone who was an experienced and varied reader would think about it. But I'll tell you more about Freddy and how important he eventually became to me later.

Of course, the only drawback with trying to write when you're in a shop is the fact that you tend to get customers, and being a shop assistant, you have to serve them. Customers and shops go hand in hand, you can't have one without the other, or it'd soon become a bit of a dead loss. But when you're trying to write and you keep getting these cunts coming in and throwing you off your work, it gets a little annoying. I hated being continually forced to abandon my work just to serve some old git who wanted a box of matches and then spent ten minutes picking his way through bits of tobacco, old half pennies and God knows what other shite he might have kept in his pocket for no particular reason. Why couldn't people like that come in prepared with their money, pay me and then bugger off out of it? Why couldn't those people leave me the fuck alone? It wasn't always that bad, but some people just seemed hell bent on ruining my day, as if they'd planned for weeks on end to find some way of fucking me up for a few minutes every time they came in.

There were worse, though. Not dangerous, but all the same, still worse. Those were the 'Pump boys' as my brother liked to call them, and they were a pretty varied bunch. There'd be the guy who spent all day at a building site mixing cement who'd come in for a copy of something to show the lads during tea-up, and then you'd get a managing director of some big firm somewhere who ogled his secretaries and made out as if he was the big player in the whole set-up and he'd be in your shop, looking for entertainment in the form of mags which specialised in leather, chains and all the rest of that freaky shit. The bad ones, the ones who fucked me about because they didn't get it over and done with as quickly as possible, or, as was often the case, walked out without buying, came in, honed in on the top shelf and started to annoy the fuck out of me. It was a shop. We sold things. People gave us money and we gave them the goods. We committed commerce. It was capitalism. We transacted. They paid their money and they took their choice. It wasn't a fucking showroom, but some of them thought it was.

It's a pretty shitty way to operate but you've got to treat everyone the same way in a shop because every fucker's capable of being a thief. I actually caught a few and just told them to fuck off and not to bother coming back. I was never one of those liberals who believed in all that softly-softly shit. I just know there isn't a lot you can do if you catch someone shop-lifting. Letting them off with nothing more than a wagging finger is just plain weak and calling the coppers is a bit over the top. So you mete out your own punishment. You mug them for what they've got before you finally go and fuck them off out of it. The bad ones usually come in and you watch them, because it's been known for these characters to casually slip a mag or two into their tan overcoat pockets on account of them being skint and desperate for a wank or simply because they'd rather not pay for the material that will aid their whacking-off session. It makes no difference to me because a thief's a thief regardless of what he or she's nicking because the intention of thievery is still there. You watch them because you have to, it's your livelihood, and you get more and more angry about them and the way they're ruining your display of top shelf material. Grabbing a hold of a copy with their grubby little hands, flicking through it and putting it back on some other, totally unsuitable shelf is nothing out of the ordinary for some of these wank mag enthusiasts. Like slapping wank mags on the same shelf as all the gardening or women's interest mags is the perfectly logical place for wank mags to go. Dopey gets, all of them. Some of them carry on for about ten minutes trying to memorise all the pictures of all those birds in a whole host of sexually explicit poses so that once they get home, they can get their dicks out and get busy with what they can manage to recall from what they've seen in the shop. It annoyed me because they'd walk out with nothing more in their hands than their dicks. I'd usually wait for them to get out before I'd start swearing my head off and I'd vow that the next time they came in I'd tell them it wasn't a fucking library. It was a shop, for fucks sake! The idea was for them to buy that shit. They weren't supposed to hire it free of charge. I could have throttled some of those tossers. But I never said a word to any of them. Fact of the matter was, sometimes the most unlikely-looking fuckers actually went ahead and bought that porno shit, and besides, you don't want to put people off by swearing and shouting at them, do you?

There was this one guy though, who really got on my tits like that. He looked just like the classic, model wanker. I mean, if you had a line up with a load of fellers and you were told that one of them was a wanker, you'd pick this guy every single time because he just fitted the bill so well, like it was all he'd been doing his whole life. He must have spent years getting that look just right so that when people would see him they'd think, 'Hang on a sec, I bet that bloke's a right wanker...'. The guy wore a green kagool, checked trousers, and those black-framed glasses with the coke bottle lenses. He also had this constantly fucked-up expression on his face, like he was trying to focus hard on something. He'd come in and scan the top shelf, then start to go through the mags. He'd stand there, his belly sticking out and his head in the pages of some Reader's Wives-type thing, staring at the photos like a fucking lunatic, holding the magazine only a couple of inches away from that mug of his, putting one hand in his pocket and having a quick tug when he thought I wasn't looking. I'd allow him to carry on doing that for a while, as if nothing else in the world mattered to him, before clearing my throat to get his attention. He'd stop, and turn to look at the source of his distraction. Only I wouldn't be looking at him any more, but it would be enough, because he'd get the message and put the mag back in its place and get himself out of there pretty bloody sharpish, which was just as well. Otherwise he'd have had me coming up behind him and looking over his shoulder and giving it ten to the dozen with the deep breathing. Wanker.

There were also plenty of other people who came in and couldn't make up their minds about what chocky bar they wanted to spend their pennies on. And then there'd be the silly sods who came in pissed up wanting to buy yet more booze and trying to look really clever in front of their giddy little pissed up girlfriends while they were at it. Like coming out with the odd 'paki', 'Punjab' or 'sabu' remark was the funniest thing in the world. Like try telling me something I haven't heard, you daft cunts! You'd deal with them all in the best way you could. You'd get them served and get them the fuck out of there as quickly as possible, which is a bit of a sin as far as your average marketing man is concerned, because the longer you keep the old punters in there, the more they're supposed to see, and hopefully buy. But sometimes, especially when I was writing, I just didn't give too much of a rat's arse about that marketing shite. I had other, better things to do.

get up, stand up

Up until the age of about fifteen, it always seemed to me that coppers only had it in for those people who messed them around, that colour or race didn't really mean anything and it was more of an attitude thing with the pigs. If you fucked them around, they'd have no problem giving you some back, which – even though I dislike the idea of siding with uniformed swine these days – was fair enough. A cousin of mine who was a plod over in Birmingham attempted to reaffirm this view. He'd joined up when he was about twenty and had been doing it for nearly ten years by the time he decided to drop some law enforcement pearls of wisdom on me. He'd tell me about the times he and his colleagues had had no choice but to fuck some people up simply because they wouldn't come quietly or because they were giving the arresting officers too much grief. The only thing that worried me, which I voiced with him one time, was what if some poor sod was innocent and the coppers were out there, gunning for him as if he was the Yorkshire Ripper?

"It's natural to protest innocence if you're innocent," I said, "I mean, who wouldn't be feeling pissed off if they hadn't done a thing and found a small army of these tits in blue accusing them of everything under the sun and generally fucking them around?"

My cousin started going off about the number of times that sort of thing didn't happen and how ace coppers were at doing their jobs. On the whole, coppers didn't hassle the law-abiding members of the populace, he said. The police were there to protect the innocent and all that shite that nobody, not even the coppers, really believes. He was just coming out with the stuff they taught him to say when people asked. But some coppers, I told him, had their own little secret agendas and swore by them. I was talking about real miscarriages of justice and what have you. My cousin didn't know what to say when I mentioned a few actual cases. As far as he was concerned, those incidents were nothing like what we were talking about because we were talking about everyday crooks. Thieves, muggers, pimps, drug takers and drug peddlars. The low life, the shit and the scum of this world were the ones he was concerned with. Above all, he rattled on about the fairness of the justice system and how, if suspects were indeed innocent, they'd be found innocent and no harm would be done to them. But what about the ordeal of arrest, I asked him? What about the stress of being locked up and awaiting trial? What about what family and loved ones went through as a result of the coppers being wrong in the first place? None of that stuff mattered as far as he was concerned.

"The police have powers to arrest anyone they want, any time they want, anywhere they want. You know that, eh? Did you?"

"No, but I say it's still full of shit." I told him, "What about bent coppers? What about coppers fixing stuff and getting away with it?"

"There might be some that do that sort of thing, but there can't be that many."

"That make it all right, then?"

"I didn't say that. The force has its own way of sorting out the idiots from the rest."

"Yeah, I bet it does. A slap on the wrist and a 'don't do it again', I'll bet."

"I'm not saying it's perfect, but what is, these days?"

"Perfection."

That cousin of mine was right about nothing being perfect these days, least of all coppers. I got a few smacks sitting between two of those fat bastards in the back of that very roomy Ford Mondeo squad car the night they arrested us. I wouldn't say anything, and that was why they hit me.

"You bin up to no good, then, eh? Eh? Nasty little bleeder, you, aren't you? Eh?" said the driver, who'd started the whole thing off.

No comment, pig.

"Not speaking, wog?" said his mate.

No fucking comment, pig.

"Cat got yer tongue, eh? Woggy-woggy!"

No fucking comment, pig!

"Chris?"

Chris duly obliged by bopping me one on the top of my head.

Fuck! It felt like the cunt was wearing a lead glove! Did that hurt or what? Made my fucking eyes water, it did.

"Still not speaking?"

Nope. Go fuck yourselves!

"Dave?"

Another one, this time from the fat bastard sat on the other side of me. It was more humiliating than it was painful. It's pricks like Chris and Dave you pray to meet down some quiet alleyway during the darkest hour of a dark night. What I wouldn't have given for that to have happened right there and then. If only Rod Serling and The fucking Twilight Zone would come along and happen to someone like me! I felt like killing them and I would have done if I'd been given half the chance, and if my hands hadn't been cuffed behind me. Those cuffs, digging into my wrists, were hurting like a bastard.

As I sat in the back of the car and did my best to ignore what the pricks were saying and doing to rile me, I wondered how my brother was getting on. It was the first time he'd ever had any real bother with the law. Not that he was a model citizen or anything, he was just good at not getting caught. My brother had a nasty temper, a streak a mile wide, which was why I was worrying about him. I remained silent when they tried on their taunts but I knew my brother would not be as passive. I'm the kind of guy who prefers a quite life, in all honesty. If it means being weak by saying nothing while being called names and everything else, then, so be it. I'll be weak but one day, I'll get you bastards back. One fine fucking day, you'll regret fucking with me like that. I imagined my brother giving them some of their own shite back, offering each one of them out and then getting a couple of cracks across the head for his insolence. That was all that I could think of and I hated myself for making this shit happen. Because, I thought, it must have been my doing.

The car my brother was in tailed ours. The driver of my car kept looking in his rear view mirror, smiling and telling his mates that the driver in the other car, Stevie-Boy, was being a right arsehole. Stevie-Boy was weaving about the road and trying to make out as if he was losing control of the car. These coppers, they sure knew how to make the most of this power they had. I turned around to look and was swiftly put back into position.

"Eyes front! Paki!"

For a few terrible moments I thought that Tahir was giving them some trouble. Even though like me, he was kept at bay with a pair of handcuffs, I imagined him to be wreaking havoc in the back seat of that cop motor. I imagined them giving him the same shit they'd given me, only worse, and Tahir getting really pissed and nutting the coppers by his side and then kicking through the gap between the front seats and making contact with the two pigs in the front. I imagined them, all four of the fat bastards, getting caught off guard and then losing a grip on the situation and that was why the car was swerving around like a dodgem on ice. And then, when they'd realised what was going on and regained their senses, they'd got even more upset with this suspect and started lacing the fuck out of him for his bravado. I feared for him and feared for myself, knowing I'd be powerless to react when I saw them drag him out of the car with blood, bruises and cuts all over his face. I felt bad knowing that he'd actually put up a fight until the end whereas I had been so fucking calm about it all. As if I should have expected this sort of thing to happen to people like us, at a time and in a place like this.

We were headed towards Central, the biggest cop-shop in Bradford, which was right in the middle of town and where the serious or more cosmopolitan and diversified criminals (the ones who operated all over the place which meant their activities were not limited to the attention of one particular area cop-shop) were brought. Town was quiet. But then, it was three o'clock in the morning and the only things you'd see if you were out and about at this time were lights; street lights, traffic lights, the driving lights of an occasional taxi flying along the roads and that special light from the stars and the moon in the rich Bradford sky.

I didn't see a single person as we drove along, but as soon as we got to the car park that led us into the major pig sty, all we could see were people. Well, coppers, actually. In and out of the car park they walked. It must have been change-over time for them and they were all looking thoroughly pissed off about something or other. Even the ones who were walking alongside a partner seemed to look as if they really couldn't give a toss any more. Maybe the ones who had finished had worked a hard night and the ones who were just about to start knew they were going to have a hard shift on their hands from the very off. I might think that coppers are bastards but it doesn't mean they don't have their off days and it doesn't mean they always have it easy. Even someone like me can accept that much. But none of that mattered to me right then. All I was bothered about was my brother and what they had done to him. And, I reckoned, he was bothered about me in the same way.

The two coppers in the front of my car nodded to each other and then got out but they did it in a way that intimated they'd done this sort of thing before. They'd done this thing all the time and they were now brilliant at it. Like this thing, what they were just about to begin, was just one part of the drill. They stood by the rear doors and opened them, one door apiece, like they were performing some weird ritual. Chris and Dave, sat on either side of me, got out without saying a word. I just sat there, waiting for their command.

"Out! Paki!"

The thing that these characters didn't realise was that for me, and very probably most young Asians, the term 'paki' didn't mean too much any more. All right, I know it's direct racism and all that, but I'd been hearing it for fucking years by the time these pricks had picked up on it and it was all too familiar to me, which made its effectiveness smaller and less significant. At one time I'd have gone apeshit at the very mention of such a term, but not now. These days, a name like that is old news and the only ones who ever make a fuss about it are the right-on middle class white liberals who think it a duty to make out they care and want to put the world to rights. These days you even get to hear young Pakistani kids calling each other paki this and paki that, so why should other people be so bothered about it? I suppose I'm the arsehole of the piece because shit like that does matter. More than anything else, saying things like that is just not nice. It's ignorance as well, I suppose. Most of the time people don't even realise they're being offensive and even when they are offending people on purpose, they don't know the meanings of the words they're saying. It didn't mean shit to me, but that just goes to show you how bad things are. Shite like that should mean something to me but I won't let it. Anyway, these pigs must have thought they were really getting me down by calling me a paki or a wog every time they got the chance. Like it would break my spirit or something. All they had to do was tell me I had bad breath and that would have worked a treat for them. I suppose it's kind of dangerous, me having such an attitude. Not giving a fuck about racist terminology and almost giving into it is something I should be ashamed of. Sadly, that's the way I am. One of these days the term 'paki', and hundreds of others like it, will cease to mean anything because that's the nature of language and the nature of people. Both of them have got more faces that the town hall clock and both of them are a million times more mercenary than I'll ever be. But those coppers weren't getting me down and they wouldn't get me down by being racist. If anything, trying to hurt me with their words made me stronger, so maybe I'm not as fucked up as I think I am.

I remained seated in the car, thinking. I didn't give them anything. No reaction either way. They could go fuck themselves for all I cared.

"I said out! You black bastard!"

"What?" I said, pretending to be dazed.

"Don't give me that shit! Get out of the fucking car! Now, y'little black…"

"Watkins! Over here! Right now!" shouted a new, strong and reassuringly honest voice.

"Shit!" hissed Watkins and stared at me as if he had the right to hate me.

"Watkins!" shouted the voice again.

I sensed something was wrong so I waved him good-bye which, hopefully, would really piss him off.

"I'm gonna fucking have you!" whispered Watkins.

I smiled but I said nothing. This Watkins, the one who had taken it upon himself to give me as much shit as he could, turned and walked over to the new voice and then followed its owner into the building. That was the last I saw of Wishy Washy PC Watkins. But I was going to see the new copper – the one whose command Watkins had jumped to – plenty of times.

broken stones

The car my brother was in had pulled up behind ours, which was when I decided it would be a good idea to get out and face whatever music these people had decided to play at us. The coppers who'd been chaperoning my brother went through the same motions my escorts had done a few moments earlier, but rather than asking, they just grabbed my brother and pulled him out. He looked bad. He was hunched over and he must have sensed me looking at him and then been lost for words. He lifted his head and I saw more of the same, blood coming from his nose and top lip, glistening in the night. There was a large and darkening swelling over his left eye. Slowly, he got out and he took even longer to straighten himself up. He looked at the coppers and then limped a couple of small steps. I could have fucking wept.

"Tahir! You all right?" I managed to shout.

My brother looked up and at me through his one good eye,

"Yeah, you?" he said without moving his lips too much.

"I'm all right, man! What they want?"

"Fucked if I know!" he said and then turned to the coppers again. "Bastards!"

"That's enough ladies," said the driver of my brother's car, "We can make this quick and painless or slow and painful. The choice is yours," he said as if he was some gameshow host asking us to pick a question card.

This copper annoyed me just as much as the prick called Watkins had but for different reasons. Watkins was a cruel and nasty bastard but this guy was different. A smooth prick who thought he could control people with his voice and manner. This guy, like all these pricks, was intent on thinking he was something special when in actual fact, he was nothing but a prick. Not even a special prick at that. The worst thing about this guy was the way he had given us that ultimatum. It was as if he'd been rehearsing the line all day and couldn't wait any longer to come out with it.

My brother looked at me and I shook my head. He'd had enough, and even though I'd had very little by comparison, I wanted no more. Easy living suits me every time and that was how it would be. As close to easy living as these pigs would allow, anyway. They led me in first and I could hear my brother follow. He was walking between a couple of those nice, considerate, coppers who were doing nothing more than keeping an eye on him. They didn't want anything 'unfortunate' to happen to either one of us, did they?

The sound my brother's feet made as he limped forward was as new to him as it was to me. Normally he was a solid walker, the kind of guy who made bangs as he walked through the world. Good, firm and solid steps, like he's got a purpose in life, like he wants you to know that someone's coming and you'd better get out of the way if you know what's good for you. But now his steps were pained and weak, hardly steps at all, more like the shuffles of an old and incontinent woman.

"You all right?" I shouted back as we walked along the corridor.

"Yeah. I'm okay," he said.

"Shut it!" a copper shouted.

And we did.

I stopped walking all of a sudden, like I'd just woken up out of a sleepwalk. I used to sleepwalk all the time when I was younger and sometimes I'd wake up outside the house, sometimes at the end of the street, sometimes waiting at the bus stop and every time that I did wake up, it felt weird, like I didn't know where I was and how I got there, but at the same time, I knew exactly what I'd been up to because I was the one who'd done it. That was just how it felt in that cop-shop. I just stopped and looked around before one of the coppers by my side digged me in the ribs.

"Move it!"

I was bent over, trying to get my breath back and speak at the same time.

"Why? Why? What the fuck are we doing here, man?" I managed to moan, in between breaths.

Then the answer darted into my head like an arrow. Bang! Straight in there out of nowhere. I decided then, that I needed to start thinking differently about the situation. That I needed to be ready for anything because something had begun and it was up to me, and no one else, to make it end. I took a deep breath and only then, did I really begin to react to the urgency of this phase. I got the gig. Now I understood. They were thinking we'd done something bad but they were wrong. We were innocent.

"We haven't done nothing!" I yelled and the copper by my side gave me another elbow to shut me up.

What the fuck was I doing here? Just what was it that I had gone and missed? People just didn't get knocked out of bed, get the shit kicked out of them and then carted off to a pig sty. I hadn't done anything, and neither had my brother. Especially my brother. And it was obvious now that this had nothing to do with the shop. And that must have been a relief for my brother. But still, it didn't answer any of the questions on either of our minds. There was no reason for us to be here.

Fuck! We were more or less model citizens. They had the wrong men, that was the long and short of it. That was the fact of the fucking matter but I figured telling them that wouldn't have done me any good and perhaps it was better to save that little detail for later, when they accused me of whatever they thought I was guilty of. Maybe it would have pissed them off some more if I'd started protesting again. Were these dicks going to pay for their foul up or what? I laughed then and got another belt in my gut because of it. Some of these coppers! Did these dildos really love to play at all that cop show shite or what? These wankers should have stuck to being security guards or whatever else they did before they decided on law and order as the career for them. Why? Because they were shit at it. Riots started because of divs like this.

work in progress – the will

He was sat on a deck-chair, in the garden one sunny day. Spread out on his lap was a newspaper, but he wasn't reading it. He was looking at it but nothing registered. He was too busy thinking to bother reading stories of vicars having sex with transvestites, cheats who did old aged pensioners out of their life savings and footballers who had dependency problems of various types. Other things were on his mind and that was a shame because the weather had turned for the better a couple of hours ago. A nice day but not nice enough to make him smile. Life was lousy and there was no getting away from it. Twenty-one years old and already, his future was sealed. A nothing he was and a nothing he'd stay for the rest of his life.

At times, he blamed his parents for this life he lived. They should never have had him if this miserable existence was all that waited for him. But how were they to know? All they were interested in was seeing miniature versions of themselves which they would make perfect through better upbringings than the ones they'd had. It was a mistake, though. He wasn't suffering from depression and the word 'suicide' had never entered his mind but still, he'd always been one to think he should never have been born. He was a realist, he used to think. His life was the way it was because of what his parents were. His parents weren't wealthy and that, he knew, was the key to happiness. Happiness was the only thing that mattered in life. Some found it, others thought they did but most spent most of their lives seeking but never seeing. It was money that made it happen, he noticed. People always said money wasn't everything but those people were usually millionaires. Money was everything and it could buy you it all, including happiness, love and even a longer life. However, knowing that was counter-productive because he didn't have any money and it never looked like he would. A job would pay him a wage but he wanted more than just a bloody wage. He wanted big, big, money. Money close to the size of a half decent lottery win. Something that would always be there, no matter how hard he tried spending it. Or at least, an amount that he could run away with. Enough money to give him a new lease of life. It was a dream and one that had been repeating itself over and over in his head for years and it would stay in there, still as a dream, until it became real or until he died.

He sighed and began looking at some of the small ads in the back of the paper, when next door's door opened. Wonders never ceased to amaze him.

Hussain looked up from the paper and watched.

It was a strange house, next door. It was the same shape, size and style as Hussain's dwelling but it looked awful. For one thing, it looked like the place hadn't been decorated in years and for another, the garden was used as a dumping ground by anyone who felt like it. It was the house that everyone turned their nose up at because of the way it looked. It brought the whole neighbourhood down, he'd heard little old ladies say as they'd walk on by.

Hussain and his parents had moved in over six months ago but they'd never seen anyone go in or come out of the house next door. As far as they were concerned, next door was either waiting to be inhabited or the inhabitant was an urban hermit. That was until she opened the door and shielded her eyes against the sun. It seemed, to Hussain, from the way she reacted, that this was the first time she'd seen the sun in years.

Hussain watched her and felt more than a little uneasy about what his prying eyes were showing him. She must have been ancient, he guessed. A few streaks of grey white hair combed across her head and a face that looked defeated, tired and haggard. Miserable, even. Her back was stooped and her fingers were all skin and bone. And her legs were even worse. Thinner than his arms and just slightly stronger than matchsticks. It was a wonder she could support herself with those two tan-tighted stalks but then, perhaps not. She couldn't have weighed more than six stones at the most.

She was struggling with a chair. She couldn't drag it out onto her doorstep where, he thought, she was preparing to sit and catch some cancer giving rays. Hussain was no saint but he felt sorry for the old dear. There was no one around to see him do this very un-Hussain-like deed so he got off his deck-chair, hopped the wall and landed in her garden as gracefully as a gymnast,

"Do you want a hand with that love?" he asked.

"Ooh!" she said and held her hands to her face in alarm.

"Sorry," said Hussain, "Didn't mean to startle you, there."

It seemed the old dear had frozen solid. Her eyes were wide open and her mouth remained O shaped. Her hands were still close to her face and Hussain could have sworn he heard her fart out of fear,

"Are you all right?" asked Hussain, doing his best to sound nice and honest, "You looked like you needed some help, that's all."

"No. I'm all right," she snapped, suddenly.

"Don't worry," smiled Hussain, "I'm not going to nick it from you. I'm from next door. I'm your new neighbour, love."

Hussain walked closer to her and held out his hand,
"My name's Hussain. We've never met before."
She looked at his hand and carried on looking at it.
"I don't bite," smiled Hussain.

hand on the pump

They put my brother in one room and me in another and I knew it wasn't just a matter of regulations or guidelines which they were supposed to follow. Splitting us up was a bonus. It was going to be their first tactic. I knew what would follow because some of my acquaintances had told me about this thing in the past. In some circles it was called the 'Prisoner's Dilemma' and in others, it was known as 'Catch the Grass'. The coppers would use this physical division, our separation, to work against us. They'd tell me my brother had implicated me in the crime, which he'd have done so he could walk free, and then they'd actually expect me to implicate him for my own freedom and also to get back at him for grassing me up. It was about getting both of us to collude with the coppers and to fuck each other over in the process. It might have worked if we weren't brothers, and even coppers and being forced to take part in their stupid fucking cop games would never change that.

I was alone, so I figured my brother must have been on his tod like that, as well. I suppose the guard on the door was there to make sure that us suspects didn't try anything funny like topping ourselves with anything that happened to be handy. A lot of that shite used to go on before they took to having these guards in place. Back then, there was a lot of talk about some of those 'suicides' not really being suicides at all. Stationing guards with prisoners was one way the coppers could show the world they were really concerned about detainee welfare. A thumbs-up to your local police force from me for their ingenuity in solving this irksome little problem. Well, you don't want little old dears taking you to court because their sons have hung themselves while they're in police custody, do you?

In all likelihood it's probably because of the way coppers go about their job that prisoners end up topping themselves in the first place. So they station an officer with the 'at risk' types, which if nothing else, makes the cops look good when it comes to counting numbers and producing headline-grabbing statistics. That's what things are about these days. You've got to reassure the general public any way you can. You've got to be seen to be doing things that make a difference. You've got to show people that you're really quite nice and considerate and not a bunch of bastards at all. Whether or not you actually want to be like that in the first place is another matter. It's the public's perception of the image that counts, that's all.

I waited in that room for one hour and twenty-three minutes for something to happen. The seconds I didn't count. At 4.49am the door opened and this huge fucking copper walked in, and like my brother, up until a couple of hours ago, he had purpose in his stride. No doubt he'd come to sort me out. That was okay. If nothing else, it would be company at the very least. He introduced himself as Superintendent Landiss, and his rank told me they weren't fucking around.

"Amjad Mahmood?" he asked and I recognised his voice from the car park as the one who'd called over Watkins. The one who sounded like he was going to give Watkins one hell of a bollocking for being such a prick.

"Nope."

"No?"

He sat down on a chair opposite me. The desk was between us and I was glad for the obstruction. I'd use it as a prop to aid my body language when protesting my innocence.

"No."

"Name?" he said, as he leaned closer.

"Yes, thanks." I nodded.

"Are you Amjad Mahmood?"

"No." I said again, through gritted teeth.

"You're not Tahir Mahmood's brother, then?"

"Yes."

"But your name?"

"Yes." I said and leaned closer to him, we were inches apart, "I have one."

I couldn't help it. I'd been sat there for the best part of two hours getting bored and worried out of my fucking head and in comes this cunt giving it the Q & A as if he was an angel of reckoning. What did this guy expect? For me to lick his balls as I answered his shite-filled questions like a good little doggy? He could kill my arse. Never mind him kissing my arse, they could all kiss my arse, whatever the consequences. Right then, consequences weren't on the top of my list, and anyway, consequences could be manipulated if you had the right way of looking at things. I couldn't have cared less who was there right then. I'd been festering and brooding over what I was going to say to the first person I saw and if it happened to be a superintendent cunt who was the size of Giant Haystacks, then so fucking what? And anyway, if it wasn't one thing with these cunts, it was another because they were always after something and thought they knew how to get to it. Like making you sweat for a while. The oldest trick in the book is making people sweat. You grab yourself a suspect, throw him in a cell and make him wait. Make the bastard suffer and by the time you eventually see him, he'll admit to the Great Train Robbery if you ask him to. That's what the sly bastards were doing, making me sweat, trying to get me to breaking point so when they thought I was ready they could just snap me in two. That would be when I was cooked. It would be over for me and this case of theirs would be as good as solved. But it wouldn't really be over at all because then they'd have me and begin to fuck me for real. Well, fuck them, I thought. I'd give as good as I got and on top of that, I'd remain like this – a pain in the arse, just to spite the bastards.

"What. Is. Your. Name?" Landiss asked.

"Am. Jad. Iq. Bal. Mah. Mood," I replied.

He sighed again.

"So you are Amjad Mahmood?"

"Never heard of him, man."

"I think I've had about enough of this," he said.

He was about to get up and do something to show me that he had, indeed, had enough.

"Oh, really?" I banged the table with the flat of my hand and he stopped. "You've had enough? How the fucking hell do you think I feel? We get knocked up in the middle of the night, and we get the shite torn out of us as we're forced into your bloody cars. For nothing. No reason, no explanation - fuck all. We get kicked to fuck on the way by a bunch of thick, racist thugs who pass themselves off as police officers and all you can tell me is what you've had enough of. Well fuck you!"

"I really think it would be advisable for you to calm down a little, Mr Mahmood," he said, still poised halfway between standing and sitting.

"I think that I've had enough of this shit. I think you owe us an explanation. Because this, all of this, is fucking bullshit!"

"I think..."

"Fuck what you think, man! Have you seen my brother yet? Have you seen what those fucking animals did to him? You know something? You pricks, you're worse than the fucking idiots you're supposed to catch."

"I think we're wandering off the track a little."

"Wandering off the track? What fucking track? You pricks wouldn't see a track if it came along and shagged you senseless!"

"I think this is getting us nowhere, Mr Mahmood."

"Just answer me this, have you seen my fucking brother yet? Have you seen what your fucking thugs have done to him? Why the fuck should you, anyway? You're all a set of racist bastards!"

"Mr Mahmood, please."

"What?! Fucking *what*? You seen him or not?"

"No, I haven't seen him. Not yet."

"Exactly."

"Calm down."

"You go see him before you come here and tell me to calm down, man. Get him a doctor or something, but make sure you sort that out first. Anything happens to him, I'll kill you all myself."

"A doctor? Does your brother suffer from a medical condition?"

"Yeah, you could say that. It's called a police force that goes around making people ill for no fucking reason. There was nothing wrong with him before he came into contact with that shite, man."

"I'm sure your brother will be just fine."

"You see him first. You go and see him before you come and tell me that he'll be just fine and then maybe you can tell me just why the fuck this shite is happening to us. You understand what I'm saying to you?"

"I'm perfectly aware of why this is happening. If I can explain..."

"Look. I'm not interested. It'll wait. You see him first, that's all I'm telling you. I think they broke his fucking leg or something, man. What the fuck are you guys anyway? Fucking Bradford chapter of the KKK or something?"

Landiss buggered off then, perhaps pissing in his pants because he might have a potential law suit on his hands. It felt great. Liberating even. I had just fucked them up with their own psychology. These lame pricks thought they could fuck me around just by making me sweat? That'd be the day. I'd show them I could wait until hell froze over.

I felt like I'd acquired some power, and even though it was a very insignificant and pissy amount of power, it gave me some kind of hope. I just needed confirmation that the pricks would listen to me if I pressed them hard enough, and maybe, if push came to shove, they'd accept my word, whenever it was called for and whatever it was going to be, without too many problems. So what if he was a Superintendent? He could have been the Queen of England in a horse-drawn carriage for all I cared. I was on a bit of a high, as weird as it sounds.

For another half-hour or so I sat around in that bare and depressing room. I ended up feeling pretty down about the place even though I'd planned on allowing nothing to get to me. It was just so bloody dull, so soul destroying. I didn't bother timing the wait this time because, initially, I thought he'd be back after a few minutes at the most. As the minutes crept by, I began to wish I'd let him tell me why I was here. At least it would have given me something to be going on with. At least I could have planned something to counter their side of the story. But I already had plans. Hundreds of plans and every one of them would have something to do with this. But still, I needed to know. I needed to be sure why both of us were there, rather than just me being there. Maybe I'd been an arsehole when I told him that I'd wait and all the rest of that macho shite. Maybe I'd gotten a little too cocky for my own good. I was always acting a little too big for my boots, my brother would warn me. One of these days, I'd bite off more than I could chew and then I'd see.

mama said knock you out

I paced the room for a bit before realising that guilty men always paced rooms in which they were confined before some smart-arse went ahead and proved them of being guilty as sin. And what's more, the copper who was on guard duty would see me behaving like a guilty man and then he'd go and tell his superiors. The pacing actions that only a guilty man would make could end up fucking me over and that'd be a tragedy. So, I stopped pacing and once again, sat down at the table, rested my head on my folded arms and hoped. Maybe I could get some shut eye if nothing else.

As soon as I did start to fall asleep the door was opened and in came that huge cunt of a copper, Landiss, again. He wasn't fat or anything. He looked like one of those blokes who took care of himself, maybe he was even one of those health freaks who worked out, went jogging and ate sensibly. He was tall, at least six foot four, maybe even a couple of inches taller and, I thought, his girth made him look even taller than he actually was. He was as broad as a fucking bus was this guy, but like I said, he didn't have a belly like most big blokes do. He also seemed older than he really was. He seemed to be in his fifties but for some reason I could tell he was probably only forty or so. He had a fair bit of grey in the short cropped hair that remained on the sides of his head. At least he was an honest man, I thought. He wasn't one of those balding cunts who grew hair on one side of his head really long and combed it all the way over a shiny bald patch that even a blind man could see. I hate it when balding people do that because they must think you're stupid. The great-baldy-cunt-cover-up. They must think people can't tell what they're up to, as if they actually think they can get away with what boils down to being nothing more than a cold and calculated lie. Anyway, Landiss looked even bigger in that navy blue/black copper's outfit. One thing that came across with Landiss was that there was no front to him like there had been with the pricks who'd brought us in. He looked, and came across, as a straight kind of bloke, which was nice. I thought maybe he might even be a fair copper.

"Your brother, he's all right," he said. "A doctor's seeing him right now."

"One of yours?"

"Ours?"

"A police doctor. One of your lot, you know."

"No such thing as police doctors, Mr Mahmood. There are only police surgeons, pathologists, forensics people and the like. No, the doctor who's having a look at your brother is a duty GP. He's got nothing to do with us. Don't worry about your brother. He's a strong lad."

Landiss nodded sagely at his own words.

"Strong enough for any one of your dogs, you mean? That is, if they've ever had the chance or wish to try someone one on one."

"If you'd like to make a complaint..."

"I am doing. Take it how you want, man. They're the ones who should be locked up! Why do you think people like me, young people, black people, poor people and anyone else who your lot have got a problem with, can't stand your lot in the first place? You think people give you lip just for the sake of it? Why do you think I feel like wringing every one of those fat fucking necks?"

"I understand."

"No, I don't think you do."

"Behaviour breeds behaviour, Mr Mahmood. I know all about it. There are always a few rotten ones in the barrel."

"Where have I heard that before?"

"I don't know, you tell me."

"Fuck it, man. It's a long story."

Landiss nodded again, and sat down.

"Okay," he said, spreading his fingers and staring down at the table, before looking up at me again. "Now. There are some things that need to be discussed."

He pressed his fingers to the side of his head, then rubbed his eyes. He looked tired.

"Oh, I see," I said. "Now you want to *discuss* things. That's funny, man."

"Is there something you'd like to say?"

"No, I don't think so."

"I gather you had some problems on the way here."

"Problems? Maybe. Anyway, who gives a shit. What difference does any of that shite make?"

"I've told your brother, you will have the opportunity and you do have the right to complain."

"Let me ask you something, man."

"Go ahead, ask away."

"You look like you're a reasonable kind of bloke, I mean, I don't know you or nothing, but you seem to be a bit better than those grunts of yours."

"That's very generous of you," he said. "I should be flattered, I suppose."

"It wasn't meant to be a compliment."

"No problem." Landiss smiled.

"No problem. That's rich."

"You were saying…"

"Okay, now, this complaints thing that you lot are always harping on about. Tell me something about it. Has anyone ever complained before?"

"Of course. People complain about other things in life, why not about the way they're treated by us? We are a public service. We're not above the law."

"Not above the law? Okay, how many of those complaints have been upheld? How many times has the party making the complaint come out on top? How many times, roughly speaking, has the verdict gone on the side of the complainer? That's what I wanna know."

"Well, from what I can recall."

"I thought as much. Any point in either of us bothering with this complaining lark? Shit, man! I don't even know why the fuck I'm in this place and here's me, busy talking about the ins and outs of police complaints statistics."

"You weren't informed?"

"Informed? Of what?"

"The reason why you're here?"

I spread my hands and shrugged.

"You mean to say you don't know? What about the arresting

officers?"

I shrugged again.

"What about them? If that's what you call them."

"Didn't they explain your rights? The reason for your arrest?"

I leaned back in my chair again now, growing more confident, trying to suppress a smile.

"I'm sorry," I said, "but I think you keep missing it. No fucker told me nothing, man."

"And your brother?"

"What about him?"

"Does he know why he's here?"

"I don't know, man." I said trying to sound fed up already. "They might have told him when they got him in the car. All I can tell you is nobody told me nothing because that's all I know. All I got was a bit of a battering as an explanation. A few smacks tend to answer plenty of questions and keep you quiet for a while, you know?"

Landiss took out a pen from his top pocket and started twisting it between his fingers. A pained expression formed on his face.

"Would you like to see a doctor?" he asked eventually, in a husky whisper.

"Look," I said, "what *is* this? I don't want to see a doctor, man. I just want to know why you're giving us all this shit. What the fuck have we ever done to deserve this? What are we supposed to have done? What are we supposed to be? Terrorists or something?"

"Okay," he said decisively, and climbed to his feet. "I'll be back in a couple of minutes. I have to speak to your brother."

Arresting officers? Arrest? They had arrested us? Is that what he'd said? That was okay, good even, because at least then I knew. I had hard information and that did help me get my bearing right. Now I knew, without a doubt, what I was dealing with. But what the fuck for? The bastard had only told me half the tale, but maybe that was still a part of the game-plan. It was getting scary but I wasn't thinking about myself. I was suss with the fuckers. It was my brother who worried me, because he was also involved in this thing. Landiss was coming across as the nice bloke and maybe that was part of the game-plan too. Maybe it was good copper first, bad copper later. Spill your guts to the good copper when the bad copper gets too much to handle and then get shat on by both of them for being such a fucking dupe. I saw my brother's face in my mind. Would he know what they were playing at? How would he react? Exactly why he was there would be a mystery and that was the real pisser about all of it. But at least Landiss seemed to be concerned about the way we'd been taken in, as if the formality of being nicked was important to him. As if it could make a difference.

Once, I'd never have dreamed of talking to a copper in the way I just had. I knew how they were and what went on in those things they called their brains. Try talking to a normal copper like that and you'll get a mouthful of fist in no time. That's it, end of story, because that's all they fucking need. Just one little excuse is justification enough for them to go to town with you. I had my own ideas about why Landiss had allowed me to get away with the verbal abuse, but then I had my own ideas about almost everything. Forced admissions used to go on all the time but there was nothing that was clearly being forced by Landiss. He wasn't the one using verbal or physical force but I was. And there was something else going on, another dimension to our little talk in the cell. It was as if he was letting me spout off so I'd go and put my foot in it and end up incriminating myself. I could have been a major criminal and anything I said, swearwords and all, could have meant something to him and his case against me. I would speak with hidden and sublime messages which would later be interpreted by some fucking head shrinker whose testimony would then end up being my downfall in a court of law. It could happen. Anything, so I'd been discovering, could happen.

Only thing that he didn't realise was that I knew the gig. I could play every misinformed, narrow-minded prick I came across and not one of them would be any the wiser. And besides, Landiss didn't know that I couldn't have put my foot in it even if I tried. I was going to be cleaner than Snow White's knickers, but I had a feeling they wouldn't see it like that. You have to expect the worst sometimes, and you've got to make sure your shit is prepared.

I waited for him to return. All the time, I was looking at the grunt who was now sitting on a chair by the door, staring right back at me.

"Something you need, pal?"

"Yeah," I told him, "I need a piss. Pal."

Landiss reappeared a good half hour later, with a younger copper at his side. Along with the guard there were now three and it was as if that was something they'd spent time calculating. I was outnumbered before and now there were three, and just that bigger number can affect some people. But not me. I was on to them and their fucking games from the off. In a way, dealing with these tossers was easy.

"Right," said the old boy, "we're going to have to arrest you, now," as if I'd been looking forward to it. Like he'd just told me some good news.

'Right, we're going to have to give you an hour with a bird who's got tits the size of water melons and who can suck an apple through a fifty foot hosepipe.'

"What?"

"You said you hadn't been arrested? You said nobody told you anything?"

"That's what I said, but…"

"Well, I'm telling you now," said Landiss.

He didn't give me the chance to say something that I hadn't even thought about. He was loving it. I could tell.

Landiss switched on the tape machine and started giving the tape player the works about who everybody was. Me, Landiss, Wilson – the younger copper – and Daley the guard. Then came the real shocker, the one that took my breath away as if some fucker had dropped a ten ton load on my chest,

"I charge you with the unlawful killing of Anne Potts," Landiss said.

Then came a silence which lasted the best part of a minute.

I looked into the eyes of Landiss, then Wilson, then down at the table. Eventually, I rose to my feet.

"What?" I said, eyeballing Landiss direct, as if nobody else was there, suddenly. "What are you on about?"

"Sit down, please," Wilson said.

I sat. I looked at him for a moment and saw that this Wilson prick was young. As young as me, if not, he was younger. I wondered what it was that made coppers become coppers. Was there something special that you had to have in order to become one? Did you have to be born differently or something? Did you have to be genetically and biologically predisposed to becoming a copper in the same way that some people are supposedly predisposed to becoming crooks? Or was it a question of upbringing? Was it how your parents and peers acted and reacted when they were around you that helped or hindered you to become an officer of the law? Was it nature or was it nurture? And did it really matter? I had nothing against the idea of coppers. In fact, they could be pretty bloody useful if you thought about it. If, for a change, they thought about it. But every time I'd had an encounter with a copper, not many if the truth be told, it had been a bad encounter leaving me feeling pretty bloody weak and useless all the same. The only time I'd been actually collared by a copper before was years ago and it was just like this. It was when I had done nothing wrong at all. When even thoughts of wrong-doing hadn't even entered my younger mind. Maybe that was how things would be for me, the guy who goes through life getting blamed for everything, the guy who's just got one of those faces that people can't resist beating the shit out of. That's how it felt at the time. That's how it feels when you're being picked on because, in all its simplicity, that's exactly what it is. Having said that, even a nazi fucker would have let me off the hook for what I got lifted for back then. The one who copped for me that day showed no mercy. He was a right bastard and that's another reason why I've always had this unreasonable hatred for coppers. I reckoned he just zoomed in on me and thought that he'd have that black bastard because that was the only thing that marked me out from the rest of the crowd in which I found myself. I won't go into what exactly happened but all you need to know is I'd done nothing wrong. That much was clear to anybody who was around. But this cunt, he just pulled me out and started battering me with his fucking truncheon. An hour later, I was in a cop shop where I got printed and warned as a first time offender. Like I was the one who kept attacking his truncheon and damaging it with my own blood and bone. Like I was the one who had been the fucking criminal. It was the last time I ever went on one of those fucking marches. I was only sixteen.

"I also inform you that anything you say can and may be used as evidence in a court of law at some point in the future. You may wish to have a legal representative present. If you cannot afford to appoint one at this time, you may wish to use the services of a court-appointed solicitor. Do you understand?" recited Wilson.

"What?"

When you try to make some sense of it all, and then, when you discover that trying to make sense actually makes even less sense, you kind of begin to get even more worked up about it than you already are. For a few moments, I didn't believe him or any of this. I told myself that this shit just wasn't happening.

"Do you understand?" Landiss asked.

"What?" I said. "I don't get this."

"Would you like me to repeat myself," Wilson offered.

"No. I heard you. But…"

Landiss shook his head, as if disappointed.

"Do you understand the charge and do you understand your rights?" he asked.

I was back on my feet again, shaking a fist at both of them.

"No! I don't fucking understand. What are you talking about? Who are you talking about!"

Landiss was up now, as well, placating me with spread hands.

"Would you like me to read you the charge and your rights once again?" he asked.

"No! Tell me what this is about. That's all I want to know."

"We're talking about murder," said Wilson.

"Do I look like a murderer to you?"

Wilson shook his head. Landiss frowned, then shook his head gently but he ignored me. Bastard.

"Look," Wilson, smarmy little get that he was, grinned. "You do understand English?"

That was funny, very fucking funny. It was so funny I could have got on the table, pulled my trousers down and shat for them.

Oh yeah, I understood English all right, too bloody well. In fact, I spoke and understood English a whole lot better than I spoke the language that was supposed to be my mother tongue. English had done its job with kids like me when we were growing up. Like everything else that was a part of the once great British Empire, the English language had found itself overtaking and replacing what there was before. What was original and what had been true for so many for so long was now rapidly disappearing.

I hated myself for being a traitor to my language but I always made a conscious effort to improve the few linguistic skills I had left. The few scraps of communicative ability I had managed to cling on to were nothing more than deflated water wings in a cold, uncompromising and vast sea of communicative deficiencies. Then, at times, I thought of the English language as a killer virus, spreading like wildfire and leaving nothing but itself in its wake, obliterating the languages that had been so foolish to even dare cross its path. It was ruthless like that because along with the language itself, the cultural baggage was also shoved onto the recipients, and most of the time, those same recipients didn't even know about it. But, to be fair, it wasn't all the fault of this killer language. Part of the problem were the new speakers of English. They themselves allowed this virus to thrive and spread. Yes, I spoke English, probably better than any of the pricks in this shithole of a place did, and what's more, I could write, twist and abuse this English like a motherfucker.

I learnt to read and write English before I even looked at those primary Urdu books or, for that matter, before the first Arabic alphabet, with its pronunciations and grammatical rules went and confused the shit out of me. I sang songs in English, I thought in English and I even fucking dreamt in English. I couldn't get away from it even if I was consciously fucked up enough to try and escape from its use. It was a part of me as much as it was a part of anyone else who said they were English. And yes, I understood it all. From the smallest of morphemes to the most complex of utterances. All of it was mine to digest and comprehend, and right then, I understood why I was in the cell. They were saying I killed someone. Someone who I'd only seen that day. Someone who I'd last seen alive and well. But for a while, the name they mentioned was just a name and nothing more.

regulate

They wouldn't tell me at first, they wanted me to be the one to tell them. It was all that cop psychology shite going off again which does get tiresome after a while. I mean, I showed them that I was shocked at the news of Annie, but the way they gave me their treatment was kind of funny. From what I could tell, they were treating it as if it was some game that kids play. They were playing by the rules of their own game but the trouble was, I knew the rules inside out, but I didn't want them to see any of that, because not letting them see was a rule of my own, invented game. They wanted me to come out with something useful so they could use that as incrimination. It wasn't working for them, though. I did my best to show them they had it wrong, they were barking up the wrong paki.

At first, when they mentioned her name, it was like some mistake they must have made. I was sure I'd heard the name somewhere, or something like it at some point in the not-too-distant past. Then, after a few moments of searching that mind of mine, they could see that it became clear to me. I knew everything then and they knew I knew but I allowed them to see that, because that was the natural thing to do. I was angry for a few seconds and Landiss asked me to calm down but I couldn't, because again, that was the expectation I had to fulfil for them. It was a performance and his requests for calm were as good as a load of *Encores!* and *Bravos!* from an excited audience. And I gave them more of the same and they seemed to love it. If only the stupid bastards had told me all of this, the important bits at the outset. None of this would have happened and I might even have been willing to assist the dozy bastards with their so-called enquiries if only they had been reasonable about it. It was their own fault.

"Annie? Dead? Shit. I didn't know her second name," I said after sitting silently for a couple of minutes.

"So you do admit to knowing her?"

"Of course I fucking know her, man. She was a customer for crying out loud!"

"How well did you know her?"

"Not very well, as well as you could know a customer, I suppose. Not too well but well enough to say hello to and that. You know."

"Anything special about her?"

"There's something special about everyone. Maybe even you."

"That's not what I meant," said Landiss.

"She'd been an actress when she was younger."

"That's a little personal isn't it?" said Wilson.

"What? Her being an actress? What are you giving it, man?"

"I meant you knowing that she'd been an actress was something personal."

"Well, she liked to talk. Liked to have a little chat every now and then and she told me about it, that's all."

"But you didn't know her too well."

"Not really."

They were such tossers. Stupid questions that just begged to be fucked over. I felt like telling them, 'Not really, I couldn't get to fuck her, if that's what you mean,' but that would have been seen as a bit on the sick side. With her being old and dead, I mean.

"But she told you about her youth. Why would she do that?" asked Wilson.

"Like I said, she could rabbit on a bit when she wanted to."

"But that's not the sort of thing people talk about, is it?"

"Depends on which people we're talking about, I suppose. Anyway, she did like to talk. She told me she worked with a few famous actor types when she was treading the boards back in her day. Maybe she liked people to know she wasn't just a little old lady."

"Anything else?"

"Like *what* exactly? You want me to tell you I killed her?"

I looked at Landiss and saw that he was staring at me.

"Did you?" he asked.

"Give me a break, please!"

"You only ever saw her in the shop, then?"

"No. Hardly ever in the shop these days. We'd deliver. She wasn't too well."

"Is that something you do for all your customers?"

"No. Not all our customers are ill. Not all of them need it."

"So, it was more of a special, one-off service just for her, then."

"Yeah, you could say that."

"But you still say you didn't know her too well?"

"That's what I say. Whether or not it'll make any difference to what you lot think is another matter."

"I just find it hard to believe that you couldn't know her any better than you say you did. If you delivered items from the shop to her, then she must have trusted you."

"She must have." I agreed.

"I just can't accept your statement."

"Which statement?"

"Your constant insistence on not knowing her very well."

"Well, that's just your tough titty, isn't it? Let me turn that around. We'd often be the ones who'd have to trust her."

"Oh? How's that?"

"When she was skint."

"So? She had a running slate in the shop?" Landiss asked.

"That's one way of looking at it."

"How much did she owe you?"

"When?"

"How much does she owe you now?"

"Nothing. She'd square up pretty quickly. She was like that."

"So she didn't have a running thing, like a lot of people do?"

"No, she didn't. She was quite decent like that."

"So why did you kill her?" Wilson said, suddenly. I'd forgotten that little toe-rag was there,

"Fuck you!"

"Don't make this harder than it is. I think it was you," he said.

"I'll tell you what I think Columbo; I think you should go fuck yourself."

"Okay," Landiss began again, with the old outspread palms routine. "Would you say she was friendly with you?"

"Yeah, I'd say that."

"And what about you? Were you friendly with her?" Wilson asked.

"What do you mean by that?"

"Just that. Would you say you got on with her? As far as customers and shopkeepers go?"

"Yeah, I'd say so. But then, you're nice to everyone when they're your customers. Doesn't do to swear and scream at them, does it? Or, for that matter, for you to go around and start killing them. That's not what you'd call good business sense, is it?"

"What sort of items did she order, then?" Landiss this time. Good cop, bad cop, I kept remembering.

"Cigs and booze mostly," I said, "sometimes a paper. A bit of grocery when she ran out, nothing too serious."

"You ever stop in for a cup of tea or anything with her?" Wilson, again.

"No, not that I can think of."

"Why's that? She never offer?"

"She might have done. I can't stand tea, and besides, I was pretty keen on getting out of there."

"Why?"

"*Why* he says! In case some bastard tried fitting me up, in case some tit thought I was in there murdering her! That's why."

"Really?"

"What do you think, Sherlock?"

"I'd advise you to state your responses clearly, for the tape," said Landiss.

"Okay. No. That's not why I never stopped in for a drink with her. I thought I'd just say it for a laugh. She had this problem, that's all."

"Problem?"

"There an echo in here or what? She had a fucking problem, all right? She was incontinent. I know I shouldn't speak ill of the dead but the place had an odour, you know."

"I see."

"No, you don't fucking see. Have you been there yourself, yet?"

"No, that's not my end."

"Well, you go there and you'll smell it for yourself and then I'd like to see you ask me why I didn't want to stop for tea and fucking biscuits."

"I see."

"Good, I'm glad you do."

"Who did her main shopping for her, then?"

"I don't fucking know! What do you think I am, her biographer or something?!"

"You were just a top-up service for her then?"

"Something like that."

"And how did you know when and what she wanted?"

"I don't think I'm hearing this right! Are you lot trying to take the piss or what?"

"Please, state your responses less ambiguously."

"You people, man, you're too much."

"Please. How did you know what she wanted?"

"And when?" Wilson asked.

"When what?" Landiss suddenly asked his colleague.

"How did he know when she wanted an order. I thought it might be important."

Wilson looked at Landiss expectantly.

"Yes, I see. Good point," Landiss said. "Can you leave us now, Wilson."

He tried to hide his annoyance, scowled at me, then turned abruptly and left.

"You people know what a phone is, yet?" I asked Landiss, now more confident. "Ever worked one of them new contraptions? They're really good you know. You can speak into it and your voice goes down a line and other people, with other phones, can talk back to you. It's great, you should try it. They're only ten pence a go."

Landiss looked at me. I sensed he was suddenly getting fucked off with the way I was taking the piss. But some of the questions, especially Wilson's, didn't even merit a response. I was trying to show Landiss how fucking stupid they were with the shit they were trying to lay on me. Interjecting my answers with a bit of humour might have livened the dozy cunts up a bit and showed them I was no pushover. I was no dumb fucking paki who they could bully around until they got what they wanted, and if it meant being a cheeky bugger to make my point, then I'd be a cheeky bugger.

They were coppers and they held the power, but it was up to me to use their strengths to my own advantage. I'd show them what I was made of. I'd show them what fuck-ups they really were and while I was doing it, I'd get my own back on a few others who thought they knew everything. I wasn't angry, I was just seeing the truth for what it was.

But alone with Landiss, things were different. As Wilson exited, Landiss looked at the grunt by the door briefly, before finally swinging his gaze over to me again. Obviously, he hadn't been very amused at me being a consistent pain in the neck. And I could tell his patience was now beginning to wear thinner than thin.

"So," he said with a deep exhalation, "she'd phone you. Only when she wanted to place an order?"

"Mostly."

"And how often did she place an order?"

"It varied. Maybe three, four, five times a week, sometimes every day."

"I see."

"Hold up. I don't see. All because a woman calls us up to place an order, that makes me a murderer then, does it? What about all the pizza places in the world? How come you haven't copped for all those guys who ride around on their little mopeds with a few boxes strapped on the back? I mean, that is what you're saying? That people who go around delivering stuff also go around killing people? How come you don't go around nicking all those people when someone else gets murdered, then? I mean, what is this? Some new theory you've got on murderers or something?"

Landiss didn't respond.

"Don't you at least think this is all a bit too much?" I tried. "I mean, it is a bit farfetched, even for you lot."

"We've got more than that on you," he said, simply, and I knew suddenly things were shifting up a gear.

"You'll need it," I told him, "because this, what you've told me so far, is bullshit!"

"We've got witnesses," he stated.

"To what, exactly? Me killing a little old lady? Me walking into her house with a sawn-off shotgun and a loudhailer telling one and all my name and address and leaving my calling card? Get real! I don't think so. You wanna know why? I'll tell you why, because it never fucking happened. That's why!"

"Maybe not," Landiss said, "maybe it was your brother."

"Go fuck yourself!"

"The truth can hurt."

"Bullshit, man! This whole thing is shit! This is a fucking scam, nothing else. Some cunt's gone and iced her and we're the only ones you could think of because we're the only ones who are handy enough to fit the bill."

"We've got enough to charge you and believe me, we don't go around charging people willy-nilly."

"Like fuck you don't."

"We're the police. We uphold the law."

"Where have I heard that before?"

"What's that supposed to mean?"

"Well, seems to me, that doing that, charging people willy-nilly and locking them up for half their lives is something your lot specialise in these days."

"That was a long time ago."

"The Bow Street Runners was a long time ago. Makes no odds to me man, can't get a leopard to change its spots."

"That's not what I'm talking about."

"I thought it was."

"Well I'm not." Landiss took a deep breath, as if bored, but determined to see it through. "You said she called you maybe once a day for an order?"

He passed over a sheet. It was a printout of times and phone numbers. The calls that were made from her number and for that day. There were five phone-calls in all, three of them to the shop.

"So? What's that prove?"

"You said she'd call you that number of times a week. She's called you that many times in one day. Something you forgot to tell me?"

"That's not what I said about her calling us."

"Oh?"

"I said she called for an *order* that number of times a week. Play the tape back if you don't believe me."

"The other calls?"

"What about them?"

"How would you account for them?"

"Let me see if I can explain this to you. She'd call once fairly early on, around about nine o'clock in the morning, just to see when a good time to place an order would be. Then, she'd call at the time my brother would have told her to call and that was usually about midday, sometimes one o'clock. Then she'd call again about ten minutes after her order had been delivered, just to tell us that she was grateful and whether she had or hadn't paid for her stuff. Then, she'd call an hour or so before we'd lock up for the night, between eight and nine, just to see what time she should call the following morning. You have to understand, she was a bit of a lonely old woman. I told you before that she liked to yab on a bit, that was what I meant. She wouldn't let you go sometimes."

"Really?" Landiss looked suddenly doubtful.

"Yes, really."

"We'll have to see how the rest of the phone print-outs match with your story."

"You do that," I said, "can I go now?"

Landiss was twirling the pen between his fingers again, looking at the table.

"No," he said.

"Why not?"

He raised a hand, then curled his fingers back around the pen, still looking down.

"We can hold you for as long as we want. This is murder. You've been arrested and you've been charged."

"This is bullshit."

"So you keep saying," Landiss said, finally putting the pen down on the desk and looking at me in the eyes. "Up to now I've heard nothing that makes me believe anything other than what we've charged you with. And, I think you should realise just how serious this is. We've got enough to substantiate our actions. We've got witnesses and we've got evidence. All of it fits. All of it points to you."

"Get a life, will yer?" I said. "This is real life, not The fucking Sweeney or something."

"I could say the same thing to you. We know it's you. Everything is falling nicely into place."

"You bang hard enough, you can make a square peg fit in a round hole."

"We don't have to bang anything. We're holding all the cards."

"This is bullshit! Witnesses? Evidence? Are you crazy?"

"No, we're not crazy. We have a witness who swears it was you. We didn't even have to press him. He knows you, and that means he can identify you, if we have to go that far."

"Oh, I see. So now it's a witness *singular*, as opposed to a million witnesses *plural*. And what did this witness, *singular*, see, then?"

"For now let's just say that he saw someone matching your description entering the house close to the time of death. That's enough, all he has to do is pick you out. And that's it, you're done, you're finished."

"All right. Lemme ask you a few things. How tall would you say I was?"

"Five ten, six foot maybe."

"Five eleven. How heavy?"

"Twelve, thirteen stones?"

"Thirteen two. Skin colour?"

"Well, brown."

"Brown. Good. Colour of hair?"

"Black."

"Right, then. There's me, five eleven, nearly thirteen stone heavy, brown skin and I've got black hair. You know how many other people there are around town who look like that? You think I'm the only one who fits the description that this fucking witness of yours says he saw? You're crazy if you think you can charge me with that shit, man. I mean, get fucking real. Do better. Work on it or do something, for fuck's sake."

"We're not stupid."

"Yeah? Prove it." I dared.

"Okay," said Landiss and leaned forward, "you have a car which has a registration number. Like everyone else, you have fingerprints. It didn't take too long to work out."

"Oh fuck! For fucks sake!"

Landiss must have thought it was over for me. That my expression was as good as a confession itself and that my career as a murderer was over with. How fucking stupid could I have been? I tossed my head back and I took in a long and deep breath. I needed to think this one out. I needed to get this shit right in my head before I told them what they thought I had just realised.

"Something on your mind?" Landiss asked eventually.

"Okay. I can explain." I said.

"Will it be good?"

"Yeah, it'll be good," I said, "don't you fucking worry about that."

He sniffed and supressed a yawn.

"Work out a decent story."

He said it like a challenge. And it was funny, when I thought about it. Stories and me, I mean. I'd been trying to work a decent fucking story for the last two years and up until recently, I still hadn't managed to do it. Not so that I could make a living from it, anyway. I laughed and Landiss suddenly shifted in his chair a little.

"What's so funny?" he asked.

"Nothing, man. Just what you said about stories."

"Oh? Why's it so funny, then?"

"That's what I do."

"What?"

"I try to write, stories and that."

"A writer?"

"I try."

"Anything I might have read?"

"'Fraid not, it's a hard game."

"I expect it is. Maybe you're just no good at it."

"Maybe. Maybe I'm as bad at being a writer as you lot are at trying to pass yourselves off as coppers."

dirty cash

I'd been writing for a good few years when it happened, when I made the break into the big-time, or rather, when the big-time made the break into me. It doesn't matter too much which way around it was, not with the way things are at this moment in time. Ambitious people will always tell you it's the here and now that means anything, and I reckon they hit that nail right on the head when they come out with lines like that. It's the result that counts and it's not how you go about getting it. The point is that it happened and, funnily enough, it happened because of this, because of what I'm doing right now. Because of writing.

I'm not going to harp on about all the disappointments writers go through, and won't waste your time with a blow-by-blow account of all the trials and tribulations they have to endure in order to be recognised as gifted people. From the start, that never really concerned me, and my initial motivation only really changed because of one person, who got me thinking and prompted my change of attitude. Forced me to devise a new plan, if you like. Thing is, from what I can gather about the few writers I do know, they're a bit too hung up on their work for their own good most of the time. They think the stuff that they've spent hours crafting away at is absolutely precious. They'd carve it out in stone if they could. There's no way they'd allow any bleeder to change a single thing about it, because it's theirs and that's the way it's going to stay.

That's definitely not the way I wrote, though. I just wrote any old bollocks in the hope that it would turn out to be okay and – who was to say? – might even have got picked up by a publisher or something. If some of the jammy and talentless cunts who have been published could do it, then why not someone like me? Other writers – so-called professional writers – insist that their work will remain as they intended it, and that's a mistake. One thing you have to do when you're writing is to compromise and adapt. You've got to give people what they want, not what you want. Money talks, but writers make out it doesn't and most of them think they'll get along fine without it. Suckers.

I used to think the old saying about there being a story in every person was true, but it's not. You've got to be able to tell a good tale above anything else. For most people it's persistence and a fair dollop of luck that makes anything happen in the world of writing. Being in the right place at the right time and all that shite does actually mean something if you're an up-and-coming writer. But that was never on in my case. I was persistent enough, but luck just never gave me a second glance. Not until the things I'm about to tell you about happened. Anyway, you know what they say about luck – sometimes it's better to make your own. So that's just what I did.

I had one mate who'd tell me all this cobblers about not selling out, about having faith in your labour and being true to yourself about it all.

"I seen this agent," he told me, "in London, right. All the best ones are down there, wankers round here. They don't know nothing around here, man. You unnerstand what I'm saying? Nothing, like, with a great big capital fucking N, man. Anyway, showed him my shit and he said he liked it, right, but said it could do with a few changes and all that sort of crap. Like here and there. The grammar and all that shit wasn't working for the guy, mixed tenses were making him wonder about stuff and shit. I just knew he'd come out with that shit, right? Anyway, the guy was prepared to offer me a retainer on the assurance that I'd do a bit of rewriting..."

"How much?" I couldn't help asking.

"Six grand. Told him to fuck off, man."

"Six grand?! You told him no to six grand? What the fuck for, man? You're fucking crazy! I mean, six fucking grand!"

Six grand? Six fucking grand? You'd have to be fucking crazy to let that go. If some bleeder had offered me six bottle tops as a retainer I'd have accepted them because it wasn't just about money. It was about being published. It was about the chance to finally become what you'd wanted to be for years. Back then, anything would have done for me. I just needed to be acknowledged, for somebody to tell me I wasn't just wasting my time, and that I wasn't as crap as other people were telling me I was.

"I ain't selling my shit out for him or any other fuck like him, man!" my mate told me. "What the fuck's he know anyway? You got to have faith in your stuff, man. You unnerstand what I'm sayin'?"

"Sure."

"You can't go round agreeing with them talentless fucks left, right and centre. You unnerstand what I'm saying?"

"Yeah."

"You can't let them fuckers tell you what to do like that, man. There's just me, and no one else but me, who knows what and where my shit is at, not them, man. All they're bothered about is a quick fucking make and it's me who loses out at the end of the day. A quick fucking buck, wham bam thank you mam! Unnerstand where I'm at on this? You dig what I'm saying, man?"

"Yeah, sure, I can dig that," I said.

Yeah, sure, like fuck I did. There he was, a guy who'd spent nearly five years on this one novel and he was turning down offers as if they came as regularly as the tides. If the truth be told, his novel wasn't that shit-hot to begin with, not as brilliant as he made it out to be, anyway. And all the time he was 'working' on this novel of his, he was being all so fucking faithful about it. He seemed to think that something a million times better than a deal like six grand in his hand was going to come along. You just can't afford to miss chances like that. The man offered him the money, and six thousand pounds is not something to be sniffed at. Especially when you were on the scrounge all the time, like this proud twat was. Six thousand fucking pounds is what most people would call serious money. Couldn't have been more serious. But no, that isn't the way you're supposed to think as a writer. It turned out funny because he told that agent he'd think about it but really wanted this autonomy shit written into this deal before things went further. He was a writer, he said, not some fucking painter and decorator who did as he was told. The agent listened and said he'd have a think as well. A few days later, the agent called this mate of mine back and told him to go fuck himself. And I had to laugh. Who in their right mind is going to offer some new writer six fucking grand and then take a load of shit for the trouble? I know what I'd have done if I'd been that agent – I'd have told him he could go fuck himself straight away, told the soft twat to go and find someone else stupid enough to pander to his egomania.

With a lot of writers, it's as if their work means more to them than just the money, as if money's not even an issue for the daft buggers. Like dying in poverty is a really happening way to go. Like being buried in a pauper's grave is the way to be buried these days. If it had been me? Of course I would have sold out. Who gives a fuck? Being noble and honourable with your work only goes so far. Being like that doesn't pay the bills, and even if you die and become famous anyway, it'll be someone else who'll reap what you sowed. The thing is, writers – real writers and not mercenaries like me – are actually kidding themselves, because deep down they actually want to sell out. They'd love to cash in, but they can't. There's this image which they believe they've got to be a part of. They have to think of themselves as writers first, and then hopefully others will think of them in the same way. The real deal with writers, though, is that they really want to be published. That's what it's all about and make no mistake, even those people who are dead modest and shy about it would love to be there on top of the best-sellers list, doing the book-signings, enjoying the fame and living forever. If ever a writer claims to be writing just for pleasure and that publication isn't something to think about, then that writer's a liar. That's why people write, to get published, to have their names on covers and to be talked about. To have status. And of course to get some money, but the status involved is the main thing. Modesty's all well and good, but what's wrong with a bit of honesty as well?

It was like this one time when another friend of mine, not a writer but a bit of a literature freak, told me about seeing other writers and hanging out at these writers' groups because she reckoned it was good to share ideas and views with other like-minded people. Sounded like a good idea to me, so that's what I did. Only thing was, it turned out to be a bit of a disaster. One evening I turned up at a school where a writing workshop was held once every two weeks. I was full of hope and ready to learn. I was raring to go but I got clamped straight away. Fucking typical. There were only three others there and they all looked like they were ready to top themselves. There was an old maid who was into writing this Sci-fi stuff, a retired teacher who looked like a fucking folk singer but was into poetry, and lastly, there was this fat bird with pierced eyebrows who was into some New Age bollocks or other. By far the most disappointing aspect of the evening was how they were so fucking paranoid about it all. I took loads of stuff that I'd written for them to see, thinking the only way to have a view about a piece of writing was to actually read it, or at least listen to it. I thought the sharing experience would actually mean something to these people. But it wasn't like that at all. It was, as far as I was concerned, a total waste of my time. These other three comrades of mine just sat there, talking about what books they'd read, what films they'd seen and anything but their 'work'. This workshop they were a part of was just a chance for them to get out and have a little chin-wag. It pissed me off no end. I could have done that with some of my mates any time I fancied, and it would have been a better laugh than with those dead-beats! I couldn't fucking believe it. I felt like a fucking sap. I felt conned, and no one likes to be conned.

Anyway, after no more than ten minutes of being there, I got the gig. I got the vibe that they were kind of worried about sharing any of their blockbusters-in-the-making in case one of their ideas got nicked. That was what it boiled down to with this trio of writers. This little crew were dying to tell each other about their ideas but they couldn't. Their 'work' was just too precious to reveal until it was in the book shops. Total wankers. Discussing creative writing was the whole point of these workshop trips but someone must have forgotten to tell these tossers. I was pretty pissed off about it, I mean, who gives a fuck about their stupid Sci-Fi, poetry and New Age cakka? People want to see my stuff? I show them, and then some.

This same lass I knew also told me about all the free books and magazines I could get a hold of simply by being a writer, or at the very least, by pretending to be one. So I got in touch with a number of writer's workshops, arts boards and even libraries and got myself put on all the mailing lists. I thought it might give me an idea of what all the fuss was about, but of all the publications I got, only one of them was of any note, and that was only in places when the guy who was editing it must have been feeling pretty brave and/or inspired. But that magazine, for all its simplicity, led to the one great thing that got me here and now.

It was printed in Yorkshire and it was supposed to encourage new writers to write and that was me, back then, a new writer needing encouragement to write. So, that's what I did. I wrote some stuff, showed it around to some friends and after a few laughs, a few words of advice and a few alterations, I was done. The job was a good one. It felt great when I dropped the envelope through the post box at the end of the road because it was the first thing I'd ever written with the express intention of having it published. That was when I became a writer, I suppose. I stopped writing for a laugh and I became a serious, career writer. But I promised myself never to have any hang ups about my art, my life and my fucking 'work'. I'd write and that would be all. It felt good because it was the first time I knew what I really wanted to do with my life. I could be a writer, I told myself, any fucking day. On top of that, I wanted to say something and be heard. When I thought about it, it was me.

What I sent to the magazine was a short story about a kid who keeps bumping into things. Not on account of him being short-sighted or thick or anything, but because he was possessed by a spirit that was pissed-up all the time. It was okay, and the few people who'd read it thought it was funny and worked quite well. Even I, the eternal pessimist, thought it wasn't too bad. It was better than some of the shite I'd seen printed in this magazine for up-and-coming writers, anyway. Miles and fucking *miles* better.

About two months later, I got the reply back in a big brown envelope. And along with all the shite I'd sent was the 'Don't call us, we'll call you,' sort of bollocks. I was prepared for the worst and that's exactly what I got. Still, I wasn't too perturbed. A small setback, if that. I carried on reading this magazine every month and soon got to thinking that maybe it was a bit too arty for me, after all. Some of the shite they printed was just plain fucking awful. Some of it I couldn't even understand because the bloody stuff was written in foreign languages like Eskimo, Swahili, Esperanto and stuff, the kind of languages you hear everyday in a place like Yorkshire. It was also a bit of a con because it claimed to be an outlet for new writers but what did the pricks who ran this magazine go and do? They printed the work of published authors. What the fuck was all that about? I didn't get it. What was it? Were they trying to say published authors were new to writing? Were they suggesting published authors wrote novels, got published and only then decided to have a go at being writers for real for the first time? Was that why it was okay for these pretend new writers to be published in magazines like the one that had turned me down? It must have been and it must have been me who had suddenly misunderstood plain English.

They might have been a bunch of lying bastards but I never got down about it and I never gave up. Perhaps they were right. Perhaps that first offering I sent them was simply shit. So I wrote some more stuff, and this time, even though I say so myself, it was fucking brilliant – crisp, clever, and boy did it say something. It was all about being a rejected writer, how it feels, what you'd say to the cunt who's fucked you off and that, and in a way, it was kind of poetic. I read it over and over again, pissing myself laughing every time I got to the funny bits. That's what writing can be like when you're on a high, when you think you're on a high, anyway. I knew that I was having a bit of a go at this editor guy who'd rejected me, but to kind of gloss over that I figured it'd be nice and polite if I wrote a covering letter explaining to him that it was nothing personal, that it was inspired by life experience and all that shite. I also sent along a few segments from a couple of other stories I'd written in between, because that's what they liked to do in that magazine – stick in a few pages from a novel between the self-contained bits of Esperanto prose.

It didn't matter. It could have been something old Billy Shakespeare himself would have been proud of, but this editor guy still wouldn't have printed it. If the next Nobel Prize winner for literature had allowed me to put my name to his stuff, I began to think, this editor guy would still have fucked me off. Rejection was much worse the second time around, because I'd committed the cardinal sin for pessimists – I had become hopeful. I knew the stuff I'd sent should have been printed, that it was good and pretty bloody worthy material. To get over it, I decided it would be better if I forgot about that editor and his pissy tuppence ha'penny magazine forever. I told myself I wouldn't wipe my arse on his so-called publication after that. Why did I take it so badly? I'll tell you why. Apart from being rejected not once but twice, it was simply the abruptness and the tone of the reply. It was like this editor guy was really pissed off at me for wasting his time with the stuff I'd written, like that was the best way to encourage new writers to write. For ages I'd think about this editor guy and why he'd done that. Why he made me feel so fucking guilty and ashamed about being such a shite writer. That was what he was trying to tell me, I thought. There were no words of encouragement, no acknowledgement, no nothing. Just a nice and short 'fuck you' letter for my trouble. I wondered how many other people he'd destroyed like that and it made me hate him more. Pretentious, poncey bastard that he was.

For a long time I imagined him to be like this little fat bloke out of a film I'd seen called *Deliverance*. It starred Burt Reynolds and a couple of other half decent actors and it was a pretty good movie, as I recall. It's all about these three or four guys out on a hunting trip who start being hunted by these rednecks. At first it's just a bit of a laugh but it gets pretty serious as the film progresses. There's a scene, a downright nasty scene in fact, that I always used to place myself and this editor guy in. The little fat guy gets caught by these rednecks, and with him being little and fat, they kind of take the piss. One of them sits on his back and makes him crawl around, shouting "Squeal little piggy!". The little fat bloke's crying because he's being humiliated with what these redneck boys are doing to him. There are serious sexual undertones in that scene which is probably why it's so disturbing. You think about all the things that could have been going through the little fat bloke's mind. And that's who that fucking editor would be. The little fat bloke out of *Deliverance*, and I'd be riding around on him, whipping him and telling him to squeal like a little fat pig.

Nothing was too bad for that bastard of an editor. I mean, it's the kind of shite that puts people off whatever they happen to be into for good. If some fucker like him had gone and told Bob Marley he was shite, the world would be a sadder place for a lot of people. If some miserable bastard had told Cassius Clay that he couldn't box for shit, thousands, maybe even millions of us might have missed out on a hero. There was no need for people to be like that. All I wanted was for him to be nice about it. It wasn't as if I was asking the bastard to let me fuck his wife or anything, was it? What hit me worse was that I knew my stuff was good. And here was this bastard, a cheap fucking editor, telling me that my stuff was shit! He couldn't write for himself, so he went around doing the next best thing which was telling other people how to write. The nerve of the bastard! Just who the fuck did he think he was? I told myself I'd show this bastard what a writer was capable of. I promised myself I'd do something that would show him exactly what I could do, if and when I put my mind to it. That's how it began. And in some ways, I suppose I should thank that cunting editor for pushing me to do what I did. But I won't. He doesn't deserve it.

Well, that doesn't matter too much these days, but (and it's a pretty important BUT right now) before I go any further, I'd just like to say a couple of things, and it's all in capitals, because I'd hate for the person it's intended for to miss it, KISS MY FUCKING ARSE YOU NERDY GET! WHO'S LAUGHING NOW, CUNT??!!

you're gonna get yours

To start at the beginning would take too long. So, I'll start from where I left off. I'd written a few stories, novels I suppose, and they were all kind of samey, kind of okay but nothing too wonderful. You'd read them if you had to. If someone put a gun to your head and commanded you to read the fucking things you'd feel obliged to read them but you wouldn't go out of your way and buy them. And that was the name of the game for me, back then. Producing something that Joe Public would go out and spend his hard-earned money on was the objective. I wanted to be published. I'm not denying it and it's nothing to be ashamed of. That's the idea when you're writing but a lot of writers shy away from it as if even mentioning success and writing in the same sentence is a sin.

I got put off sending my stuff to agents and publishers after that initial rejection from the editor guy who didn't know shit. He was nothing more than the editor of this crumby little freeby piece of shit magazine that had a circulation of about twenty. But, I thought, if he wouldn't take to my shite, then what would some big-time publisher or agent think of it? What kind of chance would I stand when I got into bed with the pros and the big boys? None. That's what I thought. But I wrote nevertheless. Every fucking day I wrote. And although writing always made my day a little shorter, my day became infinitely more worthwhile.

I was buzzing back then. Ideas and inspiration would come to me in waves. Sometimes, I'd have too many ideas at once. The result was I'd crudely finish something off in order to start something new. It felt as if I was killing something whenever I did that and I always felt as if the stories deserved a better way to end. But I never felt bad enough to go back and give them fair and proper endings because I was just too impatient to be so honourable about my work. As far as I was concerned, once one was over and done with, it was buried.

But there was this favourite story of mine and I was sure it was good enough for the attention of some professional agent or publisher. This time I vowed, I was going to do the thing right. I had a plan. I was going to aim high and if I fell, well, that was just going to be tough shit and I'd have to get up and start all over again. I thought it would be better if I showed it to a couple of friends before I sent it off, just to be sure that it wasn't only me being too involved with my work, and that others, at least two or three, actually liked it as much as they liked anything else that they'd have spent money on.

right here, right now
part two - television, the drug of the nation

My brother's been getting a bit bored lately. He's got this stall in
the bazaar that sells anything he can get a hold of but it's not
enough to keep him happy all the time. He gets on with the
people, and unlike me he's more or less fitting in. Pretty soon, he'll
be like a native and he'll go round slapping people on the back and
talking to them as if he's known them all his life. It's when he gets
home that he starts moaning about not having anything to do on a
night. I don't suppose being a shopkeeper was ever really him. I
think he did it because he thought there was nothing else he could
do. That's why we aren't too different – he used to think he was
born to be a shopkeeper and I used to think I was born to lie and
do what I now do for a living. Anyway, he's been thinking about
buying a telly to while away the evenings but I think it's a bit of a
waste of time. There's fuck all worth watching, from what I've
been told. There are only one or two local channels in Pakistan,
which to be honest about it, is just not good enough. We need
more than that to satisfy our Western, spoilt palates.

But, he argues, there's always satellite telly to rely on. It might
cost a few rupees to set up but it should be worth it. You can
watch everything you can watch over in England. Music channels,
movie channels, comedy channels, sports channels, porno
channels. If you've got enough money, you can get the fucking lot
over here. You can help make Murdoch even richer and I'm not
too keen on giving that bastard a bit more control in my life. Just
goes to show you, though, you can't get away from bastards like
that, even if you travel half way around the world. Maybe those
media magnates are the new leaders, power-mongers, creators and
destroyers of the world or maybe it's just me being paranoid again.

I don't get bored like my brother, though. I do as I please and
things are okay. I've started going to sleep a lot later than when we
first got here. Some nights I don't sleep at all because I can't. I like
to think it's the heat but I know it's not. So instead, I sit at the
computer and I write, like some obsessed fuck-up who's got

nothing better to do with his time. And sometimes, I fall asleep as I'm working, only to wake up after another dream. Usually it's about Annie, and sometimes it's about me. I keep telling myself that it'll pass but I'm not too sure any more.

I've started working on another story but this one's different because it's all fiction and even if it doesn't work I'll be okay with it. It's about time I started changing my image, about time I started fulfilling the title of writer that has been bestowed upon me by my publisher. It's about time I started lying only on paper and not lying about reality. It's about time I made things change for the better.

I got a call from Gates earlier on this afternoon. He said he's going to send me some press cuttings. There'll be some reviews of the book, most of which have been OK and he'll also send me some papers to sign; trivial stuff, he says. He said he'll send me some theories about the book, some of which are right on the money and some of which are total shite and he said he'd throw in a couple of tabloid pieces about me and what people 'allege' about me. He didn't have to tell me that Freddy was throwing in his testimonies because I always knew Freddy would be in there like a rocket as soon as the chance came along, trying to make a few quid for himself. It's all good stuff, says Gates, plenty of fuel to keep that fire burning. There might be a couple of law suits for libel in there somewhere but the best news was that the book's still selling like mad. And that, as I've always said, is the name of the game if you want to pass yourself off as a writer.

He's also got some other legal shit for me to sign. Apparently some film production company somewhere is keen on rights to the book and they want me to do them a draft of a script. They'll pay me even if the whole thing falls flat on its face. Gates is really something else. Gates is the smoothest, sharpist bastard I know and I'm glad he's on my side. He told me back then, when he first said he wanted to represent me, that it would be a good idea to work on a dramatisation but I didn't bother because I honestly thought he was pulling my pisser and making this thing sound bigger than it actually was. And now that it's really happening, I don't know where to start. I've never even seen a fucking film script before but I'll ask Gates to send me one of those 'How to write for film…' books from Smiths and I'll give it a go. It's all money in the bank and, according to Gates, it's also about keeping my career alive. If I didn't know any better, I'd say Gates and Don King were two peas out of the same pod. But that's okay because I'm no Muhammad Ali or worse, Mike Tyson, so I won't let Gates fuck me over. Gates reckons he knows the gig better than anyone. He's wrong, though. I know the gig because I made the fucking gig.

work in progress – the will

Her name was Madge. Chris, a recently retired postman, was Hussain's other neighbour and he knew everyone in this street and he knew all their stories. Chris had lived in this street for most of his life and he'd seen people move in, move out, get born and get dead. Chris told him all there was to know about Madge. It was sad, but what could you do? Her husband, Geoffrey, had died a couple of years ago and since then, she'd locked herself away behind that door and never came out. They never had kids, and as far as Chris could tell, they never had visitors. Even when her husband was alive, they were compact and lonely people. Always kept themselves to themselves but never bothered anyone, either. It was funny, but Madge had been here, in this street, for as long as Chris but she was the one person he knew least about. A bit strange, was that, said Chris, now that he thought about it.

But, Chris reckoned, her husband dying on her seemed to have made her an even greater recluse than she already was. Personal grief was something that we all had to encounter at some point in our lives but there had to be a time when the grieving stopped, lectured Chris as if he knew about these things. And she did have plenty to look forward to, winked Chris. She had money did the old dear, Chris told him. Her husband had been a working but wealthy man all his life and, from what he had heard, all he did was bank most of it. On top of that, he had life insurance policies and when he died, Madge got everything. She must have been worth a fortune. Chris didn't mean to sound so callous about it or anything but she should have done something to cheer herself up a bit. Locking herself inside the house and doing nothing for the rest of her days wasn't necessary. She should have done all the things she wanted to do. She should have spent all her money because, when she died, it would all go to the state because there was no one else who she could leave it to; she had no children, no relatives, no friends and she didn't even have any pets. It was sad, said Chris and Hussain couldn't help but to agree. Such a shame all that money would go to the waste when she died.

express yourself

"You said you were going to explain," Landiss prompted, eventually.

I looked up from the table at him. Somewhere out in the corridor some pisshead was singing an old Madonna song.

"Okay," I said. "Time of death, about one-thirty, maybe two o'clock. Am I right?"

"Something like that."

"And there'll be prints all over the place, on the door handle, on the phone table, that sort of thing."

"Go on."

"I bet you've even got some fibre samples and all that forensics shit. You don't need any of it, you know. I can tell you what happened. I suppose I should have told you but I didn't realise. I didn't think."

"What didn't you realise?"

"Not that you asked me before, but I was there all right."

Landiss didn't say anything, but his expression was urging me to continue.

"I went to deliver an order to her yesterday. It was about oneish, maybe quarter past or something. Come to think of it, I bet I even know who the witness is, as well."

I closed my eyes allowing my mind to replay the events of that fucking day. Only one person could be the witness. The witness was our Freddy. Freddy 'the ape' Fuckwitt, the biggest sleaze outside the Tory party and it was just like him to fuck you over while you were thinking he was the best thing since sliced bread. I knew he'd had something to do with this. Freddy Fuckwitt was an amalgam of many things: thief, fraudster, a user who used anything to get himself off, not a very effective piece of hired muscle and most of all, one of Manningham's biggest grasses. Anyone who was anyone in Manningham knew the gig with Freddy but nobody ever said anything because, I suppose, he was small time and no one could ever really prove anything with that cunning cunt. He was more slippery than an eel coated in oil slipping around in a bucket of piss, was Freddy. Just my fucking luck he lived a couple of doors away from Annie. Just my luck he happened to see me go in that day. Just my luck he was bound to spill the beans. Just my fucking luck!

But if he saw me go in, then maybe he also saw me coming out again a couple of minutes later. Maybe that was something they hadn't bothered asking him about, because having a witness who saw me go in must have been enough for them. And maybe Freddy Fuckwitt, slime that he was, had no intention of telling them anything as useful as that, either. Freddy and me got on most of the time, with us sharing the thing about literature but only a while ago, we had a major disagreement, a serious one that couldn't be easily rectified. It was the only time I'd ever completely flipped over anything.

Stealing some nipper's Christmas pressies is not my idea of a decent way to make a living and 'decent' was what Freddy professed to be as far as his participation in the world of crime was concerned. It was all well and good buying bent gear off the backs of lorries, but actually buying something procured from some poor sod's house was another matter altogether. That was bad. Only the really shit and lazy crooks went for jobs like those because they were so fucking easy and just so fucking cheap. Robbing people's houses was like hurting your own. My argument was simple and I thought it was justified. Freddy, fuckwitt that he was, disagreed, and I had called him a fucking hypocrite. Still me saying that never really affected either of us when we were dealing or simply in the company of each other. He knew what I stood for and I knew what he was about and we simply agreed to disagree. Until he fucked-up and got himself hurt. Until I hurt him because of what he'd done to us. And that was why he had made it his mission to get his own back on me. I had damaged him. Humiliated him and fucked him over as if I was some fucking gangster. Still, I had no regrets about doing what I did to him. It needed to be done. That's all I could say on the matter.

"You may or may not know the identity of our witness," Landiss told me. "That's not for us to worry about."

"I'll tell you anyway." I said like I was some smart-arse, "Freddy Fuckwitt, I mean Freddy MacMahon."

Landiss said nothing.

"Like I said, I did visit her yesterday," I continued, "and I even saw Freddy standing across the road, outside his yard. That's who your witness is isn't it?"

It was just like Freddy to give you a smile and wave at the same time as he cursed you under his breath with everything that he could muster. I was aware of Freddy and how he must have been scheming of some way to get back at me for giving him a new face and then slandering his name all over the place (yes, he's a bit of an Elvis fan is our Freddy). I knew he'd do something to make things equal once again and, when I thought about it, I could have done something to cover myself, but I never did. Sometimes, you just had to let things roll.

"I can't divulge that information," Landiss replied.

"Fair enough, but he's not the most credible guy in the world is he? Not with a record like his, he isn't. Anyway, Annie phoned us earlier on in the day for her order. What was it, now? Bottle of booze – a half a Bells – twenny Bennys, and a paper, *The Sun*. That's what I took her and that's all there is to it. She paid me and I left. The whole thing couldn't have taken more than a couple of minutes."

"That's it?"

"That's what I said."

"Nothing in between?"

"Nothing."

"Can you prove that?"

That was the big word. Prove. That was the bugger about it. I mean, people didn't go around bumping off little old ladies for the fuck of it. Annie was a customer and I was simply one of her delivery boys. Why would I, of all people, kill her?

"I can't prove anything," I said, "but then again, neither can you. Can you?"

"I think the CPS might hold a different view to that."

"This can't be happening. This isn't right. You can't say I killed her like that."

Landiss was watching me keenly, as if trying to assess the authenticity of my performance.

"Have you got anything more to say?" he asked, eventually.

"I don't know. I don't fucking know! What can I say? It's shit."

"That the best you can do?"

"Just stop and fucking think for a minute, will you?"

Landiss closed his folder, put the pen in his top pocket and looked at me intently.

"You'll be up in Magistrates in the morning," he said.

"Hang about! What about a fucking solicitor?"

"You waived your right to one."

"No I didn't! When?"

"When I read you your rights."

"Bollocks like! You never said nothing about no solicitor."

"I can play you the tape back if you like."

"You bastards! You really have got it in for me, haven't you?! Well, let me tell you something."

"Please do."

"You're gonna be *so* fucking sorry about this. This whole fucking thing just smells of shit! You guys, you're supposed to protect the innocent, not treat them like this. You're not supposed to keep on fucking them over until they submit."

"As I said, I can play you the tape back, if you like."

"No, there's no need. This is still bullshit, though! That's all. This is a fucking joke, man!"

"I'll see you in the morning, if you're still here."

Landiss got up.

"What about my brother?"

"What about him?"

"Why's he still nicked if you're charging me?"

"Are you saying you did it?"

"Fuck you and fuck these stupid games of yours! I'm sick of it!"

"Was it you?"

"No. That's not what I'm saying. And just stop trying to put words in my mouth. You know what I'm fucking saying."

"How about explaining?"

"Why have you got my brother locked up if you want me?"

"I'll tell you, not that it matters much. Your solicitor, if you get one, will find out anyway. He might as well hear it from you rather than pestering us for it. We know it's one of you, at the moment it looks like you but the phone-calls went to your brother's shop so there is also a chance he might have something to do with it. We can't rule anything out at the moment."

"That doesn't mean shit to me. I want a solicitor."

"I'll see. Of course, we also have your prints to go on. That's the one that's got you ahead by a couple of lengths at the moment and that could be the one that wins it for you."

"That mean you're letting my brother go?"

"We may well have to. Unless something else turns up."

"Like what?"

"You leave that to us."

"Yeah, right. Leave that to you. That's a good one is that. Fucking regular fixer uppers are you cunts."

"I'll be seeing you, perhaps."

"Hang about! What about a phone-call?"

"What about it?"

"Don't I get one?"

"This isn't the telly, you don't get a thing unless we offer it to you."

"This is bullshit."

"Bullshit?!" Landiss suddenly snapped. "I'll tell you what bullshit is, kid! Murdering an innocent old woman like that! I don't know what your problem is, but you need help. Serious help. If this happened in some parts of America, you'd be a dead man right now."

"I suppose that's what you'd like. I bet you'd really get off if they brought back the rope and all that. You liberals, you're really letting the side down with your softly-softly ideas, you know that?"

"You talk really well. You talk like a pro. Let's see how well you'll do in the dock."

"It's not going to get that far because you haven't got a thing on me. You haven't got a chance if this is all you've got. If this bollocks of a plan happens to be the best you can do then I feel

85

sorry for you, man. Shit! I've only got O-level Law and even I know you're out of fucking order. Actus reus, mens rea and all that shite. Motive, intention, you've got nothing, not one fucking thing on me!"

"Lemme tell you something, Mr O-level Law. We've got a lot more than you think."

"Meaning what, exactly?"

"Never mind. People like you make me sick."

"I tell you what, this is close to harassment, this is. And another thing…".

"No! That's it. This interview is terminated."

"Is it now? Well that's just fucking lovely!"

Something I'd said had got him going. The man meant it. Given the chance, at that moment, he'd have killed me himself.

By then, I was thinking that I'd had enough of this cobblers. Giving me the concerned copper routine was all well and good but Landiss kept overlooking the fact that they might have been totally wrong, and couldn't have been any more wrong if they'd tried. They were trying their hardest to make me admit to Annie's murder. It didn't matter that I was innocent. I was the closest I've ever been to being completely paranoid, but part of that was my own condition. When you haven't slept too well and you've been dragged in and out of a cold cell, even a nun could begin to seem perfectly capable of doing over old JFK. There was no point in Landiss telling me how he'd deal with the fuck-ups in society, how he'd make them suffer given half the chance, because he was wasting his time blowing all that shite at me. For no matter how much evidence they said they had, I was still an innocent man in the eyes of that law that he was supposed to stand for. This certainty made me smile.

Landiss had been walking away, but turned back and caught my grin.

"This is a very serious matter we're dealing with and you just seem to think that it's so funny," he said. "You're good."

"At what?"

"Acting like you know nothing about this."

"That's because I don't you arseholes!"

"Oh, you'd love it if we believed that, wouldn't you?"

"Fuck you!"

"I'm getting sick of your language."

"And I'm getting fucking sick of your fucking, bastarding shit. I'm not a fucking kid and I'll cunting-well use the fucking language I fucking want!"

Landiss put his hands on his hips and then turned away from me again. He put one hand to his forehead as if he'd suddenly got a splitting headache. He stood there and closed his eyes.

"Well? You got a problem with that?" I asked.

Fortunately, that was the last time I saw Landiss. Five minutes later another copper came in and told me to get up off my arse. Called me a black bastard while he was at it. He walked me to another cell that made the one I'd been in look like a room at the Hilton. I asked to speak with Landiss again but I knew they wouldn't let me. Still, Landiss's body might have left me but his presence was still around. He had a lot of that, did Landiss. That was what got me thinking about Annie and how I was going to miss her.

deeper love

The way I'd been brought up to look upon death was different to the way some of my white friends went about dealing with it. For us, the death of a relative, even the distant ones in Pakistan who I'd never even met, was more than a whole load of token gestures like offers of sympathy and condolences to the close family of the deceased. At first, when you don't really know any better and can't quite decide who or what you are, it can be quite confusing. Who are you? An Asian? A European? A bit of both? More Asian than European? More European than Asian? Neither of the above? The trouble with identity is that it keeps changing and growing and that can get confusing. At one time you're nothing but a kid and you're like all the other kids in the world, and then later, you realise you're not the same any more. It could be when you notice that you don't eat pork or your mum and dad don't come home pissed up on weekends. It might be that you speak two languages at home. It could be that your parents don't expect you to bring your girlfriends home for tea. It could be that you don't really have 'tea' at home, anyway. It could be, of course, the colour of your skin. Your identity is about noticing the things that make it yours. But sometimes, you just don't notice some of those things that can make all the difference.

As you get older things become clearer and inform you of what you think you are. And one of those things for me was death. Death, as daft as it sounds, was a uniter in some ways. An elder in Pakistan would die and news would get to England pretty soon. If he had any family living here, some of them would get on a plane and make it back home in time for the Janazah and the internment and they'd remain there for the next forty days until it was over. Back here, things would also be put on hold, until those duties and obligations that came with a death were fulfilled. It wasn't unheard of for people to travel hundreds of miles simply to arrive at a house of mourning to offer prayers for the one who had passed away and words of comfort for those who were left to get on with life. There were duties and formalities of course, and they seemed to mean so much more to the immediate family and the grievers than a sympathy card, a bunch of flowers or a couple of lines in the local paper once a year. Death was deep for us, and even enemies would cease-fire for a short time. Not just because it was the done thing and expected, but because we all needed to be reminded of how short, shite and unpredictable life was.

I'd been to a few houses through the years, with my dad and brother walking in front of me, and I would always be a little apprehensive about what I'd see and what was expected of me when I got there. We'd get into the house and in the hallway there'd be dozens of pairs of shoes taking up the floor space. We'd add ours to the pile and walk into the room where they were all sitting. If it was soon after the death, then the room would be packed with men and boys, who, upon seeing more male relatives, would budge up to make room for us to sit. And I'd sit there like a dummy on the floor with my legs crossed and my head bowed waiting for it to begin, so that it could be over sooner rather than later. It was the not knowing who to refer to, what to say and who to look at while I was saying it that got to me. After all, I didn't know these people. The people in the room were new faces to a kid like me, even though they might have been relatives. My dad, like all the other men, would say the words and we'd begin to pray. For the soul of the deceased and all those who'd gone before, for the living relatives, for the Prophets, for anyone who might be suffering, and, I suppose, for ourselves. We'd pray for mercy because we were going to need it. And then, in turn, starting with my dad and ending with me, we'd mutter the few standardised words of comfort we'd all spoken at some point in our lives – 'It is Allah's Will'. And it was.

But it wasn't over when we left. Sometimes we'd make another couple of visits in those first forty days, especially if it was a relative or a close friend of my parents. Throughout those first forty days there'd be a change in atmosphere and this solemnity would gradually diminish as it got closer to the fortieth and final day. If the relative was close, there'd be no music, no loud voices and nothing that showed overt joy about anything in our house. It wasn't only a respect thing that was going on because for those forty days, the one who had died would remain in the thoughts, minds and prayers of the mourners in their everyday lives. Even after that, people would still offer prayers for the dead ones whenever they felt like it but especially on Thursdays or Fridays. But for all of that, there was stuff that still kind of made things complicated for me. One particular aspect became the biggest problem for some people who had died while they were over here. The place of burial. Over here or over there? It became a problem because of different reasons. Even more problematic was the way some people went about solving it.

The burials weren't problems themselves. Nothing like that should be a problem, really. I suppose it depends on how you look at it, but the thing about our lot, Pakistanis more so than any other ethnic group, is that they have this problem with being buried in England and to me, it's just a little hypocritical. I'm not one to judge, but it just never made sense. They'd spent most of their lives here and would leave their descendants here when they died but that didn't matter. They just didn't fancy the idea of being buried in non-Pakistani soil. Most of them would be sent in a lead-lined coffin in the cargo bay of some old Boeing 747 to Pakistan. Then, the people escorting the box would head straight to the village or city they'd come from all those years ago and set about completing the task. The thing is, patriotism and nationalism is all well and good, but if you're a Muslim, all of that's not supposed to mean shit. Above all, you see, you're supposed to be a Muslim. Being an Indian, a Briton, a Yank or anything else is second place, and a pretty distant second place at that. But people somehow think that being buried back home is the right thing because it's the homeland and all the rest of it, but if Pakistan was so brilliant, then how come they'd spent all those years over here, in England? People might call me a racist but this thing is bigger than race. The thing that forces the issue even further, is that in actual fact, you're supposed to be buried as soon as possible and it doesn't matter where you happened to pop your clogs. I don't think it's true, but sometimes I can't help thinking that people seem to behave as if The Almighty only has interest in so-called Muslim nations or something. As if the rest of the world, the non-Muslim world, isn't God's earth as well. And the idea of being carted about from hearse to plane, from plane to Transit van and then from Transit van to the cemetery is appalling. Even when you're dead and not buried, there's still a tormented soul and a pained body to think about. You've got to get the body buried as soon as you can. You're not supposed to traipse half way around the world with it. But people being people don't think like that. Pakistan would be their final resting place and to add to this personal wish to be buried in the country of birth, there were also those back home who wanted to see the face for the final time. They wanted to look at the one who had once left the homeland and who had now left this earth for good. I could understand the reasons behind the actions but those reasons, all of them and more besides, still didn't make it the right thing for people to do. Not for me, anyway. There were a lot of problems with our lot and my brother also had his tuppence worth to throw in from time to time. Like marriage for example.

They'd been trying to get my brother married for ages but he just wouldn't have it, and I was right behind him on that little war that raged in our house. For one thing, he reckoned, he was still too young to be trapped by the shackles of marriage, and for another, some of the girls that were prospective candidates, were, well, to put it mildly, not entirely his cup of tea. Dog ugly, in fact. Besides, he was pretty keen on still playing the field while he was young. All that shite was a problem I never had, and in all likelihood, never would have. I wasn't the model son my mum, and especially my dad, would have wanted, so there weren't the same kind of expectations put on me as there were with my 'nice-boy' big brother. In some ways, I was kind of lucky, I suppose. My mum was all right about it, but then again, mums are always all right no matter how much you fuck around. I had a bit of a rep when I was a bit younger. When I was a schoolboy, other parents would spot me somewhere with someone, usually some girl that I might have been with and soon enough, word would get back home and fuck things up for a few days. The thing about it though, was that I never denied any of it, which was what must have made them eventually give up on me. For years people would pull my mum or my dad about seeing me here, there and everywhere in the company of some *larkhi* who might not have had any shame but obviously had great fucking taste. At the time, though, I didn't give a shit about it because I thought having a good time with some chick was easily worth the hassle I got from my folks. I mean, I didn't care too much about what they said about me, probably because it was all true, but it did get me fucked up with the way people went on at my parents instead of me. All I'd ever say to defend myself and my actions was, 'If they got something to say, tell them to come and see me'. But that kind of talk would never solve anything because this was a kin thing, a fucking Biraderi thing, an OUR mother-fucking thing that I wanted no part of. We were worse than the fucking Mafia when it came to those troublesome *family* matters. But I'd been a part of it since the day I'd been born and there was very little I could do to get out, even if I'd wanted to. Anyway, my brother always made some excuse or other about these people who wanted their daughters to marry him and he'd manage to get himself off the hook for some length of time, until another lot came along and made advances on him. One thing that got to me was how all these people were the same. Either they were relatives, or people who lived in the same village as my parents in Pakistan. Most of all, there was this caste thing going off, and that was what *really* got me thinking.

One time things got slightly fucked up, and as it turned out, this caste thing – which isn't even supposed to exist for people like us – played the biggest part. Now I look back, it was funny as fuck, but it also made me see the deal for all the mess that it was.

My brother got caught with a Pakistani bird, but more than that, she was the wrong kind of Pakistani bird to have been rumbled with. He'd taken her to the pictures in town where he'd probably snogged the arse off her in the back row. But on his way there with her, he'd been seen by some relative or other, and guess what? This relative happened to be a bit of a malicious bastard who happened to know the parents of the girl. She was all right as well was this lass, a pretty nice looking babe, if truth be told. Anyway, this relative of ours, goes and tells the girl's parents about what their eldest darling of a daughter had been up to in the middle of town and in front of everybody. At the same time, the relative gets all 'matchmaker' about it, and tells them everything about my brother – where he lives, how old he is, who his parents are and all the rest of that happy 'wedding bells' horseshit. And the next thing we know, the girl and her parents arrive at our door, giving it the love is in the air and wedding bells vibes. It was funny, though. The way my brother lost all colour in his face when he walked into the room and saw his bird sat there with her folks and all of them smiling for some reason. Both sets of parents talked some small talk about back home, about life here and one thing and another before the girl's old man decides it's time to come out with the real reason for him and his tribe being there, the real nitty-gritty. The million dollar question that he's been dying to get out since he got to our house. Marriage.

See, up to that point my mum and dad had been a little confused. I, fairly quickly, managed to work out why these people were there, and my brother, after recovering from the initial shock of their arrival, must have been pretty certain what was on the agenda. The girl and her parents sure as shit knew what they were up to, but my mum was under the impression that these people must have known my dad from somewhere and my dad thought that they knew my mum. But when the marriage thing was finally mentioned, the penny dropped, and boy did it make a loud noise when it hit the bottom. My dad went mad. He went barmy! The girl's father hadn't even told my dad that my brother and his daughter were already seeing each other yet! Shit! My brother got up and left, and, thank fuck, so did they, without muttering another word. That was a lucky break for my brother because as far as my dad was concerned, that family must have simply heard there was a son of marriageable age at our house and decided to try their luck. The thing that got to my dad was that they were a different people, a different caste. That's what fucked things up for me. These divisions weren't supposed to exist if you were a Muslim, but they did, and nobody seemed to give a shit. As a Muslim, we're all supposed to be equal, and just because they were supposed to be barbers back home didn't mean that they were lower than us. It was something that, as Muslims, went against the notions of equality and unity that Islam provided. And for another thing, once they had all arrived here, into this country, they all became the same fucking thing anyway. All of them were at the bottom of the shit tip and therefore equal, because they were all working in the mills, factories or whatever shitty jobs they could get. Over here, they were all as fucking low as each other, which was, to put it bluntly, beneath the white man, the Christian man, and the only ones who came close were the Caribbean immigrants and the Irish. Caste shouldn't have meant shit here, but it did. It seemed to me that being a Muslim and rejecting such fucked up ways of thinking didn't mean a great deal either.

These people first went to learn The Koran at the mosque from the earliest of ages, and were told to answer that they were one of Allah's people when asked who and what they were by one of the Angels of Death. But it still wasn't enough – caste, social standing and pride wrote off an answer that was as beautiful and simple as that. It was the baggage that was all around it and you couldn't get rid of. What had been around for thousands of years wouldn't disappear all because religion said so. Culture was too deep and inherent to be fucked around with for some people. That's why, I figured, my roots and just knowing who and what I was, remained so fucked-up for so long as well.

jump around

I found out later that they'd released my brother fairly quickly, and that was cool. At least I'd managed to convince them that one of us was innocent. Now he could get on with running the shop, but still that wasn't going to be as easy as it had been. There'd be customers who'd ask questions, extract information, point fingers and then spread the word, even though the word might have been a lie. Truth and lies? The same thing for some people, and mistakes are never costly for them. It's entertainment. Titillation. Gossip. All of them would be at it and I couldn't do anything to stop it. Even the fucking low lifes would be busy waxing lyrical about the latest crime in Manningham. Jamie, Jake, Bash, Gillette, Dominic and even fucking shit-for-brains Titch would be busy judging me while I was pulling my hair out in that cell.

Titch was a weird guy. Not a whacko or anything, but somebody you just couldn't work out. He was about thirty-five but he looked closer to fifty and I always thought he must have had a hard life as a kid back in Jamaica or something. But he was always very amicable about stuff, and, I always reckoned, just a little gullible. He'd lived in Manningham for years before we arrived, and he'd always been a good customer. The only thing that pissed him off was when his daily paper, *The Sun*, had sold out, or when there was some story about some black issue on the cover, like the time some black guy killed a woman down south somewhere. I'd tell him that all those fucking papers were full of shite and were never objective. I'd tell him his paper was more shite than the rest and was regularly full of inaccuracies, but he'd always tell me it was "a good racin' paper," and that was why he bought it. Not satisfied with his weak excuse, I'd tell him it was a good racist paper, and then he'd go on about how it told things the way they were, how it called a spade a spade and all that cobblers. He was okay, though. He never really got worked up about black people getting it up the arse, especially himself, and he just seemed to be interested in living from one day to the next. He worked on the buses for a few years, did Titch, but he got dismissed when he fought back with some white skinheads who decided to fuck with him, on account of him being a 'black bastard'.

A while ago, when Manningham was having a pretty bad time with one thing and another, he told me what he thought was what. At least, he tried to tell me his interpretation of the gig.

"This flamin' whole neighbourhood, man," he screeched one morning as he paid for his daily ration of printed crappola.

"What about it?"

He shook his head gravely.

"This whole flamin' harea, man."

He might have been an idiot but there were things about him that I liked. More than anything else was the way he added the letter H to certain words. I found it funny, probably because he didn't know he was doing it, or, even likelier, he didn't give a rat's arse about the way he spoke and totally fucked the English language up.

"Hat one time, this whole flamin' harea, man. Hit was totally different, you know what I mean?"

"Well, yeah. So?"

"What you mean, 'So?'. How can you say that like that. You can't say that! Flippin'..."

"Why not? I just did, man."

"You have no heyes? You don't see what's haround you? Flippin' eck, man! I don't believe the guy!"

The other thing that was funny about him was his debating style and the way he made such a big deal about everything. Whenever he showed surprise or anger, he'd look away and start pacing around and then talking to some imaginary, invisible observer. It was funny, and to milk it I'd keep on disagreeing with whatever he was saying, just for the sake of it. But I didn't have to this particular time, because old Titch was motoring away like some lunatic on a soap box at Speaker's Corner.

"So what?" I teased. "I like it like this. I mean, least shit happens, least you can talk about shit that actually happens around here."

"How can you say that, though? You saying you like seeing hall of this? What's wrong with you? There's somethin' wrong with this guy. Flippin'! Can't believe the guy, though!" he moaned to his invisible friend.

"I dunno," I continued, thoughtfully, "I like it, me. It's not that bad. It might…"

"How can you say that, though? What's wrong with you! Look hat the place, though. Flippin' look - hat - the - place! You walk down the road hand hall you see har hall these wars hall over the place. You like that? How can you say that, though?"

"Say what? What wars, man?"

"What you mean, 'What wars?'? How can you say 'What wars?' like that? You don't see them? You have no heyes? What's wrong with this guy? I don't be-lieve this guy!" he shook his head at his invisible observer again.

Old Titch, man. He could certainly give it some when he was in the mood.

"What wars? What the fuck you talking about, Titch, man?"

"I don't believe the guy! You hear this guy? That's what you want your kids to see hevery time they play hout? Flamin' wars walkin' habout hall over the flamin' place? I thought you Pakistanis were different, man! I thought your religion was hagainst that sort of thing? Don't believe what I'm hearin', man! Don't be-lieve the guy!"

I really did think he was going on about wars until he said 'walking'. I mean, you saw fights now and then, but they were usually isolated incidents that took place in isolated spots. And fights were certainly not something that kids saw every day and one thing that fights definitely didn't do, no matter how bad you were at expressing yourself, was to actually walk. I mean, what the fuck was Titch giving it?

"Walking? What the fuck you on about Titch, man?"

"You don't see them? Walkin' around with hall their legs hand backsides hangin' out hand gettin' hinto cars. Wars man, wars!"

I had to laugh. The guy was funny but the only trouble was, he didn't seem to know it.

"What's so funny? You think that sort hof thing his something to laugh hat? You! I'm talking to you!"

I laughed some more and that got Titch even more worked up,

"I don't believe the guy! I thought you'd take this sort of thing seriously!"

"No, Titch…"

Titch turned and started pleading with his imaginary friend once again. I felt sorry for this imaginary friend of his because, even if he didn't really exist, the poor bastard had a lot to put up with Titch.

"That's hall the guy can do habout it! Laugh like some flamin' nutter! Lemme hask you somethin', his that what you haar? Some kind of flippin' crazy man? I don't believe the guy! The guy's a flamin' nutter!"

"No, Titch, no…"

"I don't believe the guy! Look hat him, laughing like a flamin' lunatic! Can't believe the guy! You're a nutter, you know that? You're a flamin' nutter, man!"

"Listen, man. Listen to me."

"What? So you can make jokes hand have a laugh habout it? How can you laugh habout things like that? Oh, yeah. I forgot, you're a nutter, that's why you can laugh like that."

"No, I didn't know what you meant, man. You mean prossies, right?"

"Hof course I do! What do you think I'm flamin' telling you about? Wars, man. Flamin' wars and flamin' 'ookers!"

"No, no. That's not right, man. It's whores."

"What? What you talking habout now? The guy's funny! The guy's a nutter and he's trying to tell me something different!"

"It isn't *wars*, man. That's what I'm trying to tell you. It's *whores*. I thought you were on about fighting, you know? I thought you were on about *wars*, not *whores*."

"That's what I said, woaars."

"No, no, man. Not woaars, man. It's whores, with an H."

"That's what I said, wuhoaars."

"Whatever, man. Fuck it."

That was what I was up against. People like Titch and people who were worse would come in as if they owned the place, having already reached their verdict in respect of my guilt. In some ways, being guilty in their eyes would be worse than being guilty in the eyes of the law. I was never really a part of them and they never really constituted a great part of my life but what they thought seemed to matter to me. Somehow, I needed their support, but I was pretty sure I wouldn't get it because like me, they only had one priority in life, and that was themselves. I hated the idea of them thinking they were better than me. I hated the idea of them feeling they had the right to judge me and I hoped that my brother would fuck them off as soon as they started prising anything they could.

The first thing my brother must have done on his release was to get hold of a solicitor for me and for that, I was grateful, but the guy turned out to be a pretty incompetent legal representative as legal representatives go. I wasn't disputing his qualifications or anything, it was just I'd tell him I was innocent and he'd make out that maybe I wasn't, that maybe it was a perspective thing. That maybe something had slipped my mind and maybe I had done something to kill her. I mean, how fucking dumb can you get? I couldn't believe my luck. Here he was, a solicitor, supposedly *my* fucking solicitor, and he was trying to convince me that maybe I'd killed a little old lady, and maybe I just forgot that little detail when I gave my statement. What a fucking dickhead. I mean, whose side was this prick on? His angle was that we could change the plea from guilty to not guilty after Magistrates. But, I told him, Magistrates didn't mean a thing where charges like murder were concerned. The geezers on the bench would just look at the charge sheet and refer it to Crown straight away. They wouldn't even ask me what I thought about it or, for that matter, what my plea was. I wanted to keep my story straight, no matter how much of an inconvenience the truth happened to be.

It turned out that this solicitor wasn't a solicitor after all, but was only collecting the facts for his boss. The real solicitor had been tied up somewhere and probably wouldn't make it until an hour before I was due in the Magistrates, which was just what I needed right then. A fucking solicitor who sent his fucking tea-boy to do the recon work for him. Trust me to get a fucking apprentice when I needed an expert. But anyway, he didn't stop too long when he told me what the gig was. I nearly throttled the cunt when I found out he was nothing more than a messenger boy in a nice suit but I stopped short of hurting him. The last thing I needed was a GBH charge as well as a murder hanging over my head. I told him to make sure his boss got his arse down there right then, otherwise I'd start to kick up a real conspiracy stink. I didn't really know what I was going on about, because I was just so pissed off about things. Even the cunts who were supposed to be supporting me were being pains in the arse. I even got to thinking that there must have been something wrong with me. Why else would a fucking kid come along and make out that he was a solicitor? Why else would I be left feeling like an idiot?

I hung around, biting my nails, trying not to pace too much, asking the grunt outside if he knew where my fucking solicitor was and he'd just get more and more pissed off at me for interrupting the book he was reading (some shit called *The Fix* with a picture of a syringe on the cover). I'd ask him again, but he'd tell me the same thing as before, that he didn't know where my cunt of a brief was and if I knew what was good for me, I'd shut the fuck up. So I'd keep on asking, just to piss him off some more. I could tell he couldn't care less. And why should he have cared? If it was up to him, he'd have meted out his own punishment. Him and me, in a room. His hatred fuelling his body to hurt mine. It was depressing. I started to believe nothing would go my way, and even if the solicitor did show up he'd turn out to be some cunt who'd just passed the bar and I'd be his very first case. It was driving me mental, that room, that grunt out there and no solicitor. I got really pissed off about it and started venting my anger at the grunt even more until he just started ignoring me altogether. What the fuck was keeping him, though? Was he like all the other solicitors in the world and really into this fucking sado trip that he was giving me right now? Solicitors and pervies, same shit with a different name to me. You hear things about these sorts in a place like Manningham. Like Mr Pissy Man, a solicitor who used to cruise the Lane for action and, when he found it, would strip naked and lie in a bath. Then he'd get the girl to squat and piss herself all over him. Hence the name and hence me thinking that all solicitors were more fucked in the head than people like me were supposed to be.

I was sat on the bed, cursing the cunt for being so late, when the door opened. At last, someone who looked like he knew what he was doing and someone who looked like he might have been able to get me out of this shithole. A tall man but a well built man. A lean man but not a gangly, awkward man. A winning man but not a sports man. A well dressed man but not a flash and arrogant man. He was wearing this wicked grey suit that was more suited to professional footballers when they were busy being cat-walk fucking models. His hair was long but it was also very neat and my gaze shifted to his hands and saw a set of nails that were perfectly manicured. Image meant something to this guy and I couldn't help but to be effected just by looking at him. If I was a bird, I'd have been creaming in my knickers.

He sauntered into the cell and shook me by the hand and that was when I knew things were going to start changing. A nice, firm, happy and, above all, confident handshake that reassured me further. His after-shave was obviously not some cheap shit from the local chemist's or the open air market, but stuff that would cost most people a week's wage. There was no way I could lose with this guy. Problems he did not possess, and even if they did try to sneak into his life, he'd fuck them off just by simply staring them into a terrible surrender. The guy was something else. Slicker than cat shit and cleaner than Bryan Ferry's whistle. I could tell he was a pro, a showman even, which is what I needed most in a solicitor. It's pointless having some cunt who knows the law inside out but can't talk for shit. You need a cunt who can talk the arse off the opposition. You need a person with charisma and all the rest of the shit that made people in my position feel better. What you don't need is some timid cunt who spends half an hour clearing his throat and then sweating his arse off because he's worried about how he might sound in a room full of strangers. There's no room for shrinking violets in the game of law. They're about as much use as auctioneers with stutters. Even I know that.

"How are you, Amjad?"

"I've been better."

"You sleep?" he asked and then sat beside me.

"No."

"Good, you'll have lots of time for that later. I need you alert and fresh right now. You think you can manage that for me?"

"No sweat. I can manage anything you want right now, man."

"Okay, first things first. You've been charged with the murder of Annie Potts. You knew her, I take it?"

"Yeah, she was a customer at my brother's shop. Sort of."

"You told them that?"

"Yeah, they asked, so I told them."

"Okay. Go on."

"Not a lot to tell, really."

"How about you telling me what you think is important."

"Well, I told them she was a bit ill so we'd deliver stuff to her. That was it. That's why they think I killed her."

"I've had a chance to look at the evidence which they've linked to you."

"And? Does it mean anything?"

"It could do, but we'll worry about all of that later. It's important that you stay focused for me right now. Do you think you can do that, Amjad?"

"They've got my prints."

"Circumstantial. You made a delivery that day. You give her a receipt?"

"Always."

"Good."

"They've got a witness."

"I know."

"What do you think?"

"About what?"

"About this. Can they get me?"

"Did you do it?"

"No. No fucking way, man."

"Then you'll be all right."

"What makes you so sure?"

"Myself," he smiled.

Fuck. Was this guy something else or what? And what's more, I believed him.

"I'm good," he said, simply. "I'll try to put it into context for you, if I can, Amjad. Even if you were guilty, with what they've got here, I could still get you off."

"You're a barrister?"

"No. It won't get that far. Trust me."

"You sure about that?"

"I'm always sure. Try not to worry too much about this. Okay?"

Even if he sounded a little too sure of himself, I still couldn't help feeling reassured. I'd been brought up thinking that people like this guy were always less than they said they were and every time I'd seen a blagger, like this guy, I'd always been on my guard because it was safer and better that way. The fact of the matter is, people who go on about themselves as if they're something special, seldom turn out to be anything as wonderful as they make out. They just like to think they're the dog's bollocks, and some go to extremes to try and prove it. But there was just something about this guy that I couldn't quite get a handle on. Maybe it was how he was just so calm about it all. He seemed to communicate to me that he had the situation covered and he ate cases like this for breakfast. He just radiated optimism, confidence and, dare I say it, honesty. But even that couldn't have been too real. Bradford's not the murder capital of the world so there couldn't have been that many solicitors who were dead handy in the field. It wasn't as if he'd been doing murder cases all his life, was it? I asked him how many murder cases he'd handled and he smiled. I stared at him but he was holding strong, as if he had done hundreds of them. A couple, he said, but didn't tell me how they'd gone for him because he didn't have to. It was obvious from his smile that he'd won them, and even if it was a lie, it was a well-executed one. If he was a liar, he was one of the best I'd ever seen. Even the ones who thought of themselves as career liars back in Manningham weren't a patch on this guy.

I told him the rest of the deal and he showed little emotion throughout. Even when I told him that their witness was more of a crook than I'd ever be he didn't look up from the pad he'd been busy scribbling on after the first five minutes. I also told him about the complaint I wanted to lodge, which seemed to get his attention. He dropped his pen on his pad and looked at me.

"Go on."

"They just knocked us out of the house and told us to get in the car. No reason, no nothing."

"Can you remember exactly what they said?"

"Some of it. 'In the car, paki!' that sort of shit. You know."

"What about names?"

"I think they asked for my brother."

"Tahir?"

"Yeah."

"So why did they take you?"

"Fucked if I know. You see if you can work it out, man. I'm fed up with thinking about it. Does your head in after a while, you know?"

"I understand."

"Thanks, man."

"But you are sure about this? They didn't actually ask you to go with them?"

"Pretty sure, man. They just started into us like we were mass-murderers or something."

"Anything else you can remember?"

"I'll tell you one thing. They didn't nick us right then. The big copper, the one called Landiss, got a bit edgy when I told him, but he did it himself pretty soon after that."

"Are you saying they didn't arrest you until you got here?"

"Well, yeah. I told him about his thugs, the ones who brought us in. Excessive force and all that."

"They said you resisted arrest, Amjad. They said *you* were the one who attacked them." He raised his eyebrows like a teacher catching a pupil cheating on an exam.

"How do they figure that? They didn't say shit about arrest so how was I supposed to resist it? They didn't even tell us to go with them. I mean, it was the middle of the fucking night and they started giving us this fucking racism shit! What the fuck were we supposed to do when they started prodding and poking us like we were some fucking animals? I only poked the bastard because he poked me."

"Who?"

"Watkins, his name is. Total bastard, he is."

"Okay. That's good."

"Yeah? How?"

"You've got a name of one of the arresting officers. They're supposed to caution you or at least inform you of the reasons why you are being arrested as soon as is practicable. Now you're telling me they didn't do that. They didn't follow the law. They're in the wrong and just one look at your face tells any normal person that you haven't just fallen down the stairs. Okay?"

"Fucking great, man. I mean, you think it's enough?"

"It helps."

"That's good, man."

"Okay. Your brother. Did you see him later?"

"I haven't seen him since about four this morning. Since they brought us in."

"They let him go. He's the one who got in touch with me."

"He know you?"

"Not really. A friend of a friend."

"That's nice."

"Not really. I don't start until ten, not unless I have to. Unless it's important."

"Is this important?"

"Well, to you it is."

"What about you?"

"Every case is an important case for me. Every one I win is important."

"And you think you're going to win this one?"

He put his pad down on the bed and straightened himself up. Time for a speech, I thought.

"The first thing you have to do," he began, "is to believe in me and believe in yourself. If you tell me you didn't do it and want to tell the world that, then I'll believe you. And I'll do my job the best I can. I'll do everything I can to convince them that you are, as you say, innocent. On the other hand, if you tell me that you did do it but want to tell them you're innocent then I'll defend you in exactly the same way. If, however, you're not feeling too sure about it and even think you might change your mind at some point in the future, I'd advise you to stop wasting everybody's time. Even if you've got the nucleus of that thought in your mind, I'd advise you to go ahead and tell them that you did do it because that will make a big difference to the outcome. What I'm saying is that it makes no difference to me at this point. As long as you stay consistent and stick to your plea, I'll do my job and get you out of here."

"I didn't do it."

"That doesn't matter."

"It matters."

"Not to me it doesn't. Not that I don't believe you. I do. Right now, what matters is that I get you off and I can only do that with your support. Do you understand what I'm saying to you, Amjad?"

"I understand but do you think you can? That's what I was trying to say."

"Yes, you'll be free in a few hours."

"Yeah? A few hours? It's not that I don't trust you or nothing but what makes you so sure, man?"

"Don't take this the wrong way, but we haven't got a lot of time for me to go into the complexities of legal rights and procedures. All you have to know is that you should be out of here soon."

"But how? How are you going to manage that? I thought this was murder, man."

"We might be able to convince them your arrest was unlawful. A technicality but still quite useful."

"So what does that mean? Does that mean they'll arrest me properly as soon as they let me go?"

"Technically, yes, they could do that. But what has to be taken into consideration is that every single item of evidence they have is purely circumstantial."

"Circumstantial. Yeah, I suppose it is."

"And if the magistrates are sensible, they'll want to wait for further evidence before deciding what to do. In all likelihood, there'll be an adjournment."

"But what if there isn't?"

"Well, we apply for bail."

"I don't know. This sounds dodgy, to me."

"You'll be okay. Trust me. I know what I'm doing."

"Oh? I don't think trust has got anything to do with this. They'll only bring me back in once they go for your unlawful arrest bit. I'll be out one minute and back in the next."

"They'll take one look at you and if that doesn't convince them of your story, then nothing will. Try not to lose sight of the fact that these magistrates are normal, reasonable people. There's nothing for them to tie you with this. Fingerprints? Circumstantial. You delivered items to her house. Witness? Even you admit to being there. What would any reasonable person think?"

"But how did she die?"

"As far as I know, she was poisoned."

"Poisoned?"

"The post-mortem should confirm that. But don't worry, Amjad. If you didn't kill her, there'll be nothing to link you to her death. The truth is all that matters and it's up to me to give them the truth."

"So? You think they'll let me out, then?"

"We're going to go for unconditional bail. I might as well tell you now, if they turn us down, which I doubt, we can apply again in seven days."

"Seven days?"

"Don't worry. That's the worst possible scenario."

"And the best?"

"You know the best. The evidence is heavily circumstantial and of course there's your face which should win them over on its own. Things look good for you, Amjad. Being a first time offender won't go against you, either."

"What makes you think it's my first offence?"

"I haven't been given your file so I didn't think you had any criminal history."

"It's not my first offence."

"What?"

"I thought you should know."

"Know? What was it? And when?"

"Years ago, got nicked on this march."

"For what?"

"Nothing. Just a copper decided to pick me out and batter me."

"Did it go any further?"

"Just got cautioned for disturbing the peace or some other crap that he made up."

"Disturbing the peace," he mused, "How old were you?"

"I was about fifteen at the time. Maybe sixteen."

"That's it? Nothing else?"

"That's it. Nothing else. I thought you should know, just in case it matters."

"That shouldn't be too much of a problem. It might not show on your record."

"Here's hoping, eh?"

"Yes. Here's hoping. Right, anything else you can tell me?"

"About what?"

"About yesterday, anything else that you didn't tell the police? Anything else you think I should know. Anything at all that might be relevant?"

"I don't think so. That's pretty much it."

"You're sure? It's important that you're frank with me, Amjad. Anything you say is between me and you. You should tell me in case they spring something on us."

"Nope, nothing else."

"Okay. I think I'm just about done here. I'll see you in a while. Try to relax."

"Just one thing."

"Yes?"

"You said she was poisoned. How do they know? What if she just died?"

"They found her with an empty bottle of tablets by her side."

"What were they?"

"Temazepam."

"Right."

"Why do you ask?"

"No reason."

I was in that cell for most of the next day. Magistrates hadn't happened and the grunts still wouldn't tell me what was going on when I asked them. Gates had let me down as well, then. He said a few hours but those hours looked like they were going to turn into days. Something must have been going on. It wasn't like them to keep me hanging around. Especially if they could get the criminal procedures in operation as soon as possible. But then again, they might have still been playing that cops and robbers game with me. These things were about games. Psychological. From the smell of the disinfectant they used to mop the shit up with to the shade of paint on the walls. Designed and put together for specific purposes. The room I'd first been questioned in was different to this. Gentle pastels, soft lighting and the aroma of some pine scented forest you got in a bottle. Comfortable seats for all of us to sit on. A pleasant place. Not like this. Dysentry brown walls. The acrid aroma of something cheap and effective and a foam covered piece of wood to lie on. There'd been a clock in the other room. Pride of place. I couldn't miss it. But nothing like that in here. Again, something designed for a purpose. To disorientate me. Confuse me. Get me worried. Pity I knew about these games of theirs. They weren't really working but these games were still pissing me off. Especially the one where they tried to drive me mental by telling me nothing and ignoring me. The bastards wouldn't even tell me the time, not that I really needed to know. It wasn't as if I had somewhere to go, was it?

work in progress – the will

Hussain hated gardening. There were a lot of things that got his blood boiling but there was nothing that came close to this deep hatred he had for all things green. He'd never been a gardener, for one thing and he never knew anyone who showed him how wonderful gardening could be. It was an old person's game, anyway, was this gardening lark. Something that people only did because they had nothing better to do. Hussain had lots of things to do and all of them infinitely more enjoyable than rooting around in muck for a couple of hours once a week. So why did he do it? He had to. That was the long and short of it. To get what he wanted out of life, someone once told him, he had to make sacrifices. He had to do the things he didn't really want to do in order to progress in whichever field he was in at the time. That was why he was pissing about with weeds, lawn seed and those fucking rose bushes that kept pricking the blood out of his fingers. Like life, this gardening thing was all about sacrifice and reaping what you sowed.

It would be worth it, though. He'd been at this lark for nearly a year and, as far as the old bag inside was concerned, Hussain was nothing short of an angel. She'd tell him she wished she had a son who cared as much as he did. Hussain would turn away from her and smile an uncontrollable smile when she told him that. It was working, he'd tell himself. It was fucking working and that was all he'd need to keep it up.

Over the last year, he must have saved her an absolute fortune. To all intents and purposes, Hussain had become her slave, even though she didn't really force him to work for her. But still, this was the sacrifice he had chosen to make. Whatever the lady wanted, the lady got. Lately, she didn't even have to ask for things because Hussain had learnt to know what she wanted and when she wanted it. He knew which days she liked to have her laundry done, which day she wanted her cupboards filled with groceries, which days her house to be cleaned and of course, which day she wanted her fucking garden weeded, watered and generally tidied up. And her garden did look good, now. He had shifted all the shit that people had dumped there – the bags full of garbage, the boxes full of broken things, the knackered and old furniture and the mattresses – and then set about creating a vision of beauty right on her doorstep. Hussain had smiled through it all and even now, he would tell her how he loved gardening, anyway. How it was no big deal. How he liked the idea of helping her out if she needed it. How he was, in fact, only there to help. How all she had to do was ask. After all, he'd add, that was what friends were for.

The old bag never took the piss with him, though. She was quite honest, really. She always complained that he was doing too much for her and in the beginning, she always offered him money for his services. Hussain would never accept a penny. He'd tell her to keep it and to splash out on something for herself. Besides, he wasn't doing this for the money, he'd tell her. In reality, that was the only reason why he even spoke to her. Doing what he did was an investment and one day, he'd get the lot, in one lump sum. Who, in his right mind, would be bothered about a couple of quid for running to the shops when you had a fortune to look forward to?

She asked him, early on, how old he was. He told her and then she told him her age. She was eighty-three. She didn't look it, Hussain had said. She looked closer to a hundred but he didn't tell her that. And now, a year later, she looked the same. Just as unhealthy and just as likely to die at any minute. But she wouldn't. She'd live because now, she had something to live for. She had a friend and someone who she often thought of as a son. Someone who seemed to care for her and someone she, perhaps, had grown to love. She had Hussain and although making her feel that way had been a part of the plan, it was now backfiring on him. She should have croaked by now and the more he thought about her mortality, the more worried he got. It would just be his luck if she carried on living. If things went on like this, he'd probably end up dying before she did.

and the beat goes on

Eventually Gates showed up and he was good enough to tell me the time when I asked him. It was two o'clock in the afternoon. He was only a day and a half late but I didn't think having a go at him would do me any good. He apologised as soon as he entered, anyway. A pre-emptive strike if ever there was one. He sat down and asked me if I was doing okay and how the coppers were treating me. I told him I was all right and the coppers were still playing at Starsky and Hutch. But he hadn't come for small talk. I could tell. His voice said a lot more than words.

"It would have been nice if you'd told me about your writing, Amjad."

"What? What's that got to do with anything?" I smiled, being all bashful for some reason.

"Which one is it now?" he said to himself as he leafed through some papers, "Let me see, here we go, *Jack of all Trades*, *The Will*. You could have told me about these stories."

"About what? What are you talking about?"

"About these books of yours. You could have told me that you wrote books."

"What've they got to do with anything? I know they're a bit violent, but they're nothing too dodgy."

"You're trying to tell me that you don't see the relevance?"

"With what? Just tell me what's on your mind, man."

"The characters. This Jack person, and the one called Hussain, in your books."

"Yeah, well? What about them?"

"Well, they're both killers for one thing."

"So what? Lots of people write stuff about killers. And anyway, Jack's a bit loopy. Jack's a serial killer."

"I gathered that this 'Jack' character of yours was disturbed but people don't write books like this. Not with the way he goes about it. And the same goes for the other one. *Especially* the other one."

"The one about the will? With Hussain?"

"Absolutely, that's the one that can do the damage."

"Sorry, but I don't see how it makes a difference."

"From what my secretary tells me, it makes all the difference."

"Your secretary's read it?"

"Some of it. She likes reading so I thought I'd let her digest what we had."

"And she thinks there could be a link?"

"That's exactly what she thinks."

"Come on, you seen any of the films you can get these days? The stuff I wrote about Jack and Hussain was nothing. That shit's mild compared to some of the stuff you see these days."

"That's not what I'm saying, Amjad. Think about it. Annie Potts?"

"What about her? What's she got to do with the books?"

"Annie Potts was an old and ill woman and it looks like she was killed. There was an old and infirm woman in *The Will* and she gets killed by the central character in *The Will*. He did it for the money. That was his motive. On top of that, he was a young Asian man. Someone not unlike yourself?"

"This is a wind up, right?"

"No. It's not."

"Shit! I wrote that stuff ages ago. Oh man! This is just too much. You're sure? I mean, how could that be?"

"Of course I'm sure. We could argue that it was a coincidence."

"Of course it was a coincidence! You don't think I'd write a story about a nutter who kills old women for money and then go out and actually do it, do you? I mean, why would I do something as stupid as that?"

"I know. But the prosecutors wouldn't look at the information in the same way."

"How'd they get a hold of that stuff, anyway? I mean, it's not as if any of it's ever been published, has it?"

"They searched your house and the shop. They went through your computer and pulled out all the stories you've written."

At last, what every budding writer dreamt of – an audience taking his stuff seriously.

"Well, that's good."

"Oh? How so?"

"Between you and me, all my stories are like that."

"They're all about killers?"

"Well, I suppose so," I said. "There's one about this Pakistani hit-man, one about an arsonist, one about a bunch of thugs who go around thinking they're something special, one about a guy who's running from some hit-men, one about these guys who spend everything they can on getting doped up, another one about a guy who goes around killing gays because he's a repressed gay himself, one about a guy who's into football violence. Yeah, almost every one of them has some killing in it, and nearly all the central characters are young Asian guys. People not unlike myself. A couple of them are even worse than the stuff that Jack gets up to."

'Jack wasn't quite right...' That was how the story about Jack, the seriously fucked in the head maniac serial killer, started. All in all, it was a pretty shite story and even before all of this stuff started I regretted having anything to do with the fucker. Jack as a character was all right, but the shite he got up to just didn't make sense. The explanations for what he did were a bit, well, shit, to be honest about it, but that's all part of the skill of being a writer. Those in the know say you have to keep on writing and refining your style and learn to be critical of what you're putting onto paper. I'd written about Jack early on, and hadn't looked at the piece for at least a couple of years. I'd been meaning to go through all of my earlier work to see if anything could be improved or salvaged but I couldn't be arsed, and besides, I was motoring away with a piece about these guys from Pakistan who panelled out vans for a living. I know 'guys from Pakistan panelling vans out for a living' doesn't sound like such a big deal, but there was a lot more to it than that. That was, until I got thrown into a cell and accused of killing one of my brother's best customers. And that was weird. Hussain and me were kind of in the same spot. He wanted to get out. He wanted to make some money and he could think of no sure-fire way to do that. Hussain's little tale was all right as a piece. I thought it was anyway, and so did a couple of acquaintances who had shown an interest in my work.

"Well, that could be something," said Gates.

"Hussain killed his old lady for the money." I informed him.

"Did Annie have money?" Gates asked.

"Well, she had enough to keep her in fags and booze."

"A will?"

"How the fuck would I know?"

"Good."

"So? What's the fucking problem?"

That was a stupid question. I was not going to be all right like he had at first thought. If Annie Potts had been killed like Hussain had killed his rich old woman, anything like that at all, then I was obviously in line for a fall. It would have taken Annie Potts absolutely no time at all to croak. Just grab a hold of her and shove a few tablets down her throat and hang around until she stopped breathing. You'd leave and a while later, you'd inherit the money. What made this as bad as it could get was the witness to back the theory up. I'd been there. I could have done it and as long as the coppers had one person to pin me to that time and to that place, it would be enough.

smells like teen spirit

I was feeling pretty shagged out by the time another two coppers came along. One of them stood in front of me while the other grabbed my hands and forced them behind my back where they were cuffed. They had to do that to make sure they and the rest of society were protected from me for the duration of the short walk from the cell in the cop shop to the holding cells underneath the Magistrates Court. It was weird. They were acting as if I was dangerous and as such, they had to keep me contained, secure and simply could not risk fucking up. I knew that game like I knew all others they played. They were still trying to break me, dehumanise me by treating me as if I was deranged or perhaps, even subhuman. Me knowing the way they worked was one of the few things that gave me comfort in that place.

The only good thing about those cells was the graffiti. Most of it was pretty childish stuff, but it still helped pass the time. There were the lines that I expected to see, *'All coppers are bastards!'*, *'Pig Scum!'*, *'Coppers eat my shit!'*, *'Pakis out!'* and *'Niggers go home!'*. That shit was all over the place. Then there were also other scratchings which weren't as nasty; *'G. Smith was here! OK!'*, *'Jason 4 Louise. 4 ever.'* and lots of other lines like those. There were a few remarks about the legal system, observations on life, sex and anything else that you could think of. There were even conversations, which started off with something like: *'Bradford City Rule! OK!'* to which someone else had added, *'Do they fuck like!'* which was followed by, *'Yes they do! Go fuck off!'*, *'No they fucking well don't! They're shit!'*. And so on. I sat on the bench-cum-bed and waited for them to take me up, thinking it would be only fitting if I carved my very own personal record into the wall, which would remain until the next time they gave it a face-lift. *'A. Mahmood woz ere! OK!'*. When in Rome...

I had to stick around for another half hour or so before I was told to move my arse once again. I thought they were going to escort me to the actual Magistrates and once we would get there, Gates would give it his best shot, punch himself out too quickly and as a result, he'd get me screwed. I was quickly losing every ounce of that precious confidence Gates had instilled in me. Blaggers, I remembered, promised the earth but delivered nothing. Suddenly, Gates wasn't as shit hot as he used to be.

I thought Lady Luck had betrayed me forever that day. I'd see her again but I wouldn't see her in court. I'd see her in all her glory, and she'd be mocking me for losing faith. And fuck, when she'd show up like that, she'd make one hell of a royal entrance. She'd make it better. I was on such a low as I waited in those cells. And when that shard of luck would glimmer at the end of the corridor, it would blind me. I had been thinking it was the beginning of the end. I had been thinking it would be Magistrates and then, in a few weeks or perhaps even months, it would be Crown or County or whichever stage of the judicial system came next. It didn't even get as far as the Magistrate's door but how was I to know?

I rose and put my hands behind my back for them to be cuffed by the grunt who was assigned this most important of duties. I was led out of the holding cell, one copper in front of me and the other behind. Even in my wildest dreams, I wasn't even bordering on being dangerous, but these coppers must have thought I was some sick monster who killed for pleasure. Sure, I'd get physical if I was ever pushed hard enough but so would anyone else. Everyone's got a breaking point when it boils down to it but only some people actually get close to being broken. I could easily have gone through my life without ever having been in a scuffle, even at school, but there were just times when it was expected of you. Sometimes, you just have to do things you wouldn't ordinarily do. For show, or to save face. You just have to do what you feel is necessary in order to carry on living. Sometimes it doesn't do to ask too many questions about your actions because questions can start fucking with your mind. Everyone, even the nicest person in the world, has the potential to be dangerous. It's just that there are different reasons why people get dangerous and more importantly, there are different *ways* that people get dangerous. They could be acceptable or unacceptable reasons but the result is always the same. You get what you want, at whatever cost.

I was dreading it. Walking into a court to be faced by a bunch of strangers was more than intimidating. I was shitting it something rotten because the beaks, or whatever modern-day crooks called them, would look at me as if I was some sort of model for them to pick at and to inspect. They'd do it at their leisure and on their own terms. They'd all be oldies, these magistrates. There'd probably be two men and a woman and all three of them would look exactly how I expected them to look – smartly dressed and probably retired from some job they'd stuck to all their lives. One of them would be a bit younger and get more of a kick out of it than his colleagues, but they'd all look like they hadn't had too bad a life, with their posh designer frame glasses and even posher wine sniffing noses. Not dead rich, but reasonably well off. What you'd call 'nice' but 'a bit too posh for your taste' if you had them as neighbours. And these people were supposed to be somehow better than people like me. But how were they? They weren't qualified to be magistrates, were they? It wasn't as if they sat tests to become magistrates and every aspect of their lives had been scrutinised before they were allowed to sit in judgement of others, was it? For all I knew, they might have been worse than me. They could have been accountants for the mob, psychopaths, perverts, rapists or even child pornographers. But there they'd sit, judging me and judging all the other shit in this town. And I knew they had no right to. Not only because of what they might have been, but because of what they could never know about me. So fucking what if they were model husbands, fathers, grandfathers and all the rest of that shit? What did I care of their lives and of their reputations? Bully for them if they happened to be fine, upstanding citizens. They didn't know me and what I'd done in my life. They had no right to think of me as a killer, or for that matter, as anything. None of them knew a thing but there they were, judging people as if they were quality control inspectors and people like me were just objects on some conveyor belt passing in front of them. They knew nothing and fuck them all for trying to dominate me and my future. I'd show the bastards. I'd show them what I was made of. I'd fuck them all and their precious fucking justice. They, no matter how wise they thought they were, didn't know what the word meant.

I really don't like the idea of people judging others, even though I do it all the time. I suppose the difference is that my opinions, no matter how irrational, one-sided or full of shit they might be, don't mean anything most of the time, whereas the judgements of these so-called model citizens could mean everything to people in the dock. And that was where I would be. A victim and a suspect. A victim of my environment. They'd think I was a bad one and me ending up in the dock was bound to happen at some point in time. I'd been brought up in an inner-city, I was Asian and obviously, my life chances would suffer because of those little details. Still, there was the issue of murder to consider. They might have understood me turning to crime because things were destined to be hard for someone from my many backgrounds, but murder? Of an old lady? That wasn't an ordinary crime and surely that would mean I wasn't an ordinary criminal.

Gates was waiting at the end of the corridor with another copper standing beside him.

"Good news," Gates said, and turned to the copper, who had sergeant's stripes on his arm, underneath which was a black clipboard.

"Erm. You're free to go," the copper tapped his board a couple of times and said. "Just a few formalities to sort out."

"What? I thought I was being charged with murder."

"There's been some new evidence that's come to light."

"Such as? Another witness, is it?" I said, hoping to goad him into a verbal battle because I was still pissed off and a bit hyper at hanging around, but he wasn't into that right then.

"Erm, no. I don't think I can tell you any more than that, at this moment."

"What? I think this is bullshit. I think you, your lot, owe me more than that," I said as one of the escorting coppers uncuffed me.

"Well, you were a suspect. We had to treat you like one."

"And now I'm not?" I asked as I rubbed each sore wrist in turn.

"It looks like it."

"I think we should leave, Amjad," said Gates.

"I don't think so. What's this new evidence? Who was it?"

The officer looked at Gates.

"Off the record?" he asked, in a hushed tone.

"Erm, sure" said Gates, "go ahead,"

"Suicide. They found a suicide note in the bin."

"Suicide? Bullshit. No fucking way!"

"Well, that's consistent with the coroner's preliminary findings."

"Not Annie. She might have been ill, but she wouldn't have topped herself."

"It's not up to me," said the copper with a shrug of the shoulders and off he walked, into court, ready to fuck some other poor bastard in the arse.

"I don't believe that." I said as the two escorting coppers buggered off.

Gates shrugged.

"Why not? Suicides happen all the time."

Who gave a fuck, now that it was over? It looked like my part in the story was about to end. But fuck, it would have been nice if Gates had warned me then about what was to come. What I walked into, on leaving that place, was one hell of a shock.

firestarter

In another world, in another dimension, things might be the other way around. In another world good might be bad and bad might be good. In another world things might be better. Things might be fair. Things might be right. And people like critics, editors of fucked up little magazines that mean less than shit, the press and above all, people like me wouldn't exist as we do in our world. In another world, things might be different.

Fool that I was, I always thought you were innocent until proven guilty in England, or for that matter, in most parts of the world. Except, perhaps, for Pakistan. Maybe that's not quite a fair thing to say. Pakistan's a place like any other place where there are bad things and good things, only the bad things are really bad and the good things aren't too shit hot to begin with in a place like Pakistan. Then again, maybe it's a perspective thing, or it might be just me again, judging when I have no right to judge. The thing I was grateful for was that I had my dad to tell me it could have been worse, much worse. No matter what tragedy visited you, it could always be worse. My dad's good at that, reassuring you and telling you things aren't as bad as they seem. He'll always give you an example of some other poor sod who's a lot worse off than you are and he'll try to make you feel a little better about your own current predicament. Not that you don't know that sort of thing, but you don't particularly think like that when you're getting it bad yourself. If I'd been in Pakistan? That didn't bear thinking about, because they'd have hung me first and asked questions later.

I didn't quite believe him because he can exaggerate a bit when it comes to Pakistan, especially when it comes to Pakistan, can my dad. But the fact is, and I've heard the same sort of thing from others, that it it can be a pretty depressing situation for some people but then again, maybe it's more to do with the very nature of poverty and what it actually means to be a part of a society where poverty is so blatant but at the same time, so normal. You could always blame destiny for where you are, though. Like me, you could always say that you were meant to do what you've done in and with your life.

My dad told me about this guy who got fitted up for murder in Pakistan a good few years before I was even born. Maybe things have changed for the better since then. This guy did nothing, and there were even witnesses to prove he was nowhere near the murder scene for days before and after the actual deed. That didn't matter, though. The guy still managed to get the rope around his neck in the end. Like the poor cunt was destined to go like that. He was only young, about twenty, from what my dad told me. He'd just got married and his wife was expecting their first kid. The guy who he'd been accused of topping was his older brother, which was just a little too much for me to swallow. How could anyone do that to their own fucking brother? They say brothers get up to all sorts of shite amongst themselves in Pakistan. Cunts have been known to go and off their own fucking parents for the sake of money but that sort of shite happens over here too, so it's not really too much of a surprise, I suppose. The brothers had been arguing over some land for a few months and that was why the Pakistani coppers made the arrest.

Land's a big deal in Pakistan. It can be the only thing some people have, and it gets passed down from father to son forever. Funny thing about this passing down of land is that I reckon the land's got to run out sooner rather than later. Say a father's got three acres of land, and before he croaks, he splits it up between his three sons. That leaves each of them with just one measly acre a piece. Then, years later, when the three ageing sons are ready to pop their clogs, they split up only an acre apiece between each of their three sons. Which means the third generation only get a third of an acre each. Pretty fucking soon, we're looking at a square foot apiece. I mean, how do they get out of that? That's pretty much besides the point, but the other thing about land, especially in the rural areas, is that it stays in the family and the ownership of that land is like a symbol of existence for some people. These people exist because of the land that was owned by their ancestors before them, and as a result, they see a reason for their kids to exist after them. Not something you get in Bradford I'll grant you, but it's a bit like a fair inheritance system, without the bloodsucking solicitors and all that capital gains shite. But what, I hear you ask, about gender? About women? About daughters? Well the thing about daughters, is that they're transients in some senses. You love them just like you love a son but you know that one day, they'll get married and leave you. So what do you do to give them security the sons get through land inheritance? You give them nothing except a husband who, with any luck, will have inherited his own land and will also be able to support his new wife, and, if God wills it, the kids who'll follow. I know it isn't what people think of as a totally equal system but on the surface at least, it seems to work. Unless people start killing each other over bits of land, of course.

So, these two brothers, they have a bit of a barney about the land and end up not talking. The next thing you know, one of them is offed. The only mystery, as far as the younger brother can tell, is who'd do a thing like that? Who would stand to gain by killing his elder brother? By the time he and everyone else had worked it out, it was too late. There were three brothers in all and the third one, younger again than the other two, had an iron-clad alibi but he was the one who pulled the strings. This third brother, the youngest, really deserved to hang, having hatched a plan while working in Dubai. All he did was write a letter to one of his mates back in the village to do the dirty work for him and by doing that, he'd just trebled his share. One brother murdered and the other one taking the blame and being hung meant he got the fucking lot. And, to prove that the place is such a fuck-up, the cunt shrugged it all off and lived happily ever after.

That was what my dad told me, and everyone who knew this third brother fucked him off after that, even though he never admitted to a thing. My dad was pretty sure it was him, but my dad wouldn't put anything past some people. My dad was right about not having it too bad, of course. If I'd been in Pakistan, I'd have been dead. Maybe England wasn't too bad. Still being alive was a consolation, if nothing else.

I stood outside the courtroom for a few seconds and took it all in. Never in my wildest dreams had I been at the centre of such attention. Not in a million years would I have expected it. You just don't think of things like that happening to you. Lights! Camera!

Action! Fuck! It was like a mad person's city all of a sudden with all these cunts who were carrying cameras, microphones and tape machines, all of which were being shoved in my face as if they wanted me to eat the fucking things. Shouting their questions at me, like they were going mad about something. Off guard? You could say that, because I just stood there, blinded by the flashes and deafened by a thousand heated, urgent voices that just wouldn't stop. I felt an arm around my shoulder and turned, half expecting some cunt to bottle me. Thank fuck for slick and smarmy solicitors like Gates. He told me not to worry and to let him do all the talking. I said nothing, didn't even nod but Gates had this thing covered. Slick twat silenced them with nothing more than a raised hand. He kept his word because I stopped worrying as soon as the first sound came out of his mouth. He talked, and then some.

"At the moment," he said, "my client has not had the chance to prepare a statement. As you can imagine, the events of the last few days have been extremely stressful and traumatic for him, and for his family."

"Did you do it?" somebody shouted.

"I would like to point out," Gates continued quickly, "that my client is considering filing an official complaint and pursuing damages for verbal, physical and psychological abuse which both he and his brother suffered at the hands of various police officers, and also for wrongful arrest and subsequent unlawful detainment."

"What about the stories?" moaned some cockney bastard who probably wrote for *The Sun*.

"What about the will?" some other idiot screamed.

"My client would greatly appreciate it if the press behaved in a thoughtful, responsible manner and allowed he and his family some peace and calm. Thank you for your time. No more questions."

"When can we see the novel?"

"That is all. No more questions. Thank you."

"Who's publishing it?"

"*No* more questions. Thank you." said Gates, sounding suddenly annoyed.

By the time we'd finished shaking the media cunts off we were standing by a car which he'd arranged to pick us up.

"Thanks, man," I said, once we were in and off. "You're good."

"I know," he said.

"Why is there all this fuss, man? I don't get it."

"You're news." Gates rubbed his eyes and leaned back in the seat. "Some local TV reporter picked the story up and it just seems to have grown."

"What?" I said. "A suicide?"

"That's not the story, Amjad. You are. A writer who writes about a crime before he goes and does it. Think about it."

"But that's not what happened."

"Does that matter? The papers are going mad. Especially the dailies."

"Oh shit!"

"Some of the broadsheets are in on it as well."

"What? They wouldn't stoop to that level, would they?"

"A newspaper's a newspaper at the end of the day, Amjad."

"What are they saying? That I did it?"

"In a round-about sort of way. But the broadsheets don't seem to be too concerned about that."

"Yeah? Then what have they got a gripe with?"

"Somehow, don't ask me how, but they managed to get a hold of some of your stuff. It was leaked to them. It might even have been the police."

"And they think I murdered her?"

"That's not important, Amjad. The big papers, they're going down a different avenue."

"Don't tell me."

"You've guessed it. They're trying to print segments."

"Can't we do anything about that?"

"I've done what I can already. But the critics, they've already done their bit."

"How?"

"They've reviewed some of your work."

"What? How the fuck can they get away with that?"

"You sent your stories to a magazine for publication. That puts them in the public domain as it were, opens them up for criticism."

"I don't believe that. When did they print?"

"This morning. I didn't find out until I read them for myself."

"And?"

"And what?"

"What did they say?"

"Well, to be honest, you got slated."

"Shit! Anyway, critics, what the fuck do they know? They're like a bunch of over-the-hill porn stars suffering from premature ejaculation. And anyway, they haven't seen my best stuff."

"Maybe we could do something about that."

"Maybe."

We got out of the hub-bub fairly quickly. I couldn't believe the nerve of those fucking critics, though. Most of the stuff I'd written was only first-draft material. It certainly wasn't finished product and there's a lot of shit that goes into the finished product. Structure, consistency, relevance and even stupid stuff like punctuation.

"Listen," I said to Gates, "it's not that I'm ungrateful or anything…"

"You want to know how much this is going to cost you, I suppose?"

"It'd be nice to know how much I'm going to have to scrounge."

"Don't worry. It'll be okay."

"But still."

"You're a student?"

"Yeah, trying to be."

"You work in the shop?"

"Yeah, but it's a helping out thing more than anything else. I don't get paid as such."

"We'll sort something out. Don't worry, publicity like this, you cannot buy. If you know what I mean."

"Yeah, I know what you mean. That's very honest of you."

"Honesty is my middle name, Amjad."

He smiled tightly.

"That's got a ring to it."

"Besides," he continued, "you shouldn't have too many problems on the money side of things any more."

"You mean with the papers being interested and that?"

"Erm, not quite."

Gates was full of surprises. He wasn't being his blunt and to-the-point self all of a sudden.

"Go on," I prompted.

"Erm, well." He looked out of the window. "It seems you might have come into some money. It was just a quick conversation. I don't know all the details myself."

I glanced at him briefly, then looked down at the floor. I didn't want to make eye-contact, right then.

"What?" I managed to say.

"It seems you've been named in a will. Three guesses who. An old lady, recently deceased."

I kept looking at the carpet.

"Is this some kind of joke or what?"

"Your father contacted me today. Not long ago, actually."

"He phone you?"

"No, he came down. He was a little upset but I had to be with you as soon as I could. I'm afraid I didn't get a chance to discuss things in greater detail with him."

"What? Why? Can you just slow down a little here?"

I pulled my head up from the floor. I wasn't smiling. Gates looked at me like he knew everything but he didn't. He just thought he did. A couple of moments later he started explaining. It wasn't that I really needed an explanation but I thought I'd let him go through the motions because it might have made him feel good. It didn't take a genius to work out the cobblers he was thinking, but still, I felt I had to contest it. I mean, there were insinuations being made. The will would suddenly change a lot of things, and all of them would seem to be for the worse.

"Hang on, just hang on one second."

"Problem?"

"Yeah, there's a problem. I don't believe it. That's the problem."

"Well. It's the truth."

"What about family? She must have had some family."

"It's possible that she has relatives, the police are checking databases, but as yet, they've come up with nothing. Not that it makes much difference to you, or to the police for that matter," said Gates, sounding as if it was over.

He was thinking I'd fucked him over. I could tell simply by the way he looked at me and from the pitch of his tone. He was probably feeling a little lost, but also absolutely betrayed, because I'd told him I was innocent. Shit, I'd even proved my innocence to him. The will really fucked things up for me. What else could someone like him think?

"Of course it makes a difference!" I spat. "It lands me right back in it. Fuck, man! I don't fucking believe this!"

"No it doesn't. Just think about it. The CPS will check all the statements once again and the police will probably see your Mr MacMahon as an unreliable witness and they'll take it from there. There really is nothing for you to worry about any more."

"Where have I heard that before?" I said.

"There is absolutely no reason for you to be worried, Amjad. Think about it. What would you do? You'd check out the credibility of the only witness against you. You'd look at the suspect, his record, the fact that he admitted to delivering goods to the victim's house as a service. They'll decide that they haven't got a case. Not with you they haven't."

"But what about the will?"

"Just get on with life, Amjad. Forget about all this. You have some money now, her solicitor's number has been left at the reception for you. You go and see him, you can collect, eventually."

"What's that supposed to mean? What're you accusing me of?"

"That's not what I said…"

"But that's what you meant. Right?"

"Perhaps I should have phrased that a little better. You're a free man, and, as you say, you're innocent. Annie Potts isn't your problem any more."

"Yeah, but you have to admit, it kind of stinks, though. You don't really believe any of this, do you?"

"That really doesn't matter."

"Does to me. You think I could do a thing like that?"

"I really have nothing further to say. I've done my job, that's all that matters."

"Look, I know what you're thinking, it's obvious what you're thinking. Shit! Even I'm thinking it. But this isn't right. Someone's set me up."

"Set you up? For what? You're not making sense about this. This isn't the crime of the century."

"Why would she name me in her will like that? People don't do that kind of thing."

"Well, she did, apparently."

"She wouldn't have done, though. That's what I'm saying. This whole fucking thing doesn't make sense. Don't you get it?"

"No, I don't think I quite follow you."

"Someone's after me. First they try and frame me for doing her over, then they make sure the coppers see I'm in the will because then, the fucking coppers will go and put two and two together."

"And make four. There's no crime in being left something in a will, Amjad."

"Don't tell me that! You know what I'm talking about, man. You know how it looks."

"Well."

"Don't tell me you're not thinking it. I know you're thinking it, that's why you seemed so pissed off when you looked at me just now."

"What is there to think about?"

"Don't. Please. I know you do it for a living but don't try to be like that with me. I'm not stupid, you know."

"Perhaps you should spell it out for me."

"Okay, if you insist. You're thinking I did all this thing by myself. I planned everything from the beginning for the money. That's what you're thinking, and what's more, you're thinking I've got away with it."

"It doesn't make any difference what I think."

"It does to me. It makes all the difference in the world, man. What do you think other people will think? People who know me won't say it makes no difference. They're not as easy going as you seem to be. I'm as good as buried with this shit, now."

It was going to be hard, and the hardest part would be going back home. It wasn't just home, though. It was to do with community. I knew the way people's minds worked around my end of the world. They were suspicious and very rarely fair, but that was okay because it was consistent and they were like that with everyone. The old man who got accused of abusing kids was their target as much as the young bucks who went around nicking stereos out of their cars. One thing they all hated though, for various reasons, was the government. If they were crooks, they were only being crooks because there were no jobs they could live on. If they were straight, then they were at the hands of the crooks and the only reason crooks were around was because the government was too wimpish in banishing crooks to jails. And if it wasn't that, the government wasn't doing enough to give the bent population enough money to live on, or decent jobs to do. If the people were employed then the government taxed them too much. If they were on the dole, they didn't get enough. If they signed on as well as making a few quid on the side, they only did so because they were forced to do so by the government. And all of these people always took things to be gospel that were not necessarily proven to be truths. And sometimes they couldn't bring themselves to admit to being wrong even if someone had been proven innocent. The trouble was, they had believed that the person was guilty before the truth emerged and their truth was so much stronger than that of the government, the police or the law. That local and rough justice would happen with me. They thought I was guilty in the beginning, and regardless of evidence to counter such an accusation, I'd stay guilty because the ones who had decided it could never bring themselves to backtrack once they had reached their own unjust verdict. And that was going to mean bad news. Not just for me but for the whole family. We were all going to get that treatment.

"Look," Gates said, "she's left you some money. You can always say she must have liked you."

"Bollocks. She might have liked me but she couldn't have liked me that much."

"You need a rest," said Gates, sounding as if he was being

genuine about it. "More than that, you deserve a rest. Take some time off, you can afford it now."

"I don't think I should. I mean, I just don't fucking get it. Why would she do that? Why would she leave me all her money? I mean, all I ever did was deliver shit to her."

"She had no one else. There are no known relatives."

"She had a daughter. That's what she told me a while back."

"No she didn't. And even if she did, they haven't been able to find her. She never married, you know."

"I know, she told me. I thought that maybe she'd had this kid out of wedlock or something. She only mentioned her the once."

"There was no one, Amjad. Just you. Look, this sort of thing has been known to happen before. People with nobody leave everything they have to the few people who might have shown them some kindness at some point in their lives. It is possible that she liked you. Anything is possible."

"What? Are you trying to be funny?"

"No, of course not. She had no children of her own and perhaps you were the closest thing to the son she never had. Your guess is as good as mine with this but it really is nothing to worry about. If you're innocent, what difference does it make what I, or for that matter, what anyone else thinks?"

"That's easy for you to say. What about the press? Wait till they start going to town on this shit. You know what those bastards are like. Fuck! And what about the coppers? They won't leave me alone now. Why'd she have to go and do something like that? I mean, why me, man?"

"You'll be fine. No one will be able to harass you for one thing. The press and the police have guidelines to follow."

"Guidelines? Are you serious? You think that'll stop them?"

"The point is…"

"What? The point is that this shit is just as bad as being convicted."

"It'll all blow over soon enough. My advice is to get yourself sorted out. Put your family at ease and forget about it. By the way, your father sounded as if he was quite concerned when he came in."

"About what exactly?"

"Look, this isn't doing any of us any good. I have to get back to the office and I do have other clients to see."

"I see."

"Look, if it makes any difference, I do believe you."

"But you didn't at first."

"I had my reservations. But murder isn't what you're about."

"And you can tell?"

"Perhaps."

Gates didn't look me in the eye when he told me that.

"Fuck! I wish I never set eyes on the old bag! What a stunt, eh?"

"Believe me, she must have liked you," said Gates, still sounding friendly but also a little worried.

"I don't know, she wasn't like that."

"Don't take this the wrong way, Amjad. But you said in your statement that you knew her as well as you could know any customer. Did you know her better than that?"

"Well, I suppose so. Maybe I did know her a little better than that. I didn't love her or anything. We'd just talk sometimes, you know. Just talk. There's no crime in that, is there?"

help the aged - part two

"Would you like a cigarette?"

"Go on then, you're trying to kill me, you are."

"You are a one!"

"And so are you, sweetheart."

"How much is it?"

"It's on the receipt. Pay us later if you want."

"Ooh, no. The home help went to the post office today. I've some money in the purse."

"Pay day, eh? What are you gonna do with it? Blow it on a cruise or a week's worth of fags and booze?"

"You are a tease! I don't know why I put up with you."

"I do. Because you're after my body."

"Stop it!" she laughed and then started coughing her guts out.

"Sorry, Annie. You want some water?"

She nodded her head. I went into her kitchen and got it.

"There you go. Nice and slow."

"Thank you."

"No problem, Annie. You sure you're okay?"

"Yes, thank you."

"Right. I'll be off then."

"Just a minute! The money!"

"Shit. Forget me head if it was loose."

"There you are. A nice crisp twenty pound note."

"It's not that much, is it?"

"Keep the change."

"No. I'll knock it off the next bill."

"It's all right. It's only money."

"Makes the world go round, though, Annie."

"For some of us."

"I suppose so. Listen, I'll see you tomorrow."

"Would you like a drink?"

"Bit of a rush on. Maybe tomorrow, eh?"

The next day.

"Would you like a cigarette?"

"Go on then, you're trying to kill me, you are."

"You are a one!"

"And so are you, sweetheart."

"How much is it?"

"It's on the receipt. There's yesterday's change knocked off as well."

"You shouldn't have bothered."

"It's your money, Annie. You shouldn't be so generous with your dosh like that."

"Well, you deserve it. Young rascal that you are."

"Rascal, is it?"

"Well, sometimes."

"Okay. I'll let you off this time."

"Would you like some tea, today?"

"Yeah. Why not?"

"I won't take long."

"Tell you what, you stay where you are and I'll get it. Sugar? Milk?"

"White and two sugars. Thank you."

The day after.

"So. What's happening in the wonderful world of Annie?"

"It isn't wonderful any more. It used to be."

"I'm sure it still is, in its own way."

"I'm sure it's not."

"Well, isn't this jolly?"

"Stop it."

"Sorry. How's your health?"

"Mustn't grumble."

"Why not?"

"I haven't got the strength these days."

"I suppose a game of squash is out of the question, then?"

"Stop it."

"How about a quick game of footy, three and in?"

"Stop it."

"Sorry. How's the home help?"

"A bitch, as usual."

"I've told you before, Annie, you should change her. Put a complaint in, Annie. Show a bit of spirit."

"You can't show what you haven't got."

"You're not dead yet, Annie."

"Might as well be."

"Oh please. Stop telling me this."

"I'm sorry, I shouldn't burden you with my worries."

"No. I'm sorry."

"Have you written any more stories, lately?"

"Bits and bats. I wrote this one about a bald guy you might like."

"Yes, I would like to see it."

"I'll let you have a look-see some time."

"Lovely, I can't wait."

"It's not that good, Annie."

"You're too modest for your own good. Have you tried any more publishers?"

"Nah, not really."

"You mustn't give up. It would be such a waste."

"And neither must you, my dear."

"No. I expect not."

"I best be off."

"Five more minutes."

"For you Annie? No problem. If it was anyone else, I'd charge them."

"You are a one!"

waterfall

"Where can I drop you?" asked Gates.

"Home."

"That isn't such a good idea at the moment," he said. "They'll already be camped out there by now. This is big news and it would be better if we kept ourselves out of the limelight for now."

"Shit, I forgot about those pricks and the way they can pick up a scent!"

"Don't worry. It'll all work out. Trust me, Amjad."

"Okay. I do, man."

"Anywhere else you'd like to go instead?"

"Yeah. How's Brazil sound?"

"I don't think I can quite manage that. Somewhere closer to home, perhaps?"

"Yeah, I know a place."

The first thing I ever said to her was okay.

"Do you wanna dance?"

"Yeah, all right then," she replied. "If you want."

The second thing I ever said to her was not okay. It was a mistake as soon as I let it out of that mouth of mine. I was a bit of an idiot back then and didn't even realise it was a mistake so instead I did what was expected of me. I just stood there and tried hard to keep a straight face and not piss myself laughing.

"Go on then," I said. "Off you go love."

It was a put down line, the kind of shite young lads on a night out on the town came out with. It was entertainment, something you'd do for a laugh before you had an even bigger laugh by getting into some bother with anyone who fancied something to make the night even more memorable. You'd say crap like that to ugly and fat birds in order to get a laugh out of your mates. But Shelley, I was to discover she was called, was neither fat nor ugly. She was just a bit of a Plain Jane back then, but even that can be appealing in the right time and at the right place.

She put her hands on her hips.

"I suppose you think that's funny," she said, through half-shut eyes. Most lasses would have told me to go and fuck myself. It was a shitty thing to say to any lass, but I'd heard a lot worse and I'd seen far worse reactions. Maybe that was why I thought it wouldn't harm me to stick around for a couple of minutes.

"Yeah, well. It was funny, sort of. They thought so anyway," I said as I looked over at the rest of the lads who were standing by the bar, giving me the thumbs up, shaking their heads at each other and probably telling each other what a prick I still was.

"And that's it, then, is it? That's all? That best you can do?"

"Well, for now. I suppose it is, yeah."

"I don't know why I'm wasting my time talking with an idiot like you," she said as she tossed her head and began to turn away.

"I'm not asking you to, love!"

That got another laugh from the lads. She just shook her head and started to walk off. I didn't blame her. It had been known for other lasses to stand there giggling as you were taking the piss out of them and they'd only stand there because they wanted you. Some of them were that keen on getting bounced they didn't even listen to what you were saying and those that did listen were too fucking thick to realise they were being humiliated. The ones who did understand and had some sense of dignity would stomp off before tears could well in their eyes and those were just as bad as all those tarty slappers because, you thought, they really should lighten up a bit. It was only a laugh, after all.

But a lass who stood her ground and gave you something reasonably decent in the way of a response? A lass who didn't go for the bait but went for the hand that held the bait? That was different. That was nice.

"Look, sorry," I said, as I stepped up behind her.

I was thinking she didn't look too bad and that maybe she was the wrong kind of lass to have said shit like that to, and I was the wrong kind of lad to have said it, in all honesty. I was always doing things like that when I was younger, just to be a little more popular than the others. I wanted to be the centre of attention, but it never really suited me and got to be a bit of a burden at times. It was always me who was supposed to pull crazy and childish stunts which was fine at the time until I started getting paid back in kind.

I got sick of being an arsehole and Shelley had a lot to do with me seeing that. I was better off sticking to being a part of the furniture like most of the lads I was with, I realised. It was easier, for one thing. All they had to do was to laugh at my pranks and move out of the way when some boyfriend offered me out for looking up his girlfriend's skirt while she was dancing around her handbag. I mean, it was only a laugh, but sometimes it got dangerous.

"I didn't mean nothing by it, honest."

Shit, when the light was right, she didn't look half bad. She wasn't the most beautiful girl in the world, but she didn't seem to care. Some birds who are a bit short on the looks will pile on the old war paint as if it's plastic surgery, whereas others forget about such nonsense and let every bloke in the vicinity know they'll drop their knickers as soon as someone buys them a cocktail with a little umbrella stuck in it. There were all sorts of people in those clubs. Those who wanted a good time with the music and a bit of dancing and those who wanted to get pissed up with their mates. People who wanted to cause hassle and the majority, from what I could tell, were those who wanted nothing more than a shag with a total stranger. At least, that was one of the reasons we'd go into town and most times, half of us would get lucky. But this lass wasn't about any of that. Shelley was strictly a music and dance girl, and getting a shag at the end of the night probably never entered her mind. I felt bad about being a presumptuous twat, and besides, she had made me feel a little low. Asking her to dance for real was one way of reversing things. Well, I thought so, anyway.

"You still wanna dance?"

"Yeah, right! So you can come out with that same crap line again, go annoy someone else, will you. Kids!"

I smiled at her and grabbed her hand and she still didn't think I was being serious. We hit the floor (everyone used to 'hit the floor' back then for some reason) and we danced. She was all right was Shelley, a good dancer but a bit too keen on sticking her tongue in my ear during the slow numbers. I hated that. It was the squish-squelch noise that really ruined it for me. Sounded too much like a worm crawling into my ear and then not being able to get out.

She was a year or so older than me and was doing what I'm doing now. She was a student but she had a bonus on her side because she was from Lincoln or some place like that so she had her own place here, in Bradford. All by herself in her digs and bored out of her head, she said. I was in. That was the highest you could aim for and actually expect to reach in a lifetime. A bird, a shaggable bird and best of all, a bird with her own place. You couldn't get better than that, unless you were a greedy bastard and wanted a bird who you could sponge off, as well.

The best thing about Shelley, apart from being a natural blonde – which she honestly thought was the best thing about her – was that she was never clingy. With some women it's as if you're married as soon as you've set eyes on them. Never mind how far you're going to get on the first date, some of them are thinking they're going to have you all to themselves forever. All that possessive nonsense would immediately put me off. What the fuck, you're only young once, right? It was good because she was a free spirit and so was I, but when we were together, we got it on really well. It was like we'd known each other for years, like we knew everything there was to know about each other. There was never any pressure, and our relationship wasn't like others we'd both lived through before. Sometimes we fought, argued or moaned at each other but it never lasted too long and it was never too serious. Best of all, we just did our own things and sometimes we did them together.

But all that was years ago. It was, as they say, ancient history, and breaking off with her was mostly my doing. The last time I'd seen her was about three years ago in town while I was shopping for a pair of trainers. We stopped, looked each other up and down, commented on how good we both looked and agreed that it would be nice if we had a coffee. She paid because she said she was loaded then, working for some hotshot TV company somewhere as an executive producer, whatever the fuck that was. Shelley was one of the few people who'd got a job relevant to her training. She'd been a bit too rigid at times with what she thought about the world and how it should have been, but even that was kind of endearing. She hadn't changed that much when I saw her that day in town. And if she had, it had been for the better. She looked a lot better as a twenty-eight year-old than she did at eighteen. Laugh lines and the sleepy and a little bloodshot whites of her eyes seemed to have made her more attractive. While we sat drinking coffee and sharing some laughs, I actually regretted ever having split with her. We'd have been good if I hadn't been such a fucking dickhead.

We got talking about one thing and another, and then about old times. For some reason, the bad times were remembered fondly by the both of us. Shelley was still smiling about all those rows we had towards the end of the 'relationship' I maintained we'd never had. I got the feeling she felt it had been worth her while knowing me, even despite the crap. I didn't bother asking her about her love life or anything and she didn't bother asking me. But there was definitely this vibe thing going off between us. The way she looked at me as she sipped her coffee said so much more than what we were talking about. It wasn't just body language, there was something we were both thinking, but not daring to reveal. It was like that first night when we met at the club. I went with her to her flat. Ten minutes later, I started going through her crappy record collection and making comments about her taste. We spent the next two hours manoeuvring ourselves like chess pieces on a board. It was a game which would only end when one of us would get the other into bed. Until one of us would eventually call checkmate and win. I thought maybe she wanted to make the suggestion. That perhaps we should get together sometime, even if it was only for a curry or a drink. Something that would get us going again. I was playing hard to get, I thought and if she wanted it, the same as I wanted it, she could go right ahead and ask for it herself. I only hoped she still wanted to know me now as Gates dropped me off outside her yard.

"You call me first thing tomorrow," he said as I opened the door to get out.

"Here's my card."

His smile then, would have shamed Bob Monkhouse.

"I'll call you." I said.

"Good, there are some other things we've got to talk about."

"I know."

I knew plenty of other people who would have put me up for the few days it would take for the press to calm down. There was my big sister, I had a few mates who were living in their own places with their wives or girlfriends, and then, as the last resort, there were a couple of lasses I knew. The thing was, I didn't really feel like going to any one of those places. My sister had enough hassle with her kids and a great big fat bone idle husband who did nothing but loaf around and moan all day. My mates would only get their ears chewed off by their birds for accepting me, and the lasses I'd shagged at some point, well, they were just a bit too dippy to actually live with even if it was only on a temporary footing. They were all right for a good time, but anything else, like talking and discussing things, was way over their heads. Shelley was the only person I could have seen right then, and it was because I kind of missed her, I suppose. She was in many ways, the best partner I'd ever had. She was clever, funny and a good person to be with. Sex was there as well, but sex is never a problem with most birds as most birds know what they're doing. The ones that I've been with have all been pretty energetic. Some of them could have done it for a living but maybe that's a reflection on me. Maybe I'm just good at picking up scrubbers.

Gates stuck around for a minute or two. He seemed concerned about something and I thought it was little old me he was worrying over. I'd be okay, he needn't worry and I told him to go. I didn't want to take too much of his very expensive time. Eventually he gave a little half-hearted smile and drove off. If the house was empty I could make my own way somewhere else. I'd cross that bridge if and when I came to it. Anyway, crossing bridges and being fucked around seemed to have been a favourite pastime of mine for the last couple of days.

The house looked much the same as it did all those years ago. It was still owned by a housing association and the windows and doors were painted in that horrible, dull grey blue they seem to love. The main door was always open, but there was a real front door behind it. The house had four flats, and next to the inner door was a metal panel on which were the four buttons, one for each flat. Shelley lived in number four so I pressed the button which made a horrible rasping noise. After a few minutes I pressed again but there was still no response. There was only one thing for it, I decided, I'd have to play the tit and see if I could con my way in.

I pressed buzzer number three and waited for the intercom to crackle to life.

"Yeah? Who is it?" said a man's voice.

"All right? I'm ringing from number four, next door. I've lost my keys. All right if you buzz me in, mate?"

"Oh aye? We're not supposed to do owt like that, you know. Can't let you in just like that, you know."

"I know but I've just been to the office and they can't help me."

"Why not? They should be able to let folk in when they lose keys. Course they should."

"I know but the bloody caretaker's off sick. I've no key on me and neither have any of the people down there, in the office."

"How're yer goin' to get in to yer flat then? How're you goin' to gerrin without a key?"

"I've got a spare."

"What? In the flat? Inside the flat? What use is that, then? I mean, if it's in yer flat."

"No. It's outside the flat. An emergency key I've got hidden. You know, in case I lose my original."

"Well, I dunno, I shunt really. It's against 'rules, like. I shunt really."

"Look, I'll even show you the key when I grab it. If you'll let us in, that is."

"What number y'say yer from again? What's the number of yer flat?"

"Four, number four."

"How come I've never seen yer, then? There's a young lass that lives there. I've never seen no bloke in there, before."

"That's our Shelley. Look, I've not been here long. She'll go mad when she finds out I've lost her key."

There was a pause which was good. That meant he was thinking and I knew it wouldn't take a great deal more to convince him.

"All right. I'm letting yer in. But get this, pal, I'm warning yer, you try anything."

"Cheers, I appreciate it."

He buzzed me in and I belted it up the stairs to the second floor where I found the bloke already waiting outside Shelley's flat. I walked up to him and flashed him a smile that tried to say, *"you've nothing to fear from me, mate, I'm as harmless as a soft boiled egg"*. He didn't smile back but he did look at me for a minute, like maybe he'd seen me somewhere before but couldn't quite place the face.

"Well? Where's this key of yours supposed to be hidden then?" he said, squaring up. "Well? Are you gonna show us it, or what?"

"Don't take this the wrong way, but I can't really tell you that. Can I?"

"Oh yeah? Why not? Why's that, then?"

"Well, er, it'd be a bit pointless wouldn't it? I mean, it wouldn't be much of a secret hiding place any more if I went and showed it to everyone, would it?"

"So, how yer goin' to show us it, then? How are yer goin' to prove to us that you've gorra spare key in the first place? You've gorra show it us, you said you would, like, and now I'm waitin'."

Was it me or what? Was the guy a bit of a nutter? I'm not being cruel, but there was definitely something weird about him. He was wearing braces, for one thing, and his glasses were the kind that you'd associate with people who have no sense of taste or decency. He looked like Benny Hill when he was doing the old pervert routines. But the real business was the way he spoke. He kept repeating and rephrasing everything. Surely, this guy belonged somewhere else? Some place where there were plenty of men in white coats and plenty of electricity to keep him charged like that.

"Okay, tell you what, you turn around until I tell you to turn back and face me. I'll get it and then I'll show you it. How's that sound?"

"Nah, nah, mate. How am I supposed to know you won't lamp me one over the head with summat? Eh? I don't know you from Adam, do I? Y'could be anyone. Y'could be a bloody thief for all I know. You could bray us while I'm not loo-king."

"Well, I wouldn't. I'm not like that."

"I'm not saying you are, pal. But how am I supposed to know that, eh? You can't trust anyone, can yer? I don't know what you're likely to try on with us, do I? I mean, I don't know you from Adam, do I?"

"Okay, okay. Tell you what, you go back into your room, come out after ten seconds and then I'll show you the key. How's that sound?"

"Mmm. I dunno about that. Mmm."

"Well, that's about the best I can think of. I can't try anything on with you if you're in your flat, can I?"

"Ten seconds, or I'll call police on yer. Don't forget. Ten seconds, pal. No more than ten. You've been warned. Ten seconds or the police'll be here for you. I've gorra phone, you know. Don't think they've cut me off because I might not have paid me bills or summat daft like that, don't..."

"Ten seconds."

It was funny, like I was really in the mood for playing hide and seek with someone who should have had happy pills coming out of his ears as he sat his life out in some padded room. The guy was obviously a nutter. One of those poor souls that some loony bin had let out because they thought his condition had improved over the last ten years. I mean, the whole idea with the locks and the buzzers set-up was to protect the tenants from people like me. When you took on a flat in that joint, they'd actually make you sign a form stating you agreed to abide by all the rules and regulations of the housing association. And somewhere right at the top of the list of rules were the all important security arrangements and procedures. Any cunt who didn't have a key just wasn't allowed in. And if you didn't know the person who was trying to get in, well, they could stay outside and freeze their balls off. I could have been any old psychotic freak out on the loose, ready to kill the first person I felt like killing. Having said that, I was extremely grateful for him being there and for him being the one to let me in. For all his stupidity, he was still an angel as far as I was concerned. A more sane individual would just have called the coppers. Coppers I'd had enough of and one more accusation from someone sane would only help them getting one over on me. Fair enough, they'd have thought, they might have fucked up the murder charge but they could recover somewhat by trapping my balls in a vice with something stupid like this.

Shelley always had a spare key. She wasn't the type to ever lose her own but she was just cautious about things like that. I ran my hand over the top of the door frame and stopped when I moved the single door key. I grabbed it and squeezed it in my hand before I went to the neighbour's door.

"Key," I said as he opened the door.

"I suppose that's all right, then. I suppose it's yours," he said as he gazed at the bit of metal lying flat on the palm of my hand.

"No sweat."

The neighbour closed his door and then opened it again.

"'Ere, I'm sure I know you from somewhere. Don't I? I'm sure I've seen you around."

"Don't think so. You might have seen me coming in and out."

"Nah, don't think so. Nah, not 'ere."

"Maybe it'll come to you."

"Humph," he said as he closed the door once again.

Shelley's flat had changed considerably since I'd last been in it. She must have been earning some serious dosh, I thought. A few decent paintings adorned the walls where there was once nothing but painted wood-chip, and hand-painted Oriental vases were placed at either side of the fireplace. Then there was the furniture. Back in her student days, Shelley was something of an improviser. She'd get hold of some junk from a skip or a junk shop and make something really decent out of it. One time she got a hold of a really fucked-up old couch and decided to 'work' with it. It looked like cats, dogs and fuck knows what else had ripped the shit out of it and by the time Shelley copped for it, even sewer rats wouldn't have been seen dead anywhere near it. She got me to give her a hand lumbering the fucking thing up to her flat and spent the next three months or so fucking around with it. Restoring it. 'Working' with it.

The couch that she had made good – and it did look good after she'd finished with it – was no longer there, and in its place was something only rich people have. A black leather suite, spotless, shiny, perfect. It wasn't a gaff any more. It wasn't a flat. It looked like a home. In front of the suite was a nice rug, very plush and well kept and something she must have taken her time deciding on. The rest of the floor looked like hours had been spent on it. Where there was once this rotten old carpet there was now nothing. Just a bare, sanded and beautifully polished floor. The kind of floor that made a sharp and solid 'Tock!' when women with stiletto shoes walked over it. A few other pieces of expensive and tasteful furniture were tactfully dotted around the room. I didn't bother poking my nose anywhere else. The wonders she had doubtless done to her kitchen, bathroom and bedroom would have to wait until she came in and allowed me to discover her new, expensive and mature tastes in decor. I plonked myself down on the sofa and, for the first time in what seemed like years, I relaxed. I closed my eyes and felt myself falling asleep. Sleep was something my body yearned for, but a voice in my head was telling me to hang on a while longer. I had to accept what was happening to me, and that it was far from over. Gates, the pigs, the press and even a trial might still be waiting for me. I had to do something to get my shite sorted out, keep my head in check, stop myself from going under. Having said that, it was still exciting, in a way.

I decided to give home a ring. I'd tell them that I was stopping at a friend's gaff and I was okay. But there was an engaged tone every time I hit the redial button. Shit! All those so-called fair minded citizens must have been giving them abuse. Or the fucking press were asking them about what they thought about me, what I was like as a kid and what my interests were. Asking about my writing and whether or not there'd ever been any signs of me possessing an impulsive, or perhaps psychotic nature. I was hoping they'd taken the phone off the hook because that kind of hassle would have killed my folks. I called my sister and told her to tell my family I was okay and I'd be in touch again. She told me she would and said she'd pray for me. She's like that, very pious in her own way, is my sister.

That voice in my head, not one of those weird voices that tell cunts to go around killing people, but just a normal weird voice, could have been mimicking Jimi Hendrix down to a tee for the difference it made, because it seemed my body was past caring and told that voice to go fuck itself. I was asleep, but as usual my mind had other plans. I dreamt. And even that dream of mine ended up giving me a hard time.

ain't nobody

The dream I had lying on Shelley's long leather sofa was pleasant and reassured me that things were all right and none of the shite with Annie Potts had ever really happened. Everything had, in fact, been a dream and I was still just a student, shop assistant and would-be writer. But best of all, I was innocent in this dream of mine. That's the trouble with dreams. They try to trick you into thinking they're real. And thinking it was reality made me smile as I was dreaming. When I awoke and realised it was a dream after all, the smile didn't go, like it should have done. Instead, that smile spread itself even wider across my face. I told myself it'd be all right and I was just getting freaky for the fuck of it. For show. Playing the part.

It must have been well after five o'clock when I woke up again because it was dark in the room. What made me open my eyes was the noise coming from outside. I heard a few words being exchanged and a familiar voice. There were the moans and complaints of the neighbour and then, there was a not-so familiar female voice. Shelley? It didn't sound like her. There was the clinking of metal against metal, the zip of a key being pushed home, the click of a lock and then light. All of a sudden, I felt anxious. What if she'd moved out? What if someone else was entering the room and on seeing me would panic and call the police, providing them with a brilliant reason to come after me. What if the couch wasn't hers? What if none of it was hers? What if she'd got married? This flat could have belonged to anybody, I realised. I was such a fucking dimwit at times. Sometimes, I deserved everything I got.

But it was too late to worry. If worst came to worst, I'd just bullshit my way out the way I'd bullshitted my way in. I rubbed my eyes and turned to face her. And thank God it was her. I relaxed for a split second and then realised I was still far from the finishing line. It might have been Shelley's flat but that didn't mean she had to like what she saw on her posh leather couch.

"Shelley, before you say anything, I can explain."

She just stood there, a shopping bag in one hand and a handbag cast around her shoulder.

"I know this looks bad, but if you let me explain…"

"What?" she dropped her bag of shopping when she saw that I was real.

"I can explain. It's me, Ammy."

"What?"

"Don't say that. Don't just keep saying 'what' like that."

"What?"

"It's me. It's Ammy. Let me explain, please."

"What the hell do you think you're doing here!"

"Don't be like that Shelley. You've got to believe me."

She walked further into the room, closer towards me, and then looked at me, shook her head and did that pose of hers. Hands on hips and half closed eyes, a look I hadn't seen in years and never thought I'd miss. Even then, at her strongest and angriest, that look of hers made me smile and gave me reassurance. It was good to see some things didn't change.

"You've got to be joking," she said, finally. "This has got to be some kind of joke."

I lifted myself up on my elbows.

"I'm sorry, Shelley but you were the only one I could see. You're the only one I can trust."

"Oh? What about the cells? You could have spent a few more nights locked up if you were that desperate!"

"You've heard, then." I smiled and sat up.

"Heard? Who hasn't bloody heard?"

"Nothing too bad, I hope."

"That's not funny. An old woman is dead and all you can do is make those stupid jokes of yours."

"Sorry."

"Christ, Ammy, I don't believe your nerve, coming here."

"I know it looks bad, but it wasn't me."

"Wait a minute. Wait just one minute! Whether you did it or not isn't even an issue right now. Just tell me what you think you're doing in my flat."

"I need a place for a few days."

"Not here you don't. You don't just waltz into people's houses like that."

"I know but I had no choice, Shelley."

"This isn't happening, I don't believe I'm even having this conversation!"

Shelley stopped and looked at me as if I was a stranger.

"Why am I talking to you?"

"Shelley. I can explain. Just chill…"

"No. I'm not going to talk to you and I'm not going to bloody well chill! Just who the hell do you think you are?"

"Shelley, just calm down."

"Don't tell me to calm down! Why are you telling me to calm down? Why are you even talking to me? I don't even know you."

"Just pack this shit in! You think I wanted to throw this on you? I was fucking desperate, Shelley. Do you know what that means? Just let me explain."

"That's a good one. I didn't think you were the sort who ever needed to explain anything!"

"Shelley, look, I know it might be hard for you to dig, but I need you."

"Oh. I see. *Now* you need me. Thanks very much."

"Don't make it sound like that."

"Why not? That is how it is. That's the truth that you were always so bloody keen on."

"No. It's not the truth, Shelley."

"That's a lie and you know it."

"It's the truth. I am sorry."

"You? Sorry?"

"Okay. I'm sorry I never called you. I'm sorry we finished. I'm sorry it's you. But it is. You have to believe me. There's no one else I can go to."

"Don't think you can pull that rubbish on me, Ammy, because I won't believe you, not any more."

"Christ, Shelley, you're worse than the bloody pigs! All I'm asking for is a couple of days. I swear, I won't get in your way. Just pretend I'm not even here. For old times?"

"No-no-no. Don't try to put that guilt trip on me, Ammy. I

know how you work."

"You know how I used to work. *Past* tense, Shelley. Things are different now."

"And why should I care?"

"I don't know, because you do?"

"See? I knew you'd come out with that. You're a selfish bastard and you always were. This is mental cruelty, you know that?"

"I'm sorry. I better go. I thought it'd be, you know, okay."

"Just who the hell do you think you are? You can't just walk into somebody's house as if it's yours. That's illegal. I just don't believe your bloody cheek!"

"What do you want me to say? Sorry? Okay, I've said it. Right now I've got nowhere to go and no one to turn to. You're the only person I could think of, Shelley. Shit, I thought we were still friends."

"Sure, fair-weather friends."

"I was going to pay you rent or something. It wasn't like I wanted to free-load or anything."

"That's not what I meant. I meant you wouldn't have come here if you weren't being hunted."

"I'm not being hunted."

"Whatever."

That was it. I was in. Shelley always said one thing when she gave in, 'Whatever'. With her, it was the closest thing she'd get to admitting she was wrong and it was as if formally agreeing with someone diluted her strength or something.

"That mean yes, then?"

"I suppose so. Only for a couple of days. You take the floor."

"What's wrong with the couch?"

"It's leather. It'll crease."

"Fair enough."

Crease? My arse. She was just doing this to show me who was in control. I could live with that, for a day or two, anyway.

moving on up

Gates' office was quieter than I thought it would be. There was only one old dolly bird at reception. She had a small plastic ear-piece shoved into her lug with a thin wire tailing out of it and snaking into some machine somewhere. She sat typing away like some mad woman, her head bobbing to the rhythm of her striking fingers, smiling that permanent lipstick smile.

"I've an appointment with Mr Gates," I said as I stood in front of the counter which formed a protective barrier between us.

"Ah yes, Mr Gates is expecting you," she said in a well controlled and perfectly audible voice.

She was an expert, I could tell. She'd probably been telling clients this sort of thing for years and now she had it down to a fine art and could do it without even thinking. With another flutter of her heavily-coloured eyelids and a face splitting grin, she motioned me into his office.

"Thanks," I said.

"Quite all right."

The thing about solicitors and the like, is they're so fucking polite about everything. Even if they were insulting you, they'd be so fucking nice about it. It must be a pretty fucked up career to have. Solicitors, people like Gates, are the only true mercenaries in this world. I mean, I know I don't give a rat's arse about who and what I write about and I hope to get some coin in no matter how shite my writing is, but the trouble with solicitors is they don't seem to have problems with who they're defending. Like those dim-witted fucks who are clearly crooked because they get caught on camera doing the job, for instance. Or loopy bastards who go around offing women because a voice from the telly tells them to. Okay, every fucker's got to have some right when it comes to proving their innocence but if they're clearly not innocent, then what's the point trying to defend them? What, in actual fact, is the point of a solicitor trying to get some guilty-as-sin type off the hook when he should be doing his best to lock the bastard up? There isn't any fucking point, it's just a waste of time and money.

The legal system has been evolving over centuries and centuries but that still doesn't make it right or as fair as it's supposed to be. There are people who do deserve to be locked up but every now and then there's a fuck-up somewhere, so what happens? They get off the hook, and it's thanks to people like Gates. Defence lawyers. The guilty walk free and it's thanks to people who get paid for being as ruthless, mercenary and as unscrupulous as they can when it comes to doing what's supposed to be their job. Maybe I'm expecting too much out of The British Legal System. Maybe I should accept that like most things in life, justice is a lump of shite. Especially when you needed it to be better than that.

"Morning, how are you?" asked Gates as I walked in.

"Fine? You?"

"Oh, well enough. Have a seat, please," he said and then showed me the seat that he was referring to, as if I wasn't too sure about the word 'seat' or something. He waited, like all polite and thoroughly professional professionals should, for me to take my *seat* and then to get comfortable.

"Right, first things first, I suppose."

Something wasn't quite right with my man Gates. He wasn't exactly on edge or anything, but he just seemed to be a little wary and a bit too formal compared to the last time I'd spoken to him. Like he'd come down from a high or something.

"Your Mr MacMahon," he said thoughtfully.

"What about him?"

"This."

Gates showed me a pile of papers. Freddy's picture was plastered all over them. The same picture. A picture the bastard must have taken on the sly. He looked fucked, like he'd just had a scrap with a pack of wolves or something.

"Oh. That."

"Is that all you can say?"

"Well. That was a while ago now. He had it coming to him."

right here, right now
part three - rumours

I'll always remember the first time it rained. It was a while ago now, but I can still remember what it felt like as it came down and soaked me to the skin. The rain over here is like British rain, only it's wetter, faster and it goes on for a shit load longer.

Sometimes, in the wet season, it doesn't stop for weeks and that's worrying for someone like me who likes to see the sun as often as possible. I was working on my 'second' novel, the one writers are supposed to have trouble with, and the sound of the rain hitting the courtyard tore me away from the computer.

It was amazing, I'd never seen anything like it. It wasn't pissing it, pouring it, throwing it or even chucking it down. It was absolutely shitting it down in buckets the size of barrels. Rain drops the size of ping-pong balls came down and from what I could tell, this rain was actually hurting people. I could hear men, women and children shouting and screaming their heads off as they ran for shelter. It went on for the rest of the day, and then all of a sudden, it stopped. Like someone had just hit the switch. It had just gone half past three in the morning and I was still awake.

Sleeping is still a problem but eventually I get knackered and then, when I'm least expecting it, flake out. My folks are more worried about it than I am and keep telling me to go and see a doctor but I've never really liked the idea of doctors. I know they're supposed to cure you and all that, but most of the ones I've met have been, well, pricks. Like lawyers, but at least if you're on the NHS you don't have to pay them. It's the way they tell you everything and nothing at the same time that really gets to me. The ones over here will probably be worse than those back in England, so for now, I'll just have to do without some of their medicine.

It's strange, but even though I'm away from everything I wanted to be away from and have everything I want, I'm still not happy. It's as if there's still something missing. The more I think about it, the more worried and annoyed I get. This isn't what I thought it would be like. I thought success and money would help, but neither seem to be doing me any good. Maybe I wasn't so clever after all. Maybe I wasn't the man I thought I was.

Things are moving on. The second novel is shaping up and I've had some more money and some more offers of work in the post. I've made a concerted effort to be like I was before. To play a part. I'm a writer and I write. That's me and if people don't like it, then those motherfuckers know what they can all go and do. Saying that won't stop them from coming out with their shit. I know what they'll say and accuse me of but it doesn't matter to me, any more. I know the gig. I, like many writers, use my imagination and nothing more. I clearly use my own experiences and my life in my work. I give people what they want. I have nothing new to offer. I tell it like it is. I'm a charlatan. I must detest England and the language of its vanished realms. I use cliché as if it was going out of fashion. I apply the modern black American approach in my work. I am original. I must hate myself. I never mince my words. I'm callous with my use of language. I am proud of what I am. I am poetic. I use words as weapons. I'm a victim of the modern world. I make the reader my victim. I'm a rebel against nothing. I'm a rebel against everything. I'm a criminal. I'm gifted. I'm modest. I'm arrogant. I have something that is difficult to place let alone describe. I'm a stylist and I'm an interpreter of youth. I'm politically naïve. I'm a literary void. I'm a literary genius. I'm anything but what my character claims to be. I'm everything that my character says he is. I have no concept of the novel. I have the skill of writing a novel down to a fine art. I wouldn't know what a novel was if it danced along and hit me in the face. I'm a con man. A liar. A cheat. And all of that's just fine by me because, believe it or not, it helps. You fucking critics and especially you poxy fucking editors might like to think you know a thing or two, but you're wrong. You've still got your heads up your own arses and nothing, not even a dose of the shits will make you take them out and smell the real world.

We had some visitors today. A cousin of mine came over with his wife and kids. I'd never met him before, but my parents knew him from years ago, when he was a kid and used to run around half naked with snot streaming into his mouth. My mum and dad smiled, chatted and did the rest of the stuff expected of them. For some reason, this cousin of ours kept looking at me as if he wanted a scrap or something. I'd look right back at him and show him no expression which was what he was showing me. His wife looked down at the floor unless she was speaking to my mum and after a few minutes of sitting in and watching the conversation begin to live and then begin to die, I got the gig. It was money.

He wanted a bit of the old 'darr', did this cousin of ours. A loan to get his house, which had been fucked up by the rain, back into shape. My dad smiled and asked how much. My cousin said twenty thousand rupees, which works out to be about three hundred quid, and my dad said he'd have a word with his eldest son, my brother, about it. My cousin and his troupe left a while later and it was then my dad asked me to sit down.

"How's your next book?" he asked.

"Okay. Getting there."

"What's your agent saying?"

"About what?"

"Work."

"Nothing much. Just a few offers."

"Are you going to take them?"

"I might do. I don't know."

"He's a good man, that Gates."

"You can say that again."

"How much have you got in the bank?"

"A few thousand."

"We'll need some money soon, son."

"Sure, Dad. It's there. It's yours."

"We might be a little short, that's all."

"For what? Are we getting a satellite? A car?"

"Nothing like that. It's for you."

"For me?"

"You're not as young as you used to be."

"Marriage?"

"It's about time you stood on your own feet."

"I am on my own feet."

"You need a wife."

"Not yet. Maybe later but not now. Not while I'm trying to get my writing right."

"Your writing is fine. You're established now."

"How would you know?"

"I can use the phone as well. I know what they're saying."

"What do you mean?"

"Son, I know what they're saying about you."

"What's that got to do with anything?"

"There are stories. Lies about you and the old woman. How she died."

"I was innocent."

"I know but think of your sister."

"You believe them?"

"The rumours? The rubbish in the papers? What that criminal, thief and liar has to say? Of course not."

"So why is it a problem?"

"Why do you think? Other people believe those stories. Even if they don't, they'll still remember them. Who would give their son to the sister of an accused murderer?"

"I see."

"These people, once they get something into their heads, it can't be removed. No matter what you say, they still won't see the truth. It's like trying to dance for the blind or sing for the deaf. It doesn't work."

"I'll think about it."

There's a funny thing about innocence and guilt. The law proved me innocent, my family proved me innocent and even I proved myself innocent. But I was still guilty where it mattered. People still thought I was guilty. The ones I left back in Bradford thought I was guilty and the ones I'd come to were proving to be just as bad. Bad news, like they say, travels quickly, and it had arrived in what was my ancestral village, a few days after me. My brother was the first to mention it. Some guys asked him whether or not I killed a little old English lady while he was checking out the bazaar. He told them to fuck off. One thing I've learnt? Arseholes are the same all over the world.

don't believe the hype

Being robbed is never a nice thing. Back in Manningham, it happened to us twice in as many years. The first time we accepted it, put it behind us and got on with life like all law-abiding, decent citizens do. The second time it happened we were prepared to do the same, but at the same time there were rumours. One bloke in particular was walking around with money falling out of his arsehole. You'd have to be a fool to miss a signal like that. Of course, it meant action. We just couldn't sit there and take that shit, could we? We'd deserve to get robbed if we let bastards get away with shit like that.

I was going to have to see Freddy myself. The thing about Manningham is that it's a bit of a mini-society in its own right, and as such has its own customs and laws. It's all right, as long as you behave yourself. Behaving yourself means that thieves only take from those who can afford it, or deserve it, bullies treat subversives in a specifically violent way (by subversives I'm not talking about gays and cross-dressers and shite like that, you get plenty of those in Manningham) and everyone has an intoxicating hatred of the Old Bill. The only time you have call to be involved with coppers is when something totally out of order occurs, like some nonce prowling on kids, or a rapist being particularly violent. Or, for that matter, when some would-be-writer kills some little old dear for no apparent reason. But Freddy committed the biggest crime himself, and if he'd had any sense left in that fucked up head of his, he'd have scarpered.

One guy I knew through the shop was Snowy. He was all right, a couple of years younger than me and doing very nicely thank you. You could tell Snowy was smart from the way he talked, dressed and did business. He had always been one of those people who wanted to make things better for himself. At times, I thought of him as one of those blokes who treated success as a religion. He could be very up front at times but that was usually when he was in business mode. Most times he just got on with people and got on with life.

The weirdest things about Snowy were firstly his colour, and then his height. Snowy, as his nickname might lead you to expect, was whiter than white. But not really white. He was an Asian guy but an albino. That was okay, but every now and then, someone would stare at him for a split second too long.

"Something you need?" he'd ask, and jolt the starer back to reality. The guy was also a midget, wouldn't pass for a fifteen-year-old, but there he was, doing his thing and making money. He smoked heavily – tobacco as well as the old charash – and as a result, his voice was quite deep. His tone was just about the only thing that gave his years away.

Snowy was okay, but the only thing I didn't really dig was the company he kept. He and his mates would storm into the shop and start fucking about with the dirty mags and the chilled booze. But once his dickhead mates had walked out with their hands full of sweets, crisps, beer and fags, he'd apologise on their behalf and then pay, in full, for what they'd taken. Sometimes he'd hang around for a few minutes and we'd catch up on the latest news and developments around Manningham. And most times he'd offer me a deal, right there in the bloody shop, even when there were a few old customers kicking about. I'd tell him I'd see him around and maybe we could do something later just to get rid of the rabble. I never smoked much, hardly ever as it didn't do a great deal for me except send me to sleep whereas others would rave on about how mind-expanding, mellowing, or just plain pleasant an experience smoking the precious herb was. For a long time I thought I was missing out on something really important but then, I got wise. It just wasn't me and I just didn't need any of that shit.

Snowy had been dealing for a good couple of years when I helped him out. I don't really agree with dealers and what they do, but if they had a job or even the prospect of a job I don't think so many would bother peddling in the first place. If you get caught, you're pretty well fucked for a few years and even when you've done your time, things aren't too easy when they allow you back into society. But fuck it, everyone's got to live out there, and where there's a demand, there's bound to be a source of supply springing up close by. Like it or not, that's just the way it is. It's a self perpetuating phenomenon. People come into places like Manningham to buy drugs because they can, and the people who sell them do so simply because people come for them. And that's it. Supply and demand, capitalism at its best, people doing what good old Mrs T told them to do. The coppers try their best by springing raids on hotspots, but it's nothing more than an exercise most of the time. The few dealers that do get caught are only the tip of the iceberg and for every one that goes down there's another dozen waiting to fill his shoes. And even when the coppers do have what they call a 'successful' raid it ends up becoming counter productive because on the very same day of the raid the prices go and rocket. Hiked prices are no big deal for your casual user, who'll just hang about until they drop again and they're also not a big deal for the loaded user who'll have plenty of money to burn. But the ones who get it up the arse are the desperados, those who are well and truly hooked and can't do without. Price increases hurt them the most, so what do they do? They have to supplement what little income they have in other ways. Then, those who are right at the bottom of the pile of shit, lower than the hard-core users, lower than all those junkies who'll try to get off on dog shit when they're hard up, are people like me and my brother, your average Joes trying to make a living, who have nothing to do with the junk that people would sell their souls for.

Being a user and being skint must be bad enough, but when you're into that shit and you're young, it really must be something else. I've seen young girls, seventeen, sixteen and even younger doing that shite, and the only way they can make the money to score is by selling their bodies. And if you look at some of them you wonder how they manage to pay for their johnnies when they run out of the supply from the clinic. Some of them teetered into the shop on skinny, scabby legs, with bad hair, bad teeth, bad skin, bad breath and bad attitude. None of that meant shit to them. Some of them gave you grief for no reason whatsoever, and it was as if being fucked up on drugs and then annoying the fuck out of people was an expectation that they just had to fulfil for some reason. Why should they have given a fuck about what people thought of them, anyway? They knew what they are, and for all I knew, they might have been happy with the way their lives unfolded. I used to make the comments that normal people made but I don't bother any more because it's a waste of breath. I used to wonder how people so young could let that happen to themselves. Young lasses like that should have been busy doing young lass things and surely they should have got themselves straightened out before they ended up being like that permanently. It was those sorts of users who affected people like me. Ordinary, clean, paying-your-bills-on-time people got it in the arse because kids like them had no choice but to thieve and to rob. Getting themselves clean didn't even enter into the equation. What the fuck for? Substance problem? What fucking problem? People like me never actually considered how some of those people might have enjoyed being twatted out of their skulls. Maybe it wasn't even a fucking problem for them. Ordinary people – if we still existed – got burgled and walked into their pads after a night out on the town to find whatever they had of value gone and the stuff that couldn't be taken, like furniture, wallpaper and anything else that was nailed down, ruined with graffiti, stanley knives and human excrement. And that was normal. But the shittiest thing was to kind of expect it all before it even happened to you.

I used to get them all coming into the shop with their spoils. In big ruck-sacks, in sports-bags and even in bin liners. Clothing, power tools, car stereos, hi-fis, TVs, videos and just about anything that could be nicked offered at less than half price to people like me. You name it, they'd nick it and try selling it to anyone. I'm not going to get all high and mighty about it. I can understand the way things are, the world's a cruel place and people being people sometimes have to resort to acts of theft, robberies and muggings to get what they want. But some are flying a bit too fucking high when they do those little jobs of theirs. One time, a while back, a guy walked in and tried to sell me a security camera. I mean, talk about ironic. Then on a different occasion, another prick came in, stoned out of his head, not making much sense, and generally annoying the shit out of me with his pitch. Eventually I deciphered what he was on about and it was just so stupid. He was asking me if I knew anyone who was interested in a laundry basket full of some bird's worn underwear. All sorts of shit he had with him, knickers, bras, slips and even tights. I mean, what's wrong with these people? Who in their right mind would want to buy that shite?

"Use your fucking brain," I told him.

"What? Whassup, man?"

"Nothing, forget it."

It was pointless trying to talk sense to the guy, he was out of his head and looking at me as if I kept moving around or changing size. I fucked him off by telling him the fuzz was making patrols and he'd better watch out. Apparently he tried selling that shite to every person he came across during the next few days and eventually he was forced to cut his losses, so he just dumped the haul outside the local Oxfam shop. Guys like that, even when they're not fucked up with drugs, are just even more fucked up when they're clean, because when they haven't got all that crap in their system, their minds cease to function altogether. They just fall apart without that adhesive of intoxicants. It's called dependency, but fuck it, that's their tough shit.

I used to try and kid myself about it. I used to think that by not buying stolen goods I'd be making things a little harder for them. I should have known I was making very little difference at all, and in the long run, I was probably making things easier for the crooked bastards. If it wasn't me who made the buy, then it would be some other cunt down the road. After a few refusals they'd stop coming in and wasting their time by sticking to the people they knew were always interested in buying. Even though I knew it made no difference to anyone, I still couldn't bring myself to buy stuff that had been nicked from people's homes. We'd been there and experienced it for ourselves when we got robbed and believe me, it was an experience we could have done without. Having said that, I never had any problems buying first-hand, knock-off gear, which was as good as buying from the shops, except it was better because it was cheaper. I'd be in like a shot if some cunt came in and offered me a brand new, never been used before VCR or TV still in its packing. No problem, no questions asked and no fucking sweat. As long as the price was right and the gear being fenced was decent clobber. It was nice and handy if it was something I could move on and make a few quid in the process. Better still, if it was something that wouldn't have looked out of place in my own front room. The difference with first-hand knock-off is that you don't feel you're actually depriving some poor sod. In fact, it feels kind of good because to know that some multi-national cunt of a company somewhere is getting a little payback for all the pittances it pays its workers on some assembly line in a Third World country. Kind of noble, like meting your own, unorthodox form of justice to the modern day Sheriffs of Nottingham.

Snowy, like most dealers who kicked around Manningham, used to dabble in a few other sidelines in order to live in relative comfort. Sometimes he'd have an armful of dodgy watches that were supposed to be Rolexes and sometimes he'd have a really good line in designer jeans that he'd got hold of from a mate who was in the rag trade. Or, even likelier, from a mate who was in the sticking-up-a-designer-clothes-shop trade. The other thing about Snowy which kind of endeared the lad to me was that he wasn't as bad as some of his colleagues when it came to dealing drugs. In fact, he was a bit limited as he only dealt the safer shite. He stayed away from the stuff that was capable of wasting people in no time. And that was why, I suppose, I helped him out like I did. If it had been anyone else, I'd have let them fry.

On that occasion, Snowy was nearly well-fucked. If I hadn't been as quick as I was, he'd have gone down for a long, long time, along with the rest of his colleagues who were doing business that day. It doesn't matter what you sell, because as long as the courts can prove you do sell, even if it's only the herbal gear, you'll end up inside, and that's guaranteed. This is one area in which possession becomes nine tenths of the law. They had a lot to be grateful for, did Snowy and his buddies, and it all started in the shop, which happens to be a few hundred yards from the pub from where most of the local dealers would operate.

I'd been on duty for a few hours. It had been a pretty shitty day, with customers coming in and fannying about by not making their minds up, asking stupid questions like, 'How much are these penny sweets?', moaning and arguing about the unreasonably high prices, going on about the weather and how hot it was for the time of year and basically doing anything they could to really piss me off. I'd written bugger all because of the cunts being talkative and over-friendly, or moaning their heads off and what have you, and I held them all personally responsible for my lack of progress on what I was writing at the time. But then, an hour or so before I was due to be replaced by my brother, it started.

The door was always open in summer. It was a nice day as well. I was behind the counter in my summer clobber – T-shirt, Bermuda shorts and trainers – working on a piece about a guy who thought he'd been attacked by a werewolf. The first two vans trundled past, then another two followed a couple of seconds later. About five minutes later they all zoomed past again in the opposite direction. The last one parked up outside the shop with its engine idling. As the side doors opened and I saw the occupants, I got a little hopeful. I knew what the gig was. Action. Nothing like a bit of action, real life action, to brighten up another boring day in a shop. It was a fucking give-away. One of the coppers got out and trotted into the shop.

"All right, boss?" I asked. I always call people who have a certain look 'boss'.

"All right, mate," he said, a little hurriedly.

"What can I do you for, then?"

A little criminal humour wasn't really called for, but he seemed to think it was a fitting line.

"That's what I like to see," he said, "nowt wrong with a bit of a laugh, eh?"

"That's what I allus say."

It's weird, but I always end up talking in the vernacular when white, Yorkshire people come into the shop; giving it that 'allus', 'nowt', 'owt' business. I don't think I do it to appease them or anything. Maybe I do it just to prove to them that I'm a Yorkshire lad who also happens to be an Asian as well. Not that most of them give a fuck either way, but you do get a reaction sometimes. People are not as shocked as they would have been ten or twenty years ago, but there are still those who think people like me know nothing of this life, culture and language.

"Listen, pal," he continued, "is there a loo I can use? I've been bursting for ages, me."

"Erm, well to be honest about it, you could use ours but the bloody thing's not flushing at that moment. Even I'm having to use the neighbours'."

"Yer joking? In't there anywhere round 'ere?"

"Well, you could use the public ones in the park, only tek you a couple of minutes to get there, like."

"Yeah, that'll do us. Give us twenty coughers, then, will yer, pal?"

There was nothing wrong with our toilet. I just didn't fancy allowing a copper to use it. Especially a great big fat one who'd been clenching his cheeks for the last hour or so. I served him and waited for the van to move off before I grabbed my diary and hit the buttons on the payphone.

"Snowy? Where are you, man?"

"Who's this?"

"Ammy, from the shop."

"What's up? Something you need, man?"

"Nah, man. Just tell me, where are you?"

"The Arms, man. Where else?"

"Well, you better get yourself out of there, man. You're gonna get raided."

"What? You serious or what?"

"Look, half a dozen vans brimming with filth are cruising right now, and they're not sight-seeing. You hear what I'm saying?"

"Shit, man!"

"You'd better get moving, man. Like now, chief."

"Safe. Safe. Nice one, man. 'Preciate it, right?"

"No worries."

Not only did I save Snowy that day, but I had also saved every single dealer who used The Kings Arms Inn as a trading floor. The coppers got there and the place was empty except for a few drinkers and the bar staff who were also pretty pleased with the tip-off, since the landlord would have got a good fucking over for allowing all sorts of shit to be sold in his joint. The coppers couldn't get a thing and the following day in the local rag, they got a right shafting: 'DRUGS RAID TURNS INTO FIASCO!'.

Once things settled down Snowy paid me a visit and showed me his gratitude by offering me an envelope. It was a very Italian way of doing things, but that's just the way some people think they should do business. Image is everything for people like Snowy, and all of them think they've got their own little Mafia families to run. He and his colleagues had a whip round to thank me. I refused it flatly, but the favour was there to be repaid whenever I needed it. And thank God I refused the money, because later, when I wanted Freddy, I'd need that favour. Badly.

Freddy wouldn't understand the concept of doing a good deed, and if he ever appeared to be doing one, something else would be behind it. People like Freddy always work on this maxim: trust no one and act as if no one trusts you. It's the only way they know, and as long as it keeps working for them, they'll carry on being like that. They have no friends, they have no one they can call loved ones, they are islands and fuck them, that's what they deserve. All they have in life are acquaintances. That way they can't fuck each other up, even though they might like to try and think they can. At the end of the day, even if Freddy wasn't a malicious bastard, the way he paraded around after he had robbed us wasn't on. It was obvious he was the one. And just as obvious was how I'd have to do something about it.

The shop was looking normal once again. My brother had managed to borrow some money for stock and the shelves were slowly filling back up. We'd tried to get on with it and a lot of customers were quite sympathetic about the shit we were going through which was good of them. Some of the others who were just as sympathetic tried to help even more. Some of them knew things about our shop getting robbed. Those were the ones who knew the rumours and those were the ones who kept on telling us.

We'd been hearing bits and bats about Freddy as soon as it happened. A few weeks later, we were hearing the same things every day and the ones who were telling us were mystified by our lack of action. We should have fucked the little bastard over for doing that, people like Hash Bash, Gilette and even Jamie would tell us. We'd just shrug our shoulders, try to look philosophical about it and tell them we'd leave it to the law. But it did get to me. The more I heard, the more of a pisser it got. It got to a stage where I thought I had to do something. I had to have it out with the little bastard once and for all. It was Gilette who decided it for me. He came in one day and we started talking. We got on to the subject of Freddy fairly quickly.

"What's wrong with you guys? You should sort the man out, you know?"

"I know, but…"

"But what? There are no fucking *buts*, man. Just right and wrong, life and death. You hear me?"

"It's not as easy as you think. Not for people like us."

"Yeah? And what makes you so special?"

"That's not what I'm saying. We just don't do that shit and we never have." I told him.

"Well maybe you should start. Before others start taking you for a ride every time you fill up these shelves."

"That isn't gonna happen, man."

"You guarantee that?"

"No, but…"

"But nothing. Thing is, I like you guys. I know neither of you are bent and shit, but you're alright. I'm only telling you this because I like you. Sort the man out before other cunts start taking turns in this place."

"I wouldn't know where to start."

"You could pay someone. You could hire me. I could even do it on the cheap, as it's you."

"You think we're loaded? Look around, man. We're up to our eyeballs in hock, right now."

"You could see Snowy. He owes you, doesn't he?"

"Yeah, he does, I suppose."

"Think about it. Gimme ten cigs and a pack of skins while I'm here. Put it on the slate."

Yeah, Snowy did owe me. Owed me his life, when I thought about it. I did it right then, as soon as Gilette walked out of the door, in case I thought about it and changed my mind later on. Perhaps it was the right time to call in that marker that Snowy had been holding for me. I flicked through my diary and found his number.

"Hello. Who's this?" an irritated voice asked.

"Snowy? That you, man?"

"Nah, man. Hold up."

The line was bad, but I could tell the phone was being passed across to its owner.

"Who's ziss, zen?"

I might have known it wouldn't be easy. It was Clive but I thought it would be better if Clive didn't know who he was talking to.

"Snowy? That you, man?"

"Nah, man. Ziss is Clive, guy."

"I wanna speak to Snowy, man."

"You'll have to hang on, ven, innit?"

Clive was one of Snowy's arsehole mates. The kind of dickhead who'd crack a bottle over his head, 'Just for a laugh, guy, innit, guy?'. He used to be a bit of a footy hooligan at one time, did Clive. Bit of a skinhead as well, when he was younger. Then he met Snowy and out went the red Dockers, the Harrington Jacket, the Fred Perry T-shirt and those awful bleached jeans that he insisted on wearing at half-mast. Normal clothes made him look a little better but he was still an arsehole.

I heard Clive shout over the room. They were in The Arms, no doubt, doing what they did best – selling their shite at one price to the locals and ripping off every other fucker who, as far as Snowy and his mates were concerned, didn't know their arses from their elbows. Ripping people off, for people like Snowy, was the best and easiest way to make money.

"Snowy! It's someone of ver phone for yer, guy!"

"Tell 'em to call back, man! Y'can see I'm busy here and things, man. Tell 'em laters." Snowy shouted back.

"He's a bit busy and things, guy," Clive informed me.

"His loss, man. I got money."

"Hold up, guy, juss hold up, right."

"Snowy! It's business and things, guy."

Snowy came over and snatched the phone off Clive.

"What do you need, man?"

"Snowy?"

"Yeah, who's this, then?"

"It's me, man. Ammy, from the shop."

"Fuck! What the fuck you want, man?"

I didn't expect Snowy to be so pissed off about me calling him. Maybe he was busy being busy but that was his tough shit.

"We need to speak." I said.

"What the fuck for?"

"Why the fuck do you think I need to speak with you, man? You know we got done over and shit."

"Look, man. I don't even know you."

"Fuck you, Snowy, you fucking know me and what's more, you fucking owe me."

"I don't owe you shit! Why the fuck am I talking to you, anyway?!"

"Just listen to me, man. Listen! It was Freddy."

"There's a fucking surprise, man!"

"Just listen, you think I'd be calling in the favour if I wanted to fuck around, man? Just lemme see you and sort some shit out with that bastard."

"I dunno, man. I know what's on your mind but that shit isn't my scene. You know?"

"What? You think *I'm* into this shit? I don't need this shit from you, man. I need you to tell me you're on my fucking side. That you'll help a guy out like he'd help you out. You hear me, man? 'Cos I'm not fucking around with any of this shit. I don't have to look out for you, you know. I don't have to keep my mouth shut about certain things. You hear me, Snowy?"

"Yeah, yeah! I fucking hear you."

There was a pause.

"Well?" I asked.

"I've got your number. I'll call you from a payphone. Don't call me on this again," he said and flipped his phone shut.

I was about to call him on his mobile again when the phone went. I let it ring a couple of times before answering.

"'Lo."

"It's me, Snowy."

"Took your time, man."

"You try finding a payphone around here that's working."

"I need you to see someone for me."

"Not interested."

"I don't care. You owe me."

"What? Get real, man. You think I'd have anything to do with shit? I can give you some money and shit to help you stock up again but that's it. Shit, you've got insurance, haven't you?"

"Insurance? Of course we've got insurance but this isn't about fucking insurance, man. This is about something I need to do. I need to even up the score, man."

"Hey, look. I can give you some money. I still owe you money."

"I don't need any fucking money, man."

"What the fuck do you want, man? You think I'm going anywhere near a hot-headed motherfucker like you? Get fucking real, guy. Shit's hard enough as it is without fucking around with crazy fuckers with revenge on their minds."

"Don't gimme that shit, Snowy. You know me. I'm not crazy."

"I thought I knew you, man. This is too much like bad news for me to get involved. We're talking assault and shit like that, you know? I'm a businessman."

"Bullshit, Snowy, you're a fucking criminal."

"I don't have to listen to this shit."

"Yes you fucking do, man. I keep telling you this, you owe me, man. Bigtime."

"I owe you but not that much."

"Oh yeah? You telling me you'd think the same if you were inside, right now? Because that's what we're talking about. How much is a stretch for dealing worth to you? How much does liberty really mean to a guy like you, man? I saved you, man. Don't forget that."

"Shit!" said Snowy as if he'd just lost a bet on a horse.

"Try to think of this as a cause – justice, even."

"Yeah, yeah," moaned Snowy.

"This is serious, man. I'm talking about my brother's shop getting done over. We've been pegged for something we didn't deserve."

"That's what they all say."

"Fuck you, Snowy. We don't give no fucker no shit but still, that bastard goes and does something like this. What's wrong with you, man? What would you do in my shoes?"

"I don't know what I'd do."

"So? Let's get it on. The favour will be repaid and I'll be out of your hair in no time. Like this shit never happened. That's what it's about, Snowy."

"Nah, man. Not me. It's not right and I'm not buying it."

"Gimme a break will yer? You owe me, Snowy. Don't forget that, man. And you know what that bastard is like. Motherfucker would crawl over his mother to fuck his sister."

"You're funny, man."

"I'm being serious."

"I don't know, man."

"Don't fuck me around."

"You're the one who's fucking me around with this shit. This isn't the fucking Mafia, you know?"

"I don't need you to be a fucking comedian right now, Snowy. This shit matters to me."

"Okay. But I swear, any of this gets out or it turns out that some other fucker did your shop over, I'll kill you myself, man."

"That's cool, man. I can handle that."

Snowy said it would be difficult so I told him he'd have to find some way to make it easier. He'd have to tell his crew exactly what the gig was, that it was payback time and that all of them were about to do something on behalf of me, someone who most of them hardly knew. I told him to explain the facts and then to let them decide for themselves. Snowy was pretty convinced by the time I'd finished giving him the run down about Freddy being the one to have pulled the caper. Freddy had money. Freddy was spending money. Freddy was out of his head. Freddy had just won the lottery. Our lottery. Just over sixteen thousand pounds worth of fags and booze had been swiped and now, all of a sudden, Freddy was walking around as if he was Mr Money. Snowy said he'd sound his boys out but wasn't promising anything. He'd call me after telling them and only then would he tell me it was going to be on or not. Snowy was such a sucker, at times. He knew he'd have to get this thing on. He didn't have much choice in the matter.

I didn't think it at the time but this was strange. Me making those calls to criminals as if I was some big shot criminal myself. Anyone else would have called the coppers but not me. I had my own way of doing things. Doing unto others as they had have unto us. I know burglary is only burglary but this was Freddy. A fucking low-life piece-of-shit-bastard like Freddy? Robbing us? You'd have to be out of your fucking mind to let that happen and do nothing about it. But still, I honestly didn't know what I'd do to Freddy for fucking us over like that. I'd think about that particular problem when I actually cornered the cunt. Until my man Snowy sorted something out. Until I got a call back and subsequently made a visit of my own.

if you ever...

The big fancy rug in front of the big fancy leather sofa could have done with a vacuum so I vacuumed it. There I was, happy as anything, vacuuming away like some char-lady and it wasn't until I switched it off that I heard the phone.

I left it standing and skipped nimbly through the snaking flex out into the hall and picked up the phone.

"'Lo?"

"What's up? What have you done? Why are you out of breath?"

"Hiya, Shelley. I'm fine thanks, how are you?"

"No, tell me what's up."

"Nothing's up. I was in the bathroom and I heard the phone go off."

"I've been ringing for ages."

"Err, the hi-fi was on."

"It's not on now."

"I know, I switched it off, that's why I'm out of breath."

"Oh. I see."

"Everything all right?"

"Yes, just…"

"Checking?"

"Well, no."

"But you thought you'd just ring and make sure I was all right."

"Well, yes, actually."

"Right then, I'll see you later."

"Erm, actually, I wanted to ask you a favour."

"Go ahead. Anything. Name it."

"Well, I'm having this friend round for dinner tonight, and wondered if you wouldn't mind, erm…"

"Popping out for a while?"

"Would you mind?"

"It's your place Shelley. Of course I wouldn't mind."

"Good. Thanks."

"What's his name?"

"Erm, David, actually."

"Nothing like a nice interesting name like David, eh, Shelley?"

Shelley had this thing about names when we were an item. She used to hate certain people solely because of their names. Men with names like Jason, Gavin, Mick, Chris and David were frowned upon, along with women called Shirley, Angie, Karen, Dianne and Cheryl. She knew it was nonsensical and she was being completely unreasonable. And besides, she had a name not unlike a combination of Shirley and Cheryl, so who was she to talk?

"People change, Ammy. I've got to go. Bye."

"What time?"

"What time what?"

"What time do you want me to be out for?"

"Oh, sorry. How about eight-thirty?"

"Till?"

"Well, say, eleven?"

"You sure? I can make it later, if you want."

"No, eleven. Elevenish will be fine."

"I'll see you later, Shelley."

"Bye."

Good to see that some things hadn't changed about her. Her still being chased after by blokes wasn't entirely unexpected but I was even more surprised to learn that she was still single. It was weird, but a little while after we started going together, she used to get loads of offers from guys, all of them giving her all the lines young guys do, attempting to woo her away from me. It was before we started to drift apart and I always mentally thanked her for her loyalty because she never gave them a second look. It never happened to me like that, though. Birds would see me with Shelley and decide to stay away. For a while I thought there was something wrong with me, like I had an extra head or something. But it had nothing to do with me personally. It was just people and the way they are. For some reason, you hear about women being the bitches. Women are the ones who go around stealing blokes from their birds or wives, but it was the opposite with Shelley and me. It was as if guys thought she was that much more desirable because she was with someone. As if birds with blokes were somehow better than single birds. I suppose, if you analyse it one way, there's a kind of stupid logic about it because birds who aren't hooked with a partner might not be hooked because there's something wrong with them. And, as is the case with most commodities, people want what is popular, partners included.

I'd let Shelley entertain her guest and try not to feel bad about it. She and me were over and she had her life to get on with and I had mine. But I knew I'd regret it while I was out and he, this David character, was in. It's a thing about men that most of us wouldn't admit to. Being wrong or making mistakes and actually confessing to the errors we all make always remains buried with men, and most prefer to stay quiet rather than say anything to lower their own standing. Even if I was stuck on a desert island somewhere, on my own, I wouldn't let those kinds of sentiments become audible. I could never openly handle the fact that an ex-bird who I had chucked had now made good in every possible way – in respect of money, job, gaff, and even in the dating and mating game. Then again, maybe it's just me who's the sore loser and the rest of 'man' kind are thoroughly decent, nineties chaps who'll do the washing, change the nappies, and stay at home to look after the kids and the house. They'll be supportive, considerate partners and feel guilty for burdening their partners with pregnancies, coming out with lines like 'wouldn't it be so fucking great if I could give birth to kids as well?'. And they'll smile all the way through without knowing how fucked up they really are. And I thought that people like Jamie, Titch, Hash Bash, The Woodman and even Freddy had problems. Those cunts who kid themselves into thinking they're having a more 'equal' relationship with the wives or partners are just fucking weak – as weak as the twats who shove needles into their arms all fucking day. Only difference is, these new, nineties weaklings think they're strong for being like that.

I tidied some more and hung around after I got back from town. I'd been to see Gates but he had nothing new to tell me. I saw him for less than ten minutes, in all, and I got the feeling he was trying to get rid of me. So I left and came back to Shelley's and carried on getting bored.

Waiting for nothing to happen was beginning to get me down. I called home and was pleased to hear the ringing tone again. My little sister answered and sounded pleased, but upset at the same time.

"Mum's been crying," she said.

I told her not to worry and she said she wouldn't but it was Mum who'd worry no matter what I told her. She'd even worry if I came out squeaky clean. It's more than an innocent and guilty thing with our people. Just the very mention of a son or daughter and court or the law in the same sentence is enough to send some over the edge. It's a tribe thing and it's a respect thing and the only way you can really fully understand it is by actually living it. It's a religion thing, a culture thing, a language thing and just about every other fucking thing that's going, but you still can't put your finger on it. I told my sister to put either Mum or Dad on. It was Dad who picked the phone up and boy, was he pissed or what!

I'm kind of proud of my dad being like that, dead fiery tempered is my dad. My mum says it's him I take after. My dad has this habit of blowing his top but it's always for a good reason, or so he thinks. It isn't until later, when he's heard the complete story that he kind of retracts his earlier harsh words. All it takes for my dad to blow his top is a part-sentence or a partial sighting of something. He must have mega-flipped when he saw my brother and me getting bundled into the cop car that night. God knows what he must have been thinking about back then and God knows what he started ranting about after we'd left the scene. He must have really gone bananas when the coppers went in and searched the whole house the next day. He must have been just dying to give them a mouthful while they were trampling about, up and down the stairs, in and out of rooms, just generally acting as if they owned the fucking place. He must have been itching to lay a couple of the pricks out like one of his mates had done years ago when they first came over here.

My dad, I soon gathered, already knew most of the gig. My brother must have filled him in with all the actual details he hadn't picked up in distorted form from the newspapers and TV. Shit, I was getting famous, but not the kind of famous my dad, or most people for that matter, would have approved of. That was just one of the reasons he was pissed off at me. I did my best to reassure him I had things under control and it had all been one major fuck up (I didn't use such colourful language, but you get the idea) which would, if all went well, be sorted out in a few days. Still, my dad wanted to know why I wasn't home to tell them all face to face. I asked him to look out of the window and see the mob that had been camped there since the previous morning. But not even the hounds of hell guarding our front door were good enough for my dad as an excuse. If I had used my brain, if I had actually stopped and thought about the consequences, I could have gone home and took the shite off the reporters just the once and then they would have left the whole family in peace, not in pieces as we were right now. I told my dad that Gates, the solicitor, had advised me to stay away, and that if we knew what was best for me and the family, none of us would say a word to those fucking hacks. Not only would they distort and manipulate what we had to say, but actually speaking to them might make things difficult in court. My dad still wasn't too convinced but I wasn't too bothered after half an hour or so of his telephone interrogation. He's just like that sometimes. All dads are like that, to some extent. He told me my mum was too busy trying to sleep to be disturbed right then but he'd tell her I'd called and that was when he sounded okay about things. Maybe it was because I seemed to sound concerned about her. I didn't give Shelley's number. I just told him I was stopping with a mate who didn't have a phone and I was using his neighbour's phone. I imagined my mum or dad ringing Shelley's number while she was there and then going absolutely apeshit about me stopping with her. That sort of thing's a definite no-no from where I come from. Almost as bad as murder for some people.

I told my dad that I'd call again and promised to phone home at least once a day, then I put the phone down. It was weird. It was like I was in another country, on holiday and making sure things were okay back home and the people at home were making sure things were fine for me. Even though I told them I had my shit sorted out I still couldn't help feeling a little pissed off about things. Even if you know you're going to be okay and even if you're confident of your own confidence, there's still something inside you that tells you to beware.

I listened to some of her CDs and was pleased to see her taste in music had changed considerably. There wasn't a sign of Billy Bragg, The Communards or The fucking Teardrop Explodes anywhere in sight. She had mostly modern stuff now, which was okay. She had even got some sense and bought some decent reggae and soul. I didn't hear her come in because I was playing this *Best of James Brown* album full blast. And playing James any lower than full blast just doesn't cut it for me. I did, however, realise that I was no longer alone when she slammed the door.

"Err, hiya," I said as I turned the volume down to three.

"No, no. Why don't you leave it so the whole street can hear? It's bad enough with the neighbours complaining."

"About what?"

"Nothing. Forget it."

"No, tell me. What? What's the problem?"

"They know it's you, Ammy. What else would you think they'd complain about?"

Maybe the idiot neighbour wasn't such an idiot after all.

"Oh, right. I see."

"Do you?"

"Look, Shelley."

"What? What are you going to talk me into this time?"

"I'll be out of your hair in a day or so. Any sign of the press and I'll be out before."

"Whatever."

Shelley carried a bag of shopping into her kitchen without another word. She didn't want me to spoil her mood, did she? She didn't want me to stop whatever she and that David cunt were going to get up to, either. And why the fuck should she have? No doubt she had gone out to buy something special for dinner with her latest flame, that David twat. I hated the bastard and I didn't even know him. Why the fuck did she have to do it? Now? Why couldn't she have waited for me to get back out of her life again? Maybe she thought I wouldn't.

I tried talking to her but she didn't say much. Just stuff that had to be said. Like she couldn't keep me here forever and all that. I felt unwanted and decided it would be better if I scarpered for the rest of the evening. I didn't want to get in the way, did I?

"Right then," I said, "I'll be off. I'll see you tonight. About eleven, yeah?"

"You don't have to go right now. I mean, have you had something to eat?"

"Yeah, I stopped at a cafe earlier on, while I was out."

"You've been out today?"

"Earlier on. Had to see the solicitor, you know."

"How did it go."

"All right. So-so."

"Are you sure you've had something to eat."

"You don't have to feel bad about me, you know."

"I don't feel bad," said Shelley and came up to me, "I just don't want you dying of starvation while you're here. That's all."

I smiled.

"Sure." I said, "I believe you."

"Well, there was food in the fridge, you know."

"Didn't fancy it, but thanks, anyway. I'd better get off. Have a good thing, with what's-his-name."

"David," she said.

"Whatever."

She was in a right mood, I decided, and it would be best if I left her on her own to vent her frustrations, whatever they were and whoever happened to be the cause of them. Who the fuck was I trying to kid? It was me who was doing her head in. How rude and inconsiderate could you get? I dumped her all of ten years ago and then, when I was under pressure, I came crawling back. Only I hadn't even crawled to her. I'd forced my way in and she'd had to accept me or, for the rest of her life, she'd have to live with the guilt of rejecting me when I needed her. I hoped she'd cheer herself up when this David guy turned up. In fact, I knew she would. She'd be a totally different person then, but, I suppose, everyone does that on a first date.

***

I got the back of the queue at the bus stop and waited for one to show. An old dear was talking to an old bloke about how shocking the bus service was, these days. They used to come every ten minutes at one time but not now. Now, she'd be lucky if one came every hour. Aye, said the old feller who looked as if he was having his head done in.

I turned away from her and looked down the road. Cars came but no sign of a bus. Waiting was never my strong suit. I always preferred to be occupied, either physically or mentally. Perhaps that's why I allowed my mind to go walkabout and think. For some reason, it wasn't such a big walkabout as it concentrated on one area. Freddy.

Freddy had snitched simply because he was a malicious little bastard and also because of the wrong I'd done him. He was like me, but only in some ways. He robbed my brother, I got our own back on him and now, he thought he'd finish it by being witness number one against me. Difference? Of course there was a difference. He started it, not me. He robbed us. We didn't do anything to him. In fact, we treated that low-life bastard son of a bitch like a friend. He borrowed items when he was skint. He paid us back when he felt like it but there was always something left owing. He talked with us when he was bored. We talked with him when he was good enough to grace us with his presence. On top of that, I even let the bastard read my stories. So why did he break into the shop and then rob it? He must have known it was well out of order and surely, he couldn't have thought I was going to turn over and let him fuck me again.

If Freddy happened to have luck on his side, he'd come out of this dead, unlike old Tony 'Big Mouth' Hudson who, it had been proved a couple of years ago, was a total grass. The Mouth was always a smooth talking bastard. Crook and con man he was, but his main hobby or interest in life, was birds and that's how he got to have the nickname. The guy could sweet talk a nun into bed if he ever wanted to. Only difference was, the guy Tony 'Big Mouth' Hudson grassed up, Tommy Walker, ended up doing six years for rape, and when he came out, the only thing on his mind was getting the man with the charm back and hurting him in the worst possible way. That's the trouble with prison. Sometimes it can be the worst place to put some people, even if they are guilty. When they come out, they're a lot wiser and they know how much difference a well-executed job can mean and have the first hand knowledge to ensure everything is right the next time. And if they're innocent? Like the guy Tony put away? Well, that's worse because an innocent man is much more hassle than a guilty man when it comes to revenge. Imagine having to spend six years inside a prison for something that you didn't do. Imagine being known as something you never were. Imagine your wife or husband leaving you with nothing, not even a chance to see your own kids grow up simply because some bastard went and lied. That was what Tommy Walker didn't have to imagine. Tommy Walker lived through it and hated Tony Hudson a little bit more as each day passed. He just stayed in there and bided his time, bottled it all up inside of him even though he felt like exploding with anger for every minute of every day of that stretch. What happens when a guy goes through that? What happens when a guy just festers like that for such a long time? Guess for yourself.

After revenge, Tony 'The Mouth' Hudson could talk a good line, but without a dick life soon became unbearable for him. The last any of us heard was that Tony had fucked off to somewhere like Holland, hoping to make a fresh start and all that. Nobody missed him because everyone knew what he'd done and nobody, not even the coppers, really likes a snitch.

help the aged - part three

I was in the shop the day they got him. Annie had called first, for the usual – a paper, some booze, some milk and some fags. My brother teased me about being so willing to deliver stuff to the old hag. Funny guy, my brother, he thinks. I put the carrier full of her items on the counter and told him to go himself if he was that bothered but he told me he'd have rather topped himself. And he wasn't joking. He couldn't stand the sight of her. When I arrived she told me to bring it in.

"How are we?" she asked as she sat on her piss-stained couch.

"Well, we've been better, Annie. A few problems, you know how it is around here."

"Oh dear. Anything I can help with?"

"Not unless you can grab the bastard who robbed us."

"You've been robbed?"

"A couple of days ago."

"I am sorry. I didn't know."

"It's okay."

"What did they take?"

"Cigarettes. Booze. Money."

"I am so sorry. Really, I am. Animals. Nothing short of animals!"

"I know, Annie. Never mind, eh? Life goes on."

"If you need some money, I can offer you some."

"That's okay, Annie. We've got a loan. Thanks anyway."

"You should have said. I'm not just saying it, but I do have some tucked away. It was your's for the taking. You should have said."

"You old charmer, you."

"Honestly. What good is it going to do me?"

"I appreciate it. Really. And I believe you."

"Who else can I give it to? There is only you who I could call a friend."

"Give up. You've got loads of friends."

"The home help?"

"You must know some other people, Annie. There must be loads of people you know. You've got kids, haven't you?"

"I had a daughter, once."

"What about a hubby?"

"We never married. He died before we could."

She looked up and gave me that brave smile that all people give when they feel like crying.

"Cheer up, Annie. It's never that bad."

"I know. At least I've got you."

"Sure you have. You need me, you call me. Okay?"

Again, that same pathetic, weak smile.

"I'm sorry. I can't help it sometimes. It's terrible when life becomes a burden. When the only thing that keeps me alive are pills."

"Cheer up, Annie. Please."

"I'm sorry. Really I am."

"It's okay. Any time you need me, Annie."

"Thank you. I am so glad I know you."

"And I'm glad I know you but right now, I've got to be off. We've bought some more stock in and the shelves need stacking. Busy."

"I understand. Don't forget. The money. It's yours."

"You keep it, Annie. Splash out on a new catheter for yourself."

"You are a one."

"I know."

I turned to walk out.

"If there's anything you ever need, you must let me know. I mean it."

Slowly, as if I'd just thought of something, I turned back around to face her again.

"Okay," I said, "there is one thing."

"Anything."

"It's kind of silly but…"

"Say it. I insist."

"Well, you know I do a bit of writing and that."

"And very good too. The language is a touch colourful; you use the f-word a little too often for my liking but still very, very good."

"You're too kind. There was just one thing that I've always wanted to do."

"Yes?"

"I've never used a typewriter, not a real one, anyway. I just wondered if you wouldn't mind."

"Of course not! That old thing? Why should I mind?"

"Can I just have a quick bash on it?"

"Be my guest! Of course. You can even borrow it if you want."

"No. I just want a quick tap or two. That'll be fine. Thanks."

perfect day

I stopped at the shop for most of the day. I had to help out because those were heavy times back then. My brother spent most of his time on the phone, hassling the bastards from the insurance company to give him some money but it seemed he was wasting his time. They wanted to send an assessor out and they wanted a full audit of all the stock we had before and after the robbery. The bastards just wanted to stretch this thing out for us in case they thought we did an insurance job. My brother was close to swearing at them through frustration but eventually, he gave up and got on with getting the shop back up to scratch.

At ten past four the phone went. It was Snowy, and bless his thoughtful little heart, he'd managed it. I was to meet him at half five. He gave me an address of a house where small time dealings went off, a place that was safe. Safe as houses, he said. He said the rest of his boys would be there to see what happened during the session for themselves. That was cool, I told him. I could handle that and they'd see the deal for real and then they'd know Freddy was the creep who went and fucked his own.

The cabby from Zippy's Taxis – *'polite, professional 24 hour service, discounts for old age pensioners, business accounts welcome, no distance too long or short'* – wasn't as friendly as the card made out but that's the way advertising is these days. Pretty much a bag of shite that only fools believe. He pulled up outside the shop and papped his horn a couple of times and then, about ten seconds later, he gave two longer and louder blasts. Cabbies aren't noted for their patience at the best of times and I thought it would be wise to show my face before the daft bastard started working himself into a frenzy.

"Where you off?" asked my brother.

"Nowhere. Just out."

"Take the car," he said and tossed me the keys.

"Can't, now. There's a cab outside." I said and tossed him the keys back.

When I told this polite, professional cabby where I was going he told me, without even thinking about it,

"Six quid, pal."

It was more of a demand than a request which was anything but polite or professional and I thought I'd let him know, by way of protest. Consumer rights and all that shite.

"We haven't even set off yet," I said.

"Well, I'm not going down there unless I get paid first."

"Suit yourself, but it's not that much. I bet it's not even a fiver."

"I know what I'm doin' pal. Done this lark for more years..."

"Yeah, yeah. Just drive. Spare me the fucking life story."

If I was paying the cunt six quid, I was going to get my money's worth from him, miserable bastard that he was. The cabby turned around and looked at me before grabbing the money out of my hand, forcing the gear-stick into first and setting off. He was a typical-looking cabby. Big fat get with sweat streaming down his forehead. He swore like mad at other drivers and drove like a maniac. The thing with some cabbies is, when they get young people in their cabs, they get all Nigel fucking Mansell about it, tearing around corners, going through red lights and all that crazy shit just to feel a little superior and young again. What you have to do to alleviate the situation is, in fact, nothing. Act as if it happens to you every day and you can handle speed and thrills better than they ever could. If you don't, and start whining like a bruised puppy, then that's you finished, as it will only make the sick bleeders worse. If it gets to that stage, then you might as well close your eyes and begin to pray because those crazy fucking cabbies seem to think there's nothing better than getting pleasure from their job through inflicting pain, fear and even humiliations on their passengers. And that's just what this one was like. I could see the cunt smiling to himself throughout the journey. Driving like this was what he fucking lived for. Sometimes, I wonder how those fuckers cope when they lose their licenses. I reckon they must go out of their minds waiting around and doing nothing with their hands, feet and voices. They'd be counting the days before they're free to get on the road to cause untold havoc once again. They must go through some serious withdrawal symptoms because the very nature of their driving seems to be so habitual and so fucking intense. Yes, it must be as bad as that.

I got to thinking how cabbies really did have it easy, although in a roundabout sort of way. If you happen to enjoy driving like a maniac then that's what you should do. You should become a cabby because it must be miles cheaper than becoming a real racing driver. The only time the law bothers cabbies for doing sixty miles an hour in a thirty zone is when some new copper, who's a bit on the over zealous side, decides to stop them. Most coppers let cabbies off the hook, with cabbying being their living and it being a very much needed service to the community and all that bollocks. I could say the same thing about drug peddlars and prostitutes offering their services to the community and the community members that they serve really appreciating and needing them but I won't because that'd be taking the piss. Having said that, prostitutes don't get such a hard time from the filth these days, either. The old bill will just tell them to move on unless, once again it's some green kid who's out on the beat for the first time.

"Bang on six, then was it?" I asked him as the car jerked a couple of times before coasting to a stop.

"'Ere," he said, and handed me a fifty pence piece.

"Are you sure that's right, pal?"

"We charge what we want when we've to make these bloody trips. Danger money, mate. That's what it is. Danger money around here."

There were areas around Bradford cabbies weren't keen on entering. As a result they'd charge you double, but you could still argue about it if you wanted to.

"You keep charging like this and you'll be on danger money all the fucking time, mate. I'm surprised you're still driving at these fucking prices. I could have hired a fucking limo for less."

"That a fact?"

"Just watch yourself, that's all," I said.

I was being genuine. There are plenty of people about with little tolerance for fools like this cabby taking liberties. Snowy or any of his boys would have mugged the stupid bastard, kicked the shit out of him and battered his poxy little cab for his cheek.

The house was smack in the middle of one of the worst housing estates in Yorkshire. If I was forced to live there for whatever crime I'd committed (I can't imagine any other reason for people ending up there) I'm pretty sure I'd end up homeless or dead. And to be honest about it, death wouldn't be such a bad thing faced with the prospect of actually having to doss down there. It was like something out of a futuristic, post-apocalyptic novel where people ate each other and shite like that. Every square inch of it was a fucking tip. Worse than a wasteland, which made it ideal for some. For people like Snowy it was a place to make money, and ironically, it was so fucking dangerous it became safe for them. Safe from prying eyes, and especially from the coppers.

Les answered my kicks to the door. Les was another one of Snowy's tight acquaintances, who stuck around both for the pleasure of Snowy's company and for the economic advantages of cut-price product.

"Look who it is. Look what the cat's..."

"Save it, man. Where is he?" I asked, sounding as annoyed as I could.

"Who?"

"Who do you fucking think, man?"

I could handle people like Les all day long. All you had to do was sound pretty pissed off about something and then bored with them as soon as they uttered their first few words of jest.

"I dunno what you're talking 'bout, man," he grinned.

What annoyed the fuck out of me about Les though, was he had this weird way of addressing people once he started to get into his stride. Like he figured everyone was shit compared to him. Like he was so much wiser and funnier than the rest of us. He was like that with everyone though, which I suppose is better than being only like that with the people he knew he could fuck with. Les was an arsehole, but at least he was consistent about it. He'd accept a fight and take a battering if he had to, just to prove he was always an annoying little fucker who didn't know any better and couldn't care less.

"Stop being an arsehole, will yer? I've had enough fucking around for one day."

"Cabbie rip you off?"

"Good guess. Been there have yer?"

"Nah, man. I just guessed from that look on yer face. They try that danger money shit with everyone around here these days. If it were me..."

"Save it, man. Snowy. Where is he?"

"The Snowman?"

"Look. Stop fucking around."

"I ain't fucking around."

"We gonna stand out here all day or what?"

"All right. Cool it. Snowy's in the back, man."

Les led me through what at one time had been a living room and was now just a dark shell – four bare walls, a ceiling and a floor. The glass in every window of every house on that part of the estate had been broken and boarded up by the council. The wood was then prised off and used for firewood or a bit of the old DIY. Large pieces of blockboard has it's uses in these parts. A few sheets of that stuff, when cut down into manageable strips and then nailed together can be made to form a kennel for the dog that gets fed better than the kids. A few strips of wood when strung together in a row can be used as a symbol of protection. A fence tells others someone lives inside the perimeter. A fence tells people the owner or tenant of such a house is stupid enough to think a fence without a few thousand volts of electricity running through it will make some difference to the security arrangements of the property it encloses. Everyone knows the gig. Everyone knows a fence of that nature, no matter how high or how well painted, won't mean a thing to those who want to get in. If they want to get in, they'll get in and a fence of wood, metal or even barbed wire won't mean shit. It might slow them down by giving them something to piss themselves laughing about but it won't stop them. Even the most amateurish of thieves think they strike lucky when they see a fence, an alarm box or a shit load of locks because that means there has to be something worth protecting on the inside.

The light fittings, switches, copper pipes and anything else removeable had already gone. It was usually less than a day after the houses were vacated when the local scavengers got busy. Sometimes they'd receive inside information from those leaving and get to work as soon as the battered old Transit van was loaded and off. More often than not, not much thought was given to what fuckry was left to those who had an interest. The idea was to get in, get the shite and get out, and as you might guess, workmanship was never much of a priority. Once a place had been gutted, the building hardly existed. Like some of the people, the place was invisible. For most of the crooks and low-lifes, a gutted house became worthless, not even worthy of target practice once all the glass had been smashed.

Such places were still in demand. A dive is still better than roughing it in some shop doorway in the middle of winter. It's also a comfort thing. Psychological. You feel safer and less vulnerable to predators when you're inside, even if you're inside a shithole. For a small capital outlay, which would be recovered in the first couple of days of desperate tenancy, Snowy, or some other local 'landlord', would get someone like Lightning Bups to rig up a derelict house with a light and one mains outlet. A roof was a roof for some, and free light and heat was well worth the fifteen quid a week's worth of rent. All you had to do to enjoy a long, uneventful and cheap tenancy was to be careful and not open your mouth while you were out on the tap or the make. Lightning Bups was quick and would take on jobs old and well-experienced sparkies wouldn't dream of doing, even if they were wearing rubber body suits and wellies. He'd tap into the main terminal and set the power up and get a fee for his work from whoever was funding the development. He'd roll up in a knackered old Escort van – once given to him in payment – and he'd just get cracking. He had the tools, the three-core wire, the switches, the bulb holders and the rest. He was lucky was Bups, things worked both ways for him. He bought all the shite which had been ripped out by the scavengers at a fraction of their worth then sold it back to them. He could be in and out within half an hour. Lightning Bups was also a Godsend for many families. One of his most called for services was spinning the meters for a mere twenty five quid a quarter. He had his own, non-patented and very effective device for this, invented they say, when he was just a kid. Usually, he earned a tidy sum doing the meter thing, but every now and then his mobile phone would go off and he'd have to get his skates on and do a rush job. Just like the one he'd done for Snowy that very day – one light fitting and a power point. It had been known for others to try it and end up in the burns unit before they got nicked and eventually sent down. It was risky, but Lightning Bups knew the animal he was fucking with. At the same time, he still had to have balls of steel to fuck with that kind of juice.

Snowy met us in the hall, shining the beam of a torch in my eyes.

"You done it then?" I said as I guarded my eyes with my hands.

"He's through there."

Snowy pointed his torch towards the back room – what had been the kitchen the last time someone lived in the house. The knackered old handle-less door was closed but thin, smoke-filled slits of light were coming from the spaces between the body of the door and its frame.

"Nice place," I told him.

"I've been in worse," he said, his tone implying he didn't care a fuck for small-talk.

"Can't say I have."

"You gonna get this on or what?"

"Fuck yeah. I'm here, aren't I?"

For a couple of minutes I felt a little fucked up. What the fuck did I think I was playing at? I must have been mad to think I could carry it off. I almost laughed when I thought about how corny this was. I was no Snowy. I was nothing like him or any of his boys, but there I was, playing at crooks for real and keeping a straight face about it. Trying to get something out of someone like Freddy was not me. This kind of behaviour should never have been a part of me. I never had and never would run with these idiots and why the fuck should I? It wasn't as if I had no choice like some of them. It wasn't as if I had poverty, a preordained and genetic vicious streak, identity problems or any of that shite that's cited as reasons for being like this. For being a crook, a criminal, a fucking disgrace to human kind, for being anti-social or whatever the fuck being like this was classified as these days. Why did I want to ruin everything that meant anything to me? I mean, my parents taught me what they thought was right from wrong, and instilled what was dear to them into me. Okay, I wasn't a complete success, but then, who the fuck was? Sure, they'd have loved for me to turn out a Hafiz, or a model Muslim, but they must have known it could never be easy for a kid like me growing up in a place like this. Sacrifices, no matter how painful, would be made not out of choice but out of need. Sacrificing was the only way. Why would I want to risk myself and my family? Because that was what it boiled down to. That was the choice I had. I'd be an outcast and the subject of shame and I'd be fucked before I let any of that 'our thing' happen to either of them. That's what would happen if I resorted to being a crook and using a crook's tactics and methods of retribution. But still, there was no doubt, I'd have to do this.

I was a clean living guy. Okay, I'd have the occasional blast on the odd joint, but fuck, so did every cunt around here. It was even known for coppers to sample some of the contraband that they'd worked so hard to rid the streets of (in their own time and in the privacy of their own homes, of course). I'd have to do it. There was no other way to show myself. I wasn't thinking of the police and the law at the time and what they'd do to me if they found out about this. I was thinking about the people who I knew. My people. My friends, my peers, my family and yes, even the shit that came through the shop door could make all the difference. They were more important than the law. The law was always fucking up but the people who knew you, the ones who really knew you, were the ones that mattered. Those were the ones who would see the truth. Freddy had it coming to him and I was doing the right thing. It was called justice even though it was illegal. The closest I got to these characters and to being a crook was as an observer. I knew how they operated. How they lived and how they thought. That was as far as it went but now it was going to go the distance.

Acknowledging my plan of actions and dipping back into the hard world of reality wasn't going to make this easier. It wasn't as if I was actually experienced in these ways. This, all of this shite and especially this shite with Freddy, was way out of my league. This was not my turf and fuck, I felt it and what's more I knew it. It only dawned on me when Snowy dropped the beam of light so I could just about make his face out without the dazzle of the torch to blind me. Doing this would change things irretrievably and that was the bugger. This was the point of no return as shitty as it sounds. This was when I would become one of them but then again, maybe I was already one of them. I was one of them before I had set my eyes on Freddy and even before I said a word to him. I was involved and there was no escaping that. I told myself over and over again that I had to run with them and do this shite just to complete this thing. Just to finish it and get on with my life. That much was clear. Another person might have tried to talk the police into doing something like this but not me. The police were the ones who'd hand out a load more shit to someone like me for fucking with the system and giving them more work to do. Besides, the coppers would need more than just my word to go for Freddy. They'd need evidence, proof and all that shit that nobody would be prepared to give them. It didn't matter because the coppers would never be a part of this. I, for one, would have sooner swung than approach the coppers and if I had, someone like Snowy might have seen to it that I swung anyway. I couldn't grass Freddy, even though my brother and me were the ones who Freddy had fucked over. Grassing isn't a tit for tat thing. It's worse than that.

I had no other choice but it was the right choice. I was here and it was time to make my mind up and make my life go the way I wanted it to go. Snowy was as good as anybody for this. At least I'd have one witness who'd seen me get the truth out of Freddy and, if things went well, that one witness would tell the rest of my world when the need arose. When fingers would begin to point and tongues would begin to wag, I'd need this. I wanted, more than anything else, to be the same as I'd always been - innocent. But that wasn't all. I needed to do this, for my own sake and for my own future.

Freddy was a bastard and might make things even more difficult for me. It didn't mean he was stupid, all because he was a weasly little crook and a hoodwinker. From the conversations that I'd had with him in the past, in the shop, I'd have said the bastard was pretty fucking sharp. If you stood too close to the cunt, you'd cut yourself.

After it was done, Snowy and Les gave me a ride back to the

shop, dropped me outside and drove off quickly. They obviously didn't like what they'd seen, what I'd made them be a part of, and who could blame them?

I looked at my watch as I walked back to Shelley's. I put the cinema's show times down to jammy timing. I got there five minutes before the first of two flicks started and I was on my way out by half past ten. I was going to get a bus back but I couldn't be arsed waiting another hour for one to show up, once again. So I walked it all the way back from the cinema in town. A place as big and as populace as Bradford with a fucked up bus service. Tragic, was that.

At least I didn't have to doss around for a few hours before I could go back to my temporary home. Shelley said around about eleven and right now was good enough for me. I'd get to Shelley's, have a nice night's kip and then my new life would begin. It was more or less cooked and ready for consumption. In my mind it was, anyway. Trouble was, something else was in there, fucking around as usual.

Freddy must have thought he'd just stumbled into it. The coppers would have knocked on his door in the middle of the night and asked him what he knew and what he'd seen. People like Freddy know and see everything in a place like Manningham and the coppers are no fools when it comes to spotting and then recruiting eyes, ears and of course, the all important mouths. He would have told them what he knew 'unintentionally'. It would have just slipped out, and once he opened his mouth, they kept on pushing him for more. He'd tell people later that they threatened the shit out of him. All they wanted was a name and a time. They wouldn't have asked him about my writing but he'd have mentioned it anyway, just dropped it in, thinking he was doing himself a favour.

Freddy's blabbing was motivated by something that had become personal. Fucking me over because I had fucked him over. Like me, he had no physical proof and like me, he only had hate pushing him further. And the coppers must have known he had a motive. He wasn't the kind of neighbour who kept an eye on old people through the winter like the two-o'clock-in-the-morning-when-no-one's-watching-public-service-ads asked you to. He was the kind of neighbour who robbed them while they were dying of hypothermia.

I'll give the cunt one thing, though. He can think on his feet can Freddy. As soon as he copped for what was going down in the street, his mind started spinning into action. I could imagine a series of gears turning in that sick little head of his as he contemplated what lay before him. That was where I came in. That was when his chance to get me back came alive. That was when I became the murderer. As I'd known all along, Freddy turned out to be one of those people who didn't know what trust, friendship or what loyalty meant. Some rules, you just don't fuck with, but Freddy couldn't resist. So, he decided, somewhat rapidly, that I'd be the one to take the fall for Annie Potts's death. Silly bastard had no idea it was a suicide but then again, murder was just what the police thought at first.

Freddy had grassed me up out of spite rather than simply snitching on the strength of the facts. He'd seen me go in and in all likelihood, had seen me come out. But that wasn't what he told the police. A detail as insignificant as that must have slipped out of his mind. And then there was what he knew. I wrote stories and he should have felt privileged to have first gander at my stuff but what does he do instead? He reads, digests and then? And then, the bastard plays at detective and figures I could have done something like that to Annie because that was exactly what I wrote. And then the bastard goes and grasses me up. That was low. That was like incest.

At the end of the day, Freddy was more than a grass on this occasion, he was a fucking liar and there's no room for liars, especially those who lie to the old bill in a place like Manningham. After all, you don't have to go looking for trouble in a place like Manningham. You stand still long enough and it'll come along and find you easily enough on its own. And of course, when word gets around about some of your antics, trouble just seems to be attracted to you like iron filings to a magnet.

Freddy had read that manuscript of mine, the one about the will and he'd decided to make Annie's death look like a carbon copy of the book. You might be wondering why anyone would give such a low-life like Freddy one of their own books to read, but when I was writing I wanted anyone who read to read my stuff. I wanted it to be liked, I wanted for people to tell me how ace me being a writer was. I wanted encouragement, I wanted pats on the back and even people like Freddy could do that much for me even though they were the lowest of the low. Freddy could read and he intimated that he liked to read and that meant a lot to me, back then. The thing is, people like Freddy have their uses.

He recalls the plot of the book and he must have just loved himself right then. Not only could he get a little matey with the coppers but he could also screw me in the process. I always thought he hated me and maybe he did hate me. Maybe that was the key and maybe the timing of it was nothing more than a series of coincidences. Maybe him being the one to get me locked up for what I had done to him was all that mattered right then.

fastlove

The walk back from the cinema that night knackered me. I
staggered and gasped up the stairs to Shelley's and stood by the
door for a couple of seconds before entering. I was listening out
for some conversation between Shelley and her new man. He
might still have been there and Shelley would be pissed at an
interruption. There was nothing happening, though. No talking,
no light music for them to converse over, not a whimper. Nothing.
So in I went.

I walked into the kitchen. All the dishes were washed and dried,
but the room was empty. I imagined David giving her a hand with
the washing up like every new man should, imagined him standing
behind her, threading his arms through hers, kissing her neck and
covering her soapy hands with his as she washed the plates they'd
just eaten off. I was pleased neither of them were there. The
lounge was vacant and clean. Maybe they were getting it on
somewhere else, I thought, maybe going for it right at that
moment in her bedroom. But that was their business. It was late,
and I had enough problems, I reminded myself, without adding
Shelley and her taste in men to the list.

Sleep was what I needed, and plenty of it. I knew it would come
as soon as I'd had a piss and got horizontal on Shelley's floor. But
as I approached the bathroom door I heard something. Not a
voice, more like a little squeak. I looked around trying to locate the
source but there was nothing. A gaff like Shelley's shouldn't have
had mice, but that was what it sounded like – one of those nasty
little bastards that seem to be powered by warp drive motors. I
waited outside for a moment and heard nothing, but then, you
never hear anything when a woman's in the bathroom, no piss
hitting the bowl or the floor, no plops or farts, no nothing. Not
even a cough to let you know the room is being used. I walked
back into the lounge and decided to wait it out. Maybe it was
something she ate. That'd be cool, funny, even. It'd make me feel
better if her and the new fucking man had been getting all
romantic with each other and then went and chucked their guts up.

Ten minutes later, she still wasn't out. If she'd been having a bath I would have heard running water. I would have heard something. Splashing, scrubbing, singing, fucking anything that would tell me she was in there. Maybe they were both in there, I thought then, going for a soapy tit-wank and all that. Dirty bastards, I thought. What a slag. But that couldn't have been it. There still would have been some noise to give them and their dirty little sex games away. Then, I thought that maybe the door was just closed but not locked and she'd gone out with David. After all, I hadn't actually turned the handle, had I? I got up and thought I might as well check. She'd been a long time in the bog, even by a woman's standards. I cleared my throat, to warn her or something, but the door was locked, so I knocked.

"Shelley? It's me. I'm back."

Nothing. I turned the handle again and gave it an extra solid push but it still didn't budge. I was getting confused, angry and more and more desperate to empty my bladder.

"Shelley? You in there or what?"

I heard that squeak again and looked around for some little bastard baring its teeth and daring me to throw something at it but again, nothing mouse-like was visible. Maybe the little bastard of a mouse hid behind or under something every time I turned around. Maybe even something as lousy as a squeaky little mouse thought it could fuck with me and get away with it these days.

"Shelley! You in there or what? I'm gonna break this door down if you don't say something."

Something was up. People don't lock themselves in the bathroom for no apparent reason. Either she'd passed out or was dead, and neither option was what I needed right then.

"Shelley! Open the fff-! Open the door! I'm gonna bust it in, I'm telling you!"

And with that, the door opened and out came Shelley. She looked upset to say the least. She'd been crying and I felt like apologising.

"Shelley," was all I could say, "you okay?"

She didn't say anything, just squeaked a few sobs and sniffed, before pushing past me.

"Shelley, what's up? You okay?"

"I'm fine," she said, wiping snot and tears away from her face with a thick swab of white toilet paper.

"You don't sound it. You want a coffee or something?"

"No. I'm going to bed."

Shelley walked towards her room but I followed her. I'd never seen her like that. It just wasn't like her. Something must have happened. Maybe someone close to her had died, maybe David had chucked her or something. Fuck! I didn't know what it was, but I couldn't leave her in that state. I had to say something, anything, to comfort her in some way.

"Shelley, come on, you can tell me. What happened? He didn't show up? Is that what it is?"

She shook her head.

"Well?"

"He's a solicitor," she said, and looked at me for the first time.

"What?"

"Your solicitor."

"Gates?"

"Yes. David."

"So?"

"He told me about the case."

"My case?"

"Whose do you think?"

"So what?"

"He told me more than I wanted to hear before I could tell him I knew you, Ammy. He told me what he thought before I could tell him I was putting you up."

"What? What did he tell you?"

"That you did it."

"And you believe him?"

"I don't know, Ammy. I don't know you any more."

"You know something? I don't think I know me any more, either."

"I'll see you around." I said without smiling. I tried to show no expression. It was sad and I was sad but I didn't think Shelley needed any of that soppy goodbye shit right then.

"You're not coming back?"

"I told you I'd get out of your hair by today and that's just what I'm doing."

"You don't have to. I mean, if things are still bad at home, you can stop another few nights, if you want. It's not a problem, you know."

"I know, but I reckon things'll be okay. The tits from the press and all the other sightseers will have gone by now. Back to plain old boring home."

"Somehow I don't think things are going to be plain for you any more, Ammy."

"Maybe not."

"We should do something together sometime, we could go out or something, see a film."

"Maybe we could. Listen, I'll call you about it, but right now I've got to see your boyfriend."

"He's not my boyfriend."

"Yeah? Hope it wasn't something I said."

"I don't think so, Ammy."

"I'll see you around, Shelley. I've got to go."

"Right now?"

"Within the next two minutes," I said as I glanced at my watch, "you know what those leeches are like with their appointments. They charge by the minute."

"You've made an appointment?"

"No. But I'm sure he'll be okay if I pretend I have one."

"Call me?"

"Sure thing."

"I'm warning you though, it had better not be like this next time. If you ever come knocking on my door because you've got the police after you, I won't even know you. I'm not going to fall for any of that 'I need you desperately' stuff again."

"I never said that."

"Whatever," she smiled.

"Don't worry, I'll see you in a day or two. Promise."

Maybe she was thinking I wasn't such a cunt after all. And I *had* been a cunt with her before, when we were together. I was a changed man, though. I was seeing life in a different way. But one thing I would have hated would have been a sympathy fuck. Even if it came from my former good-time (make that best-time) girl.

disco 2000

The same doll-faced woman was sitting behind the counter in the same position with the same gadget sticking out of her ear. Again, she was typing away as if her life depended on it.

"Hi," I said. "I've come to see Mr Gates."

"Do you have an appointment?"

"He'll make one."

"I'm afraid he's with a client at the moment."

"I'll wait."

The woman smiled uncomfortably. She wasn't used to this. Not many people have got the balls to fuck with solicitors, really. Scared in case they get sued, I suppose.

"I don't think he'll be able to fit you in today," she managed.

"He will. Trust me."

"I'll just let him know."

"Fine."

Ten minutes later, a fat man walked out of Gates' office. He looked like he'd been short-changed and, I realised, if he had been, it was due to me coming in and fucking up Gates' appointments. Gates came out next and asked me to join him.

"So," he began, "how are you?"

"All right. You?"

"Fine. I'm glad you came."

"I bet you are."

"I feel terribly embarrassed," offered Gates, cheerily.

"Don't be," I smiled, "she's a friend. That's all."

"I know. That's what she said."

"It's the truth."

"Yes. I suppose it is."

I leaned forward and told him.

"She's told me what you thought."

"She has?"

"You still think I did it, don't you?"

"Not quite."

"Excuse me? You either do or you don't."

"Well, that could be debatable," he smiled.

"It could?"

"Tell me something, Amjad."

"Sure, man."

"What would you say if I could offer you a deal?"

"What kind of deal?"

"A publishing deal."

"Why the fuck should I go through you? They'll be queuing up at the door for me."

"I can be very good for you. I can make more money for you than you've ever dreamed of."

"You want to be my agent?"

"I want to be your everything. In a business sense, of course."

"I dunno."

"You should think about it. There are ways of making you more of a commodity. Strategies."

"Strategies? For writing?"

"Of course. You've got to be able to market a product, these days. You're perfect for that."

"Yeah? How come?"

Gates told me what I already knew. He went on for ages about what he wanted and what he thought would work best for me. I thought I'd let him feel really clever for a while because the guy was really trying his best to close the sale. He needn't have bothered because I'd have gone with that slick son of a bitch any day of the week. He thought he had me sussed but he didn't. I was the one who did all the sussing and I'd started doing it ages ago. When I started to be a real writer.

The deal was simple. First he'd rush out the book which had started all this thing off. The book which paralleled me, Annie and her death. *The Will and the Way*, he had suggested. I shook my head and told him I wasn't too sure. Fine, he said. We could discuss details later. Next, I'd write a new book. A semi-autobiography to begin with. About me, my writing, the rejection, the arrest, the murder, the escape and the ending. Gates thought it might even be a nice idea if I put in a few twists and made it into a mystery or something. Better still, it would be fucking great if I turned out to be the murderer all along. That would make a great fucking book and because it was borderline non-fiction, it would be in the headlines all over again when it was due for release. It was perfect, he thought. I told him I wasn't too happy about that and if he was so fucking clever and could dream up plot lines and events so fucking easily, then maybe he should be the one to write a fucking book.

That was when I stopped thinking in the way I had kept on telling myself to think. I confronted the truth I'd been shying away from. All of it had happened out of nothing, but it came about because of me. And now I was there, where every single fucking wanker who called themselves a writer wanted to be. I was being offered a deal. Money. I was getting what us fucking writers craved, and to be honest about it, it scared me. It was real, and right then, for some reason, the reality didn't seem to be so appealing any more. Perhaps that twat of an editor had been right all along. Perhaps I was a shite writer and perhaps that meant I was an even shiter person. Perhaps the whole thing had been one big mistake.

Gates suggested we discuss the details later. Gates was my man, though. A sharper son of a bitch you won't meet.

everything must go

Home was quiet. It was usually quiet but never deathly silent.
Usually there'd be conversation, or the telly would be on, or the
tape player would be blaring out any one of a number of popular
Indian and Pakistani singers. Rafi, Hassan, Noor Jehan, Lata,
Rehshmah, Lohar and a few more unique and soothing voices
would be coming out of the inadequate, ancient speakers that were
in opposite corners of the front room. My mum was a bigger
Noor Jehan fan than my dad was. My dad listened to anything that
happened to be playing. They didn't listen to the music from the
old country habitually or anything but when things were quiet, out
would come the cassettes. The songs would evoke plenty of
memories. Some sad and some happy. They'd tell me how things
used to be back home, what it was like to be young, and of course,
how they missed home terribly.

I only liked a few of those singers and Noor Jehan and Alam
Lohar were my joint favourites. Even when I was little I used to
dig them like crazy. Now, I only listen to that sort of stuff when
the mood takes me. When I need some of those inspirational
melodies and emotive voices to make me feel a little better.

You'd walk into the house and there'd be talking, but funnily
enough there'd never be any shouting. There was a big deal about
raised voices just being impolite in our house and my dad would
shout his head off at us whenever we fouled up, even if we were
shouting about some one or some thing that had really pissed us
off. You just didn't shout. It was rude and that was a rule that had
been around from the beginning. If they weren't saying something
then they'd be doing something. My mum and my sister would be
cooking, cleaning, washing up, doing the laundry, ironing. There
was always something that had to be done at home.

I closed the front door gently and walked towards the kitchen
but before I got there, my mum opened the kitchen door. We both
paused for a moment, and looked at each other. Then I moved
towards her and she towards me, and all the time she was looking
straight into me, as if she hadn't seen me in years, as if she had

known of me but never seen me, like I was a lost son who had, at long long last, come home and come back to her. There were tears in her eyes and torment in her words. That was all I got because I was somewhere else after the first two seconds of being with her. I was trying to think of other things but I wasn't doing it very well. I'd known it would happen and hated myself for thinking of it as an ordeal I had to go through, some initiation that would make things the same again. I hated thinking it was just so unnecessary, that there should have been rejoicing and smiles, not tears and pained frowns. But that's mothers for you, I suppose. They truly are genuine, are mothers. When it comes to their children, anyway. Mothers, man. They'd do anything for you, even though you might not think so at times and even when you think you're old enough and big enough to look after yourself they'll still be there for you. She held onto me and then kissed my cheeks over and over again like she used to do when it was Eid when I was little. She looked me in the eyes and ran her hands through my hair and all I did was just stand there. Feeling stupid but not uncomfortable because I knew this thing. It had happened before, but it wasn't exactly the same then. The last time it had happened was when my mum came back from Pakistan after spending a couple of months on holiday. Not so much an actual holiday really, more of a visit back to the homeland than anything else. And she was like that when she left us and she was like that when she came back. As if going on holiday was a mistake because we weren't going with her.

Nothing I could have said to her as I stood in the hall would have made any difference to either of us, though. Saying something might have made her more anxious, so I had no choice but to just wait and let it pass.

Dad wasn't the same. Dad could never be the same after everything that had happened, but that was just his nature. He blew his top for a while, just coming out with anything he could think of to put me back in my place. The only thing you could do when my dad got like that, which was pretty rare as a matter of fact, was to stand there and take it. You'd say nothing and take the onslaught as if you were a rock. If you started blubbering or showing any signs of protest you were in for an even harder and longer time of it because reacting like that made him think he was even more right than he already believed he was. After a few pleas from my mum he seemed to settle down, but just when I thought it was about to get better, it got worse.

It was time for an explanation, time to show him that there was no reason for him to be like that, and that there were a shit-load of pretty bloody decent and honest mitigating circumstances for all of this shit. I told them all – even my little sister was there – what had happened and where I'd been for the last couple of days. Of course, I had to reinforce some of the things I'd said over the phone about me stopping with one of my friends. That seemed to satisfy them for the time being. Then my dad started asking me about Annie Potts and why I'd been implicated in the first place. He was almost as bad as the coppers, and I suppose, he had good reason to be. You don't take accusations about your son being a murderer lightly do you? But what could I have told him? I mean, I was there, my prints were there and the coppers thought it was me. Freddy had strengthened their case. I delivered shite to her house for crying out loud! I knew what my brother must have told my dad over and over again, that things would be all right and that I was innocent, but my dad wanted to hear it all from me. Things couldn't have been much harder for me, being the black sheep of the family and all that. My brother could get away with some stuff, even if they heard it second-hand. But with me, everything meant an inquisition. When I told him what my brother had told him, about me being there and being eyeballed by a div called Freddy and all the rest of it, he bowed his head and remained silent for a while.

Then he showed me the letter from Annie Potts's solicitor. I read it slowly and carefully. Most people would have leapt for joy at having something like that drop through their letter-box, but under the circumstances, that was hardly the right thing to do. The last thing you think about when someone dies, is what you're getting out of it. It's always a loss. That's the important thing.

***

I went to the shop later and was pleased to see it was still the same shitty little corner shop, existing on a day-to-day basis as it always had been. My brother was sitting behind the counter in his big leather chair, staring into space as Barry White grunted out his lyrics.

'Your mah first, mah last, mah everything...'

Barry could fucking motor when he wanted, big fat burger loving walrus love machine that he was, and did he have one hell of a gravel-munching voice or what? The guy was something else, really. That's one of the best things about the shop. You can listen to music all day long if you want, and whichever type of music takes your fancy because customers will think it's the radio and not your taste that's being played. My brother was one of those seventies kids who was into disco, reggae and funk, and I hated all three at the time. He still listens to that stuff, even shit by Boney M, Kool and The Gang and Barry Biggs (Never heard of him? Don't worry, nor have most people, but some talentless fuck will come along soon and do a cover version of one of his top songs and make himself and old Barry Biggs famous again). It's surprising, how many songs from the seventies are still being covered, but what's not surprising is what my brother thinks of these new versions of old and untouchable classics. A fucking shame, is his opinion, to ruin a decent song, "bastards ought to be locked up for getting away with that shit". I have to admit, he does have a point.

I hadn't really thought about my brother for a while, what he'd gone through and how it must have affected him. It wasn't until the door slammed shut that he came out of his trance. I was glad to see a smile spread itself across his slowly-healing face.

"Well? What's happening?" I asked.

"Fuck all. Boring."

"You look fucked, man."

"It's not as bad as it looks. Anyway, where the fuck have you been, then? They've been worrying their heads off at home. You and your fannying around's meant I've been getting my head done in."

"Yeah, I know."

"What did Dad say to you, then?"

"Gave me the works. But he's all right."

"You should have been there when I got back. Never seen Dad like that, man. You're lucky."

"Course I am." I smiled.

"When did you get in?"

"A while ago. Just come back from town."

"So? Where the fuck were you stopping, man?"

"I was with this lass. She's got her own place."

"Oh yeah? How could you have been thinking about fanny at a time like this? You're a dirty little cunt, you!"

"No, nothing like that, man. I just know her. She's a friend."

"I bet she fucking is anall."

"It wasn't like that."

"What do I care?"

"Why you ask, then?"

"Just felt like it."

"You been all right, or what, then?"

"Yeah, I'm all right."

"You been to hospital, yet?"

"Yeah. Tried to keep me in, set of tossers."

"What about your leg? Broken or what?"

"Nowt serious. Just bruising and shit."

"You seen Gates?"

"Yeah, I saw him. He's started a case."

"Yeah? For what?" I asked.

"Damages."

"Cool." I smiled.

"Could be. Serves the bastards right. Said I should come out with a few grand."

"Bully for you," I said.

"Some people keep calling and asking after you."

"Yeah? Which people?"

"Publishers or some shit. They want to speak with you. Meet with you."

"I know. Gates told me about that."

"Thingy's been in."

"Who?"

"That fuck-up mate of yours. What's his name? Snowy. Yeah, that prick called Snowy."

"He say anything?"

"Nah, just asking after you. What you want with that idiot anyway?"

"I don't want anything with him."

"You started running with him and his mates or summat? You think you're a fucking bad boy because you've spent a night in a cell?"

"What? No. Don't be daft, man. Maybe he just wanted to see me or something."

"Like what? You do any of that shit and I'll fuck you for it. You know that."

My brother wasn't one of these people who was heavily anti-drugs or anything. For all he cared, people could pump any old dog-shit into their veins till the mad cows came home. But that was people, and not family. He caught me with a joint once and nearly knocked the shit out me. He slapped me a couple of times and then gave me a right earful for my trouble. I thought he'd never stop and it was one of the few times he'd nearly gone and battered me for real. It was fucked up, though. Hypocritical. It didn't matter that he'd have the odd reefer himself, it didn't matter that he was as guilty as I was when it came to a bit of the old social smoking. That didn't make a difference, because, the way he saw it, he was doing the right thing. It was nothing more that his duty to protect little brother. He would lecture and chastise me regardless of his own faults, regardless of the sanctimony brought about by his conflicting morals and it was still okay because he said it was. Anyway, after that instance, I was a lot more careful about where and when I smoked. Never at home, and never in the shop. Besides, it was a rare event when I did smoke as it was only when I could get hold of the stuff for next to nothing. That's what it's like when you're a student. You don't even have money for fucking food let alone fucking drugs.

"It's nothing like that. You know me, man."

"Make sure it isn't, I don't want to see any of them losers in here, asking after you like that. You tell them."

"I'll tell them. Have you seen Freddy around?"

"That bastard? That fuckwitt? What d'you wanna see that little bastard for? Wait till he comes in here. I'm gonna fuck him for all of this. Little bastard! You hear about him? You know he's the one who grassed you up, don't you?"

"Yeah, I heard about it all right."

"Lucky little bastard, if you ask me. Lucky I haven't got my hands on him, man. I'll fucking kill him if I see him."

"You don't have to. He's a fuck-up."

"Little bastard more like. Some cunt sliced him up a few months ago."

"Yeah? Who told you that?"

"Bash told me but it was in all the papers, anall. I reckon it was Gilette, me. You know how mental that fucker can get."

"Saves us doing it."

"I still owe him for doing the shop," said my brother. "I bet he thinks I've forgotten. Every dog has its day, never forget that," said my brother like some wise old man.

"Nah. Fuck him. He can't help it. It's his nature, man."

"What? Robbing people isn't fucking nature."

"Just forget about it. Just make sure things stay cool."

"Things are fucking cool. We're both getting rich out of this. You're getting the will, I'm getting paid out from the insurance any day now and we're both fucking the coppers over for being a bunch of bastards."

"Don't say that, man."

"What?"

"About getting rich."

"Why not?"

"Because. She's dead for fucks sake!"

"So what? You didn't kill her. Fuck, you must have been a fucking Prince Charming or something for her to leave you her fucking money. You see the letter, then?"

"Yeah, Dad showed me it this morning."

"What's he think, then, this Gates chap?"

"It'll be all right. He reckons I've got away with it, you know, nothing for me to worry about and all that. He reckons it's all over and done with. I've just been to hers, you know, her solicitor."

"And?"

"She left me some stuff and some money."

"Yeah, I know that, but how much?"

Titch and his invisible observer side-kick walked in, then. My brother got up to serve and Titch looked me in the eye. He was smiling but it was a fake. I was expecting something to happen and when it did, it still surprised me.

"How's it going, Titch, man?" I asked.

"Hall right, man, hall right. So. They let you hout then?"

"Of course they let me out, man. I didn't do anything."

Titch sucked his teeth.

"What the fuck's that supposed to mean, man?"

"You know what hit means. Hit was hall hin the papers, there."

Word gets around pretty quickly, and it usually reaches all quarters even though the word might be totally fucked up. Who the fuck was he to think those things about me? He had no right, no fucker did but that wouldn't stop any of them. But I couldn't say that to him. He was still a customer and business is still business at the end of the day. Sometimes, you just have to pucker up, kiss arse and let people walk all over you.

"You believe that shit, man?" my brother asked. "Innocent until proven guilty, that mean anything to you? Shit, I thought you were a friend, man."

"So? What's that supposed to mean, then? You sayin' a friend can't be doin' something like that? Hold lady like that."

"What," I said, "you think I could do some shite like that? That what you really think, man?"

"You have to keep han hopen mind with these things sometimes."

"Yeah, but I thought you knew me, man."

"Honly person who knows you his you. Don't forget that, you hunderstan' what I'm saying?"

"Fair enough. I get where you're coming from, man."

It was a blow, and took the wind out of my sails. Titch was right of course. No one knew you as well as you knew yourself, and, I suppose, if I'd been in his shoes I might well have thought the same. But it still didn't make it nicer for me. Even though the coppers couldn't do anything to me, the people who knew me could still do plenty. Sometimes words can hurt a great deal more than a few fists or kicks. Words can stick for the rest of your fucking life no matter how fucked up, untrue and irrelevant they are. I wondered if I'd end up like one of those people who get pointed out in a crowd or mentioned in light and meaningless conversations like the guys who get done for child molesting, or the ones who get caught with a shipment of powder in their suitcases, the subject of gossip, rumours and frivolous debate. *Did I do it or didn't I? Could someone like me have really done something as bad as that? Of course I could have. Anyone could do something like that.*

Titch got his daily ration of printed bullshit and went out without saying another word.

"Fuck him." I said to my brother as the door closed behind him.

"Yeah, fuck him. What's that fucking wanker know anyway?"

the score

"Well," said Snowy flatly, "your man's waiting for you. I think he's got a few things he'd like to get off his chest."

"I bet he fucking does," I replied. "Cocksucker."

"I think I might stick around for this. You got a problem with that?" asked Snowy, doing his bit to sound as if he was in control.

"I insist, man. Be my guests."

"It's you and him, though. You know that. Me and my boys, we're only here to see this shit for ourselves. We're not here to get involved. You understand what I'm saying on this?" nodded Snowy.

"Don't go out of your way will you?"

"I think I've more than repaid that favour, man."

"I don't think doing this and doing time are the same thing, Snowy. But still, the favour's been returned and I appreciate it."

And I did appreciate it. Convincing Snowy to become at all involved in something he really had no business in wasn't easy, but I should have thanked him, all the same.

Freddy's voice rode out into the hall on those low watt beams of light coming from the room. He was giving it some, but then a man in his position would be saying anything he could to try and prove his innocence, just as I did later, when the coppers had me in their clutches. But this was different. That was about me and I was innocent. I'd always been innocent up until then, and Freddy was a lying, scheming bastard and he always would be.

"Hey, Freddy, my man! How goes it?" I said as I walked in.

Freddy squinted because he'd recognised my voice but couldn't quite make out my face in that subdued and inadequate lighting. It took him a few seconds for my face to become clear and meaningful.

"All right, matey? What you doing here?"

He said it as if he was welcoming me. As if he had any clout in that room. One sly mother-fucker, is Freddy

"Same as you, I've come to see someone."

"See someone? I'm not here to see no cunt. These lads, they've fucked up, got the wrong man."

I didn't say anything. I just looked at the others for a moment.

"I don't even fucking know what it is I've supposed to have done. It's a fucking joke, is this, our lad. I'm walking along, minding me own fucking business and up pull these cunts in the big motor, you know. What's fucking going on, I ask 'em. Not a fucking word – no parlez, no nowt. They just fucking grab us and you can guess the fucking rest, our kid. What'm I supposed to have done to these lads, eh? Our kid? You fucking listening, or what?"

I looked away from him. I needed to see the faces of the others. I had to make sure they were still there. Still interested.

"I'm listening and I think you're here for the same reason as me, man. You're here to see someone. You know?"

"Nah. I hardly know any of these lads," said Freddy.

I didn't respond verbally, a raise of the eyebrows was enough.

"What's going on? What the fuck have they tied us up for? It's not as if I'm the most dangerous cunt around here, is it?"

He sounded reasonable. Believable? Not as far as I was concerned, he wasn't.

"I think you know what's going on, Freddy."

I smiled because, I hoped, that would piss him off.

"Leave it out, will yer!"

I gave him another one of my prompting eyebrow raises to see what else he had to say.

"How come you're mixing it with these lads? I thought you were like me."

"And what's that then?"

"Straight."

"You? Straight? That's rich, man."

I had to laugh. Funny bloke, was Freddy.

"No." I said, "You're not straight. Me? Now I'm straight. You? You're crooked. Straight equals me. Crooked equals you. You got that?"

For once, Freddy looked stumped.

"You know what the dictionary says under the word 'crooked'? It says 'see Freddy'. That's because you and crooked are the same things. You understand?"

"Are you feeling all right, or what?" said Freddy and looked at the others. "Is there something wrong with him?"

None of them said a word because it wasn't their place to speak. They were there to observe but not to get involved.

"Look, I don't know what these lads want with us," said Freddy as he looked at me, "You don't know what they want, do yer? Tell 'em they've made a mistake, eh?"

"No one's made a mistake, Freddy." I told him and began to pace. "They don't want nothing. It's me who's got something to see you about."

"Well fucking hell mate, there's ways of doing things."

"This is a way of doing things." I said.

"I seen you a couple of days ago, you should have said. What's with all this business? Anyone would think I went around killing and robbing folk."

"That's funny."

"What? What's funny?"

Of course, I knew he'd try the dummy routine on, that he'd start off with the lines that conveyed confusion and most of all, his innocence. I wasn't going to have any of that shite, though. I was going for the throat. He was going to tell me the truth if it took me all night to get it out of him.

"Listen, I'm not going to say a word about why you're here. You're going to tell me everything yourself. You understand what I'm saying?"

"What? What's going on? You feeling all right or what, our kid?"

"Like I said, I'm not going to say a word about any of this shit. I'm not going to be told later that I went and put words into your mouth. Now, from the beginning, if you'd be good enough to give us an explanation."

"What? What you fucking giving it, you? Divvy bastard or what?"

His expression changed. I knew he'd do that. Be the angry man. "Save the dramatics for your shitty fucking books. They could do with it."

I shook my head and laughed. Funny cunt, Freddy. Also a cunt with a good memory. I got myself together and continued from where I left off.

"You know why people like me go and piss on the graves of people like you? Because you're fucking shit, that's why."

"People like me, what's that supposed to fucking well mean when it's at home?"

I tore off the clear covering from the white plastic case that held the blades, then carefully slid one out. Dangerous things, those blades. Even the case looked dangerous. They held blades that could slice a hair lengthways. Those blades might have looked like they were nothing but small rectangular pieces of thin metal but those little bastards could be lethal if they were held by the wrong and inexperienced hands. My dad used them in his shaver, but not me. You had to have nerves of steel to use the little bastards. Even when some of their danger had supposedly been reduced by placing them in a 'safety' razor (like doing nothing more than simply calling it a 'safety' razor made the fucking things safer or something), they were still capable of pretty much fucking your face up. I scrumpled the crispy wrapper into a ball, dropped it on the floor and took a step towards Freddy. Conveniently, they'd tied him to his chair.

"You a bleeder, Freddy?" I asked.

"Go fuck yourself!"

"You know something? I bet you'll blab after three cuts."

"Fucking razor blade? What's he like, eh lads? This has got to be a fucking joke or summat, has this!"

I pulled out a packet of salt and gave it a shake.

"Something to spice things up for you, man. You know, something that's nice and savoury."

"Yer a fucking baby, man! You think I'm gonna fall for this crap? You haven't got the bollocks for it for one thing! You're out of your fucking depth with this, pal!"

"You reckon I'm wrong about you?"

"Course you fucking are. Every fucker knows that. You're nowt but a shopkeeper, man."

"Fuck you, Freddy. You're a robbing bastard and I'm gonna prove it."

"Do me a favour and just fuck off."

"I got you fucking sussed."

"And who the fuckinell died and made you king? Who d'you think you are, you?"

"I know who I am, man."

"And what's that, then?"

"I'm not like you. I'm not scum."

"Do me a favour and go tell it to the judge."

"Tell me something, man."

I stopped talking. I twiddled with a blade in between my fingers and then held it up. Freddy saw it and kept on looking at it. He wasn't scared because he thought that was the closest it was going to get to him.

"You don't think I've got the bottle to fuck you up with one of these?" I finished.

"You haven't got the bottle for anything."

"We'll see."

"Go on, then. If you've gorrit in yer, do it!"

"Just admit it, man."

"Admit what?"

"Don't insult my fucking intelligence. Every bastard knows it was you."

"I won a bit of money on the horses. Big – fuck – ing – deal!"

"Fuck you, Freddy! You're too fucking stupid to win money. Shit like you only robs money."

"You're just clutching at straws, now, pal. You've fucking had it and you're just trying any old shit on."

That was the moment for cut number one. Just a slight slit across the right side of his forehead. No blood for a couple of seconds and then a small, growing blob which broke into a deep red dribble when it got too massive to hold its original form. It was a timing thing. A second later the moment would have been lost. It was a good call because it got a reaction from Snowy as well as Freddy,

"Aaah! Yer bastard! Yer fuckin' bastard!" hissed The Fuckwitt.

"Jesus!" said Les as if he had just knocked someone over in the red BMW convertible he'd bought a couple of days ago.

"Fuckinell, man! That's out of order is that!" said Snowy as he stepped forward and then, realising his reaction was out of place, stepped back.

"You think I give a fuck about this cunt?" I asked him. "Just stay out of this, Snowy."

"Not 'ere man, I'm not having anything to do with this," Snowy protested.

"I'm not asking you to have anything to do with it, man. You said it before, you're only here to see this for yourself. So? Now, you can see."

"Bastard...fucking bastard." Freddy moaned.

"Ready to say something yet or what?"

Snowy shook his head and bit his lip. Dying to stop this, was Snowy but knew he couldn't. Knew the deal. Knew his place.

"Go fuck yourself. Bastard. Fucking bastard."

Them fucking razor cuts man, they could sting like a mother-fucker. I'd only used my dad's razor the once and that was enough for me. You had to have a steady hand and be prepared for the worst if you ever used one of those fucking things. My face was cut to ribbons when I used my dad's safety razor and I figured I just wasn't man enough to shave with one of those things yet. It must have been even worse when it was just a bare blade glancing off your face, neck and anything else that it cared to skim across. Those things could cause damage in the wrong hands. Serious damage and, when I think about it, they're a much under-used device in those gangster films. Baseball bats, cut-throats, guns, throwing stars and all that shite's all good and well, but a nice little razor blade? That's got a bit of thought, and fuck, a bit of first hand experience that many people could easily appreciate and relate to.

"You want some more, then?"

"Fuck you!"

The top right hand side of Freddy's face was looking pretty red. He looked just a bit like one of those Harlequins from medieval times and I always thought those guys looked slick with their two tone faces and fancy but sleek costumes. All I needed to do was to give him another slit so the blood would dribble down and cover the bottom left side of his face. Then, the new look for this season would be there. A face that would be divided into four. From left to right in a clockwise motion; white, red, white, red. Like a portion of a chess board but instead of black, there'd be red. That'd be okay, I told myself, but it would only look good until the blood ran down one half of his face and spoiled the whole thing.

"Aaah! You fuck-ing bas-tard!" screamed Freddy.

Oh shit! He looked terrible. I'd just gone and ruined it. Should have been a little more careful. Should have took my time but it was too late to worry because it was only Freddy. Missing my target by a couple of inches and getting him right on the nose wasn't the end of the world. Just meant this year's new look would have to be something else. Still, being cut on the bridge of the nose just had to hurt. It just had to. Looking at the guy made the others turn away and moan as one entity. But not me. That motherfucker had started it and now was the time for his comeuppance. I was in control. On top of things. On my game. I even thought I was getting handy at that business. And I didn't feel as bad as I thought I would. You never knew with some things, until you tried them.

"Ready for something different, Freddy? Ready for a bit of spice in your life?" I asked and shook the packet of salt I'd been holding in my other hand. Sometimes, it was better to be prepared.

"Jesus, man, this ain't fuckin' right," said Snowy.

"Who the fuck asked you, man?"

"This guy's a fucking sicko, man," said Les to the others who couldn't help watching. They nodded and hummed and hah'd a bit, but they didn't protest. Maybe they were enjoying it.

"You don't have to be here, man," I told him. "If you can't stand the fucking heat..."

"Fuck-in' bas-tard!" yelled Freddy.

"Try playing another record, man. You listen to me, and make sure you understand what I'm telling you. I'm gonna keep on doing this until you tell me. You understand what I'm saying? You tell me!"

"Fuck-in' bas-tard!"

Another one, and more cursing and screaming followed. I could hear him acting up but I wasn't listening any more. Nothing he could have said would have mattered. I'd done the right thing, I told myself. The bastard deserved everything he was getting not just for what he'd done to us but for all the other cunts he'd mercilessly screwed over in his fucked-up and selfish life. Freddy was a bad person. Freddy was a bastard to the world and always would be and that was the thing that mattered most. Unlike any self-respecting crook, Freddy had a habit of boasting about some of his criminal adventures, especially the violent and stupid ones. Those sentimental trinkets that weren't even worth a quid at the flea market but were the only thing some old dear had to remind herself of her dead husband. The little three wheeler Johnny Briggs had been given by his dad the Christmas before Dad was killed in a car accident. And other similar stories of pointless theft. Freddy wasn't totally stupid, and he was quite versatile. I had the problem with him when theft was a subject of discussion. Nicking was nicking, as far as I was concerned and nicking off people was just down right nasty. People worked for a living. Worked for the finer things in life and if Freddy wanted to deal in stolen goods, he should have dealt in stolen goods that hadn't quite reached the consumer. Stolen goods from stores. From wagons but not from people's homes. You had to have some heart for people who were like you. Freddy didn't give a fuck about any of that, though. Criminals aren't the most compassionate people in the world but they do have standards. Ninety-nine out of a hundred would only go for stuff like robbing Joe Public when they were truly desperate but not Freddy. For him, everything was business, and I figured, a fair dollop of pleasure as well. Sometimes he'd change his mind and it seemed to me that even his morals and ethics had mercenary qualities. He'd go with the flow. If the company he was with disapproved of hanging he'd also get all liberal about the subject, and if the company changed, so did his views. Freddy had probably upset thousands of people in his life. Most of them were everyday normal people and even crooks like himself had been stung by his tail. He was nobody's friend and that day, he certainly wasn't going to be mine. If it had come to it, he'd never have worked his wrangles again.

"Lighten up, man. I'm not going to stop until you tell me."

"Tell you fucking *what*? You fuck-ing bas-tard! *What* can I tell you?"

"Now, now. That's not nice, Freddy. It's nice to be nice. Remember?"

I gave him another one to show him, but also to show Snowy and his boys that I really didn't give a fuck any more, which was a pretty good way of describing how I felt at the time. Snowy and his normally loud and merry crew were looking on as if they were longing for it to be over and done with. Snowy even looked like he wanted to get in and stop me himself. But he couldn't. It wasn't his place.

"You mad fucking bastard! This isn't fucking right! This is bollocks!"

"And, you know what the sad part is? There's no need for it, man. You just tell me and that's it, forgive and forget."

Freddy took a deep breath and I thought the moment had arrived, that he was ready to tell. But he didn't, he just tilted his head back and showed everyone in the room the pain he was feeling. I grabbed the packet of salt and tore off a corner.

"Sting like a bugger, eh? Wait till I shake some of this stuff on it. It'll be like getting salt rubbed in a wound."

I smiled at the piss-poor pun but my captive audience didn't get it. I continued with this cause of mine because it was the only thing I could do.

"Last chance Freddy. I mean it, man."

Freddy closed his eyes, as if he'd been working two shifts in the mill. As if the bastard was dog-tired. If he hadn't decided to talk that night, which seems so long ago now, Snowy and his boys would have been wise to get themselves out of that shithole. Either that, or they'd have wished someone gave them something to shove in their ears.

right here, right now
part four - countryman

Pakistan had always been on my mind one way or another. Pakistan was like Georgia in that song by some old soul singer who was probably dead and buried now. It was a good time for me to go and start all over and all that shite. Only thing that took some thinking was how to go about it. Eventually I managed to convince myself that doing it wholesale, lock, stock and barrel would be the best way. But everyone else, my mum, dad, brother and my little sister had one advantage over me, and as advantages went, it was a fucking corker. They'd all been to Pakistan before and they all knew, to some degree, what to expect. Me? I'd never been anywhere at all. I'd never left England and never thought I would – Yorkshire lad, born and bred, strong in arm and thick in head. Except I wasn't as strong in the arm as some of my fellow Yorkshiremen were supposed to be and I wasn't as thick, either.

Everyone was worried about me. What if I didn't like the weather, the food, the people, the way of life, the smells and aromas? Well, as far as I was concerned, burning my bridges would be the best way of going about it. No way back to England meant I had to like it, and besides, Pakistan had always been there for me. Pakistan had always been something to aim for, but never to reasonably expect.

For most of the first ones to arrive in Britain the idea of return was one of the premises that they left with in the first place. They thought they'd go over to Britian, earn some dosh and leg it back to Pakistan once they felt loaded enough. That didn't happen, and the idea of return became a myth. I heard this old bloke tell my dad what he thought had gone wrong. We had a sweet taste in our mouths, he said, and we couldn't do without it any more because we liked it so much and had become so used to it. It was like an addiction, he said. The sweet taste was there, all right. In Bradford, Birmingham, Dewsbury or wherever the fuck you happened to be. But he was also right when he said England was nothing more than a habit for most of us and as such, could be dropped. That's what I wanted to do. I wanted to make the snake eat its own tail. To come full circle. I wanted to be the one to finish off what my father had started over forty years ago and that, thanks to Annie, was just what I did.

We sold the shop first. Then the house went for a song, and for a week or so, we stayed at a rented gaff until it was time to go. The day before we went I saw Shelley for the last time. I might have been a shit heel with her in the past but not then. I owed her and told her I'd always owe her before I kissed her goodbye. A nice, affectionate peck on the cheek. That tongues-examining-the-back-of-her-throat shite didn't seem appropriate somehow. She was pleased for me, but still a little sad to see me go. We kissed a friend's kiss and that was all.

Yes, I do feel better, though. Now that I've made the move, I feel all right. I took the liberty of bringing all my CDs, tapes, PC and anything else that I thought I couldn't do without. I write a letter to Shelley once every month or so and she writes back. We're a bit like fucking pen-pals but it's still kind of nice to hear about some of the shite that's going off back in England. The last letter I got from her was all about Freddy and how he's on remand somewhere and awaiting trial for mugging some OAP or something equally distasteful. There are still some people who ask questions about me but I'm not too bothered about people and what they think any more. I've got other things on my mind, these days. Lots of things to keep me occupied.

These days, things are okay. We've got our own house, our own fucking courtyard that's as big as a five-a-side pitch and now that my brother's set up business in the local bazaar, everybody's happy. Gates is still all right and he's even set me up with a proper agent because he can't handle all the work I've made for him. It's some woman in London who I've never even met but that doesn't matter. She'll carry on where Gates left off and make all three of us a fortune with the newspaper deals and the rest of the books I'm churning out for them like some cheap plastic product. She writes to me at least once a week and rings me every other day to see if things are all right. She thinks there's a shit load more where the first book came from, but she has to be quick before I dry up.

Annie Potts? Sure I still think about Annie, and yes, I thank her for what she left me. I still owe her, but the trouble is, it's not too easy to pay her back now that she's worm food.

On Thursdays I light some incense and say a prayer for her soul. Her death wasn't nice, but as fucked up as it sounds, it sure as shit helped. I couldn't care less about the fact that I killed her these days. I mean, I'll think about it and I might feel a little bad about it but nothing else really comes to mind. I know I did what I did for the sake of money and ambition and there are even moments when I go through all that guilt trip shite but at the end of the day, I still feel it was worth it. And besides, I could always say that it was Annie's idea in the first place. I could always argue that I was just the one who carried her wish out for her. Seemed to me she'd had enough of living and she thought that death wasn't necessarily a bad thing to happen to her at that time of life. She could die but I could live. I could get something out of doing her that one great favour. Like I said in the beginning, coming to Pakistan was the second best thing I ever did, but what I did to get here, that was the best.

The plot came to me as soon as I found out she had money. The plot was born and all I had to do was act it out and then write it down. The robbery was my own and Freddy just got blamed for it. The suicide note was mine, as well. I left it where I did on purpose and I even used her typewriter, with her own blessing, to write it.

She didn't struggle or anything. She didn't say anything as I held her mouth open and shoved those chalky white babies in there. I watched her die and then I left. It was just a delivery, that's all, and Freddy was there. Watching me walk back to the shop car and hating the fucking sight of me. I knew he wouldn't be able to resist getting me in trouble. If only that dim bastard knew who was really in the driving seat.

I don't have any real troubles accepting what I've done. Except in my thoughts and my dreams. But I'll settle for that because I know it's nothing more than my own conscience trying to trip me up. I tell myself that Annie gave me her blessing, but sometimes I start to crack, and it's only my family that acts as a sealant. Yes, I'll settle for what we've got right now, even though for some it might sound like I'm settling for less. And who knows, I might make the trip back one day, even if it's a holiday. I might need to remind myself about what all those, who haven't realised the truth about that myth of return, have to put up with.

work in progress – the will

He had to do it. No choice in the matter, really. He'd made the sacrifice but where was the reward? It hadn't arrived and it would never arrive, at least, not in his lifetime. He had to do something to get things moving. To get what was his by torturously earned rights.

He'd known her for just over fourteen months when she did die. She didn't die, though. Killed, was more like it. Slain, they said in the paper the next day. Some sicko had broken into her house and done her over for the sake of a couple of quid. Pitiful, Chris had said the following morning while Hussain got all choked up just by talking about her. Chris patted him on the shoulder and said he was sorry. He knew how well Hussain and her got on and how her going like that must have been really painful for him.

All he wanted was her money and fuck, he knew she had money and that was thanks to her being a silly cunt and still hoarding it after all these years. Sometimes people said things that they thought meant nothing; she told him she had always been a little 'careful' with money and sometimes, she regretted it. Especially after her Geoffrey had passed on. In a way, she was saying she didn't deserve wealth any more. And in a way, Hussain agreed with her.

He took his shoes off and left them on the doorstep. Then, he took his socks off and put them over his hands. Wouldn't do to have his prints where they shouldn't have been, would it? He walked into her hall after he had allowed himself in with the key he was now trusted with. He'd smash the glass panel in the door when he was done to make this look like a break-in. He walked in and went to her room. With any luck, she'd be asleep.

She was a little deaf and she probably didn't notice much of a change in his voice as he called to wake her. The balaclava over his head sent the craps up her but Hussain was in no mood for giving her yet more sympathy. As soon as she woke, he slapped her a couple, thinking he had to tell her who was boss from the beginning and to tell her that he meant business. That way, there was less chance of her trying anything funny on. But exactly what Madge, in her state, could have tried on with him was beyond him but Hussain didn't care too much about that, right then. She fell out of bed and onto the floor. He cursed and then picked her up by the neck. He told her what he wanted, why he was there. Money. Nothing else. Just that fucking wad that she had stuffed under her mattress but, just like he knew she would, she denied all knowledge of it. All she said was "please…". "Please" didn't mean shit to Hussain any more. She could have called Hussain God and he wouldn't have given her a second chance or given a shit. He slapped her again and told her that he'd rape her if she didn't give him what he wanted. He was a sick bastard for doing this to her, he thought but still, it might have proved to be a means to an end. If he was lucky, she might have had a heart attack, keeled over and that would have saved him from really getting his hands dirtied. Above all, it was just another one of those sacrifices that he'd been making.

A bit of money. That was sad. That was terrible, the papers commented the next day. A human life for a bit of money. It was working out well because no one knew that it was a lot more than just the few quid he'd got from her before he beat her to death. Everybody wanted to live. Everybody had to have something that kept them going. Everybody had this will to live a better life and Hussain was no different.

Her last few moments with him were uncomfortable. She had no idea it was him, the closest thing she had to a son, who was doing this to her. As he looked at her pathetic body in a pink nightdress that was two sizes too big for her, he thought about getting the next few actions perfect. He thought about doing her nice and slowly, like some deranged fuck-head would. Then it would become one of those sicko killings but going that far wasn't necessary, really. He didn't want this thing to bring more attention than was needed. He'd stick with plan A – a bungled robbery. Some tripping crack head who didn't know what he was doing was going to get the blame for this shit. He cracked her a couple more times and then throttled her. She tried to put up a fight but he'd seen babies with more strength. After he'd finished, he rooted around some more but found fuckall that would have been worth nicking had he been a real thief and had this been a real robbery. There was an old radio, a telly that she had owned for the last thirty years and a couple of bottles of booze. The booze he decided to take and the other shit, he'd leave. Before he did that, he messed the whole place up as if he'd been looking for goods of value and then got pissed because he wasn't finding any. He did that quickly and he did his best not to look her way as he was doing it. It would have been nice if she just died of her own accord but what the hell, he thought, some people were stubborn like that.

discography

right here, right now	Jesus Jones
	Doubt (1991)
	SBK
paid in full	Erik B. & Rakim
	Paid in Full (1987)
	4th & Broadway
sound of da police	KRS-One
	Return of the Boom
	Bap (1993)
	Jive Records
help the aged	Pulp
	This is Hardcore (1998)
	Island
get up, stand up	Bob Marley and The Wailers
	Burning (1973)
	Tuff Gong.
broken stones	Paul Weller
	Stanley Road (1995)
	London
hand on the pump	Cypress Hill
	Cypress Hill (1991)
	Ruffhouse/Columbia
mama said knock you out	LL Cool J
	Mama Said Knock You Out (1990)
	Def Jam
regulate	Nate Dog & Warren G.
	Regulate… G Funk Era(1994)
	Def Jam
dirty cash	Adventures of Stevie V.(1990)
	SPV
you're gonna get yours	Public Enemy
	Yo! Bum Rush The Show (1987)
	Def Jam
television, the drug of the nation	Disposable Heroes of Hiphoprisy
	Hypocrisy is the
	Greatest Luxury(1992)
	4th & Broadway
express yourself	NWA
	Straight Outta Compton(1988)
	Priority Records

deeper love	Aretha Franklin Greatest Hits 1980-94 (1994) *Arista*
jump around	House of Pain House of Pain (1992) *Tommy Boy*
and the beat goes on	The Whispers Greatest Hits (1997) *The Right Stuff*
smells like teen spirit	Nirvana (1991) *Uni/Geffen*.
firestarter	The Prodigy Fat of the Land (1997) *Maverick*
waterfall	The Stone Roses The Stone Roses (1989) *BMG/Jive/Novus/Silvertone*
ain't nobody	Chaka Khan Life is a Dance – The Remix Project (1989) *Warner Bros*
moving on up	Primal Scream Screamadelica (1991) *Sire*
rumours	Timex Social Club(1994) *Jay*
don't believe the hype	Public Enemy It Takes a Nation of Millions to Hold Us Back (1988) *Def Jam*
if you ever	Gabrielle & East 17(1996) *London*
perfect day	Lou Reed Different Times – Lou Reed in the 70s (1996) *RCA*
fastlove	George Michael Older (1996) *Dreamworks/SKG*.
disco 2000	Pulp Different Class (1995) *Island*

everything must go	Manic Street Preachers
	Everything Must Go (1996)
	Epic
the score	The Fugees
	The Score (1996)
	Ruffhouse
countryman	Fun da mental (1993)
	Nation Records

M Y Alam was born in Bradford in 1967.
He is currently studying at the University
of Bradford. He is married with three
children.

other titles from springboard fiction

Dark Places
by Margery Ramsden
ISBN 1 901927 02 4   Price £6.95
Laura is a woman in crisis, drinking and dreaming. Her father is dying and Rod, her belching husband, is poking at his toenails. She finds comfort in the pub and narrow-hipped Phil. A series of flashbacks leave her in a state of confusion. Rod blames it all on the drinking. Phil keeps supplying the comfort. Her father sucking on an empty pipe and wandering the streets in search of a lost grave, holds the key to the past that could free her.

The Righteous Brother
by Adrian Wilson
ISBN 1 901927 00 8 Price £6.95
For Crown prosecution solicitor James Turner there is a clear distinction between right and wrong, and before the local magistrates he's usually right. But what of his wife Sally, and her admirer Kevin? Or his courtroom adversary Colin Chatterton and the ambitious journalist Jo Hinchliffe? How have these people forced James Turner to be so suddenly and murderously wrong?

Miasma
by Chris Firth
ISBN: 1 901927 01 6   Price £6.95
Deserted. Lonely. Sad. Going bad. Going slowly mad. Anna Fisher can only take so much. In this darkly humoured first novel, Chris Firth leads us into the murky world of Anna Fisher - where nothing is quite what it seems.

The White Room
by Karen Maitland
ISBN: 1 898311 23 4   Price £6.95
They have surveillance cameras in the White Room, watching every move you make. In a Britain of the future where social and cultural conflict has sharpened, Ruth is drawn into a disturbing exploration of the forces that shape her life: her cultural identity, her family history and a society that she no longer feels a part of.

Flood
by Tom Watts
ISBN: 1 898311 12 9   Price £4.99
Bob is back in the home town he hasn't seen for thirty years. A remarkable first novel which moves us into an adolescent world fraught with underlying passion and danger. A demanding, disturbing and rewarding read.

The Labour Man
by Jim Wilson
ISBN 1 898311 01 3   Price £3.00
Can there be honour in politics? Harry Beamish, a lifelong socialist, wrenches a marginal seat from the Tories in an election which returns a Labour Government with a majority of one. Unfortunate then he's done a bunk. A pre-Blair Mania novel where the future of the Government and socialism depends on Harry.

Tubthumping
ISBN 1 901927 04 0   Price £5.95
Short stories from a selection of the most promising young writers in the Yorkshire region.

Ordering

Annie Potts is Dead	£6.95
Dark Places	£6.95
The Righteous Brother	£6.95
Miasma	£6.95
The White Room	£6.95
Flood	£4.99
The Labour Man	£3.00
Tubthumping	£5.95

Title: _

Quantity _ _ _ _ Price _ _ _ _ Total _ _ _ _

Title: _

Quantity _ _ _ _ Price _ _ _ _ Total _ _ _ _

Title: _

Quantity _ _ _ _ Price _ _ _ _ Total _ _ _ _

20% discount on orders of 5 or more of any individual title. Postage and packing free in the UK only.

You may pay by cheque or postal order made payable to Yorkshire Art Circus Ltd. We also accept payment by Access or Visa.

Card Number (Access/Visa): _ _ _ _ _ _ _ _ _ _ _ _ _ _ _ _ _ _

Expiry Date _ _ _ _

Name _

Address _

_ _

_ _ _ _ _ _ _ Post Code _ _ _ _ _ _ _ _ _ _ _

Address to: Yorkshire Art Circus, School Lane, Glasshoughton, Castleford, West Yorkshire, WF10 4QH. Please allow 28 days for delivery.